MW01294487

Black Cotton II

Ted L. Pittman

authorHOUSE®

AuthorHouse™
1663 Liberty Drive
Bloomington, IN 47403
www.authorhouse.com
Phone: 1-800-839-8640

First published by AuthorHouse 11/16/2011

ISBN: 978-1-4670-6627-3 (e)
ISBN: 978-1-4670-6628-0 (hc)
ISBN: 978-1-4670-6629-7 (sc)

Library of Congress Control Number: 2011918818

Printed in the United States of America

Dedication

Black Cotton II is dedicated to my brother Dean. He fought the good fight and now rests in God's hands.

And to my sister Beverly. She was an angel here on earth and Heaven is a better place for her being there.

Preface

The stories in "Black Cotton" were mostly about events that happened in my life as a child growing up in Southern Oklahoma in the 1950s. "Black Cotton II" continues that style, but most of the stories center around an older, though not necessarily wiser, 'Petey'. I've also included a few stories from the 1950s that I thought readers would enjoy. I was pleasantly surprised at the popularity of my stories and it is my sincere hope that the stories in "Black Cotton II" are received so generously.

Most of the stories included are true stories and are documented as well as my memory could recall them. A few of the stories are what I will call bonus stories, and may or may not have happened in exactly the manner I describe.

I've also included a section called "Short Takes" that contains shorter stories or happenings that have stuck in my mind over the years. I hope you enjoy this section.

While writing the stories included in "Black Cotton" and now "Black Cotton II," characters that were a part of my life as I was growing up came back to mind. Some of these folks I hadn't thought of in many years. One thing is certain; folks were different back then. Not so much in looks or stature, but in their beliefs and behaviors. I believe people were more set in their beliefs fifty or sixty years ago and not so easily swayed by popular opinion or the current trends and fads. We would probably be better served if we were more like that today.

As I drive through Mill Creek, Oklahoma today, little has really changed over the forty-five years since I graduated from high school. The new school is nice and was really needed; there is no real grocery store anymore, just a convenience store and gas station. There are a few more brick homes scattered around. I remember when Mill Creek had four gas stations operating at the same time. Somehow, all of them managed to stay in business, at least for a while. Shine Waller had the Deep Rock Station on the south side of town on the highway, Doc Spears had a station where the convenience store is located now. Emory and Grace Sewell had the station down by the tracks west of where the post office is now. Lastly, Roy Damron had the station on the highway on the southwest corner of Main Street and highway #1. It was between the highway and where the post office is presently located.

Across the highway east from Roy's station, the sidewalk was raised about two feet from ground level and was a popular place for the old men to gather and talk. It was one of the 'spit and whittle' benches scattered around town. They could sit and watch the traffic go by on the highway that went through town. For a few years in the 1950s, there was even a traffic light where Main Street bisected the highway. There was another spit and whittle bench in front of Clément's Grocery and still another under the tame Mulberry tree at Shine Waller's Station. I could sit and listen to those old guys for hours. Some of the stories they could tell were hard to believe. I sometimes thought they spiced them up a little bit just because I was listening. I hope readers enjoy the stories in "Black Cotton II" as much as I enjoyed writing them. Petey is at it again and gets into some pretty good messes in some of the stories. I'm just glad he finally grew up and settled down.

Disclaimer

Any association of characters in "Black Cotton II" with people who lived in and around the Mill Creek Oklahoma area in the 1950 to 1975 time period is strictly intentional. However, it is my sincere desire that folks take the stories as they are meant to be, humorous and entertaining. If any were to be offended by anything in any of the stories, please accept my deepest apology. I have not used real names except in the description of places and businesses operating at the time. Be aware that some of the stories are spiced up a little to clarify the subject matter. Most of the stories happened just as described. You decide which ones.

Table of Contents

The Big Bang

It was the summer after my fourth grade year of school. My brother Dan had just graduated from high school and had a job working at a Phillips 66 station in Oklahoma City. The last time he had been home, he had secretly told me of a big surprise he had in mind for July 4th. He had always liked fireworks and he had been saving up money to buy fireworks for the biggest display anyone around Mill Creek Oklahoma had ever seen. I could hardly wait.

True to his promise, the day before the July 4th holiday, he arrived home with a huge suitcase full of every kind of firework I had ever seen and a lot I hadn't. There were regular "black cat" firecrackers, roman candles, bottle rockets, cherry bombs, and several larger rockets and missiles all packed neatly into that huge suitcase. It was so heavy I couldn't even lift the thing.

Now Dan was feeling pretty good about himself. He could hardly wait to put on the fireworks display the following night. Mom had a big to-do planned with homemade ice cream, watermelons, and hot dogs. Aunt

Em and Uncle Jasper were coming over, several of the nearest neighbors were invited, and I knew there would be a lot of mine and my sisters' friends there as well. It was going to be the most exciting thing that had happened around our place in a long time.

The long awaited day finally arrived. We had a fire going in the back yard to roast wieners and marshmallows. Dad had set up a couple of long tables and three or four huge watermelons were sitting there just waiting to be cut. Two big freezers of ice cream were under way with me sitting on one and my little sister Virginia sitting on the other while Dad and Jasper turned the cranks.

It was still an hour or so 'til dark when we all sat down to eat. I was just about too excited to eat anything until I tasted those roasted hot dogs. There were at least forty or fifty people in attendance and everyone was having a good time. Dan had taken the big suitcase full of fireworks out of his 1956 Plymouth and sat it near the back porch where the display was to take place. Dad had placed a big sheet of plywood in front of the porch to use as a launching pad for the fireworks.

By the time everyone had their fill of the ice cream, Dan was ready to begin the fireworks. He had the suitcase open and lying on the bottom step of the back porch. The back steps were made of cement and had a small apron of cement at the bottom of the two steps going up to the screen door. The screen door was just an ordinary wooden screen door like was common in those days.

As it neared time for the display to begin, everyone had positioned chairs in a semi-circle about fifty or sixty feet east of the back porch so as to have a good view of the fireworks. Dan was busy sitting up the first three or four items he was going to shoot off and I could see he was reveling in all the attention. After all, he had spent around a hundred dollars on the fireworks and in that day a hundred dollars was a lot of money.

Finally, Dad told him to start the display. Dan started off with a couple of smaller rockets and roman candles to get everybody in the mood, then he reached into the suitcase and pulled out a huge rocket about eighteen inches long and sat it up on the plywood. You could hear the oooohs, and aaaah's from the crowd as everyone anticipated the lighting of the big rocket.

Dan looked sort of like a master of ceremonies as he carefully adjusted the rocket on the plywood. Then as everyone held their breath, he lit the fuse with the punk he had been holding in his hand. I climbed onto the hood of Mom's car to have a better view.

With a loud screech, the rocket left the plywood headed for the high heavens. When it was only about a hundred feet off the ground, that thing took a sharp turn to the right and headed back to earth even faster than it left if that was possible. It was headed right for the circle of chairs in the back yard. Folks were running and screaming, trying to get out of the way of the thing when it made another abrupt turn to the west. It headed straight toward the back porch, and with a downward turn, landed directly in the open suitcase full of fireworks Dan had placed on the bottom step.

Holy Jehosophats!! You can't even imagine the chaos that took place. With a loud roar, the contents of the suitcase began to explode. Rockets and missiles were going every direction. Bottle rockets and roman candles were going off as were the several bundles of black cat firecrackers that had been stored in the bottom of the suitcase. It looked like the re-enactment of a Civil War battle I had seen on the television just a few days earlier. Folks were running for their lives and falling over each other in their attempt to get out of the way of the flying projectiles. I couldn't believe Aunt Em could run so fast but she went by my perch on the hood of the car looking like an Olympic sprinter.

Just about then the screen door caught on fire. It was blazing pretty good by the time Dad got the water hose hooked up to put it out. He got it put out just before the back door to the house caught on fire. Smoke hung in the air so thick I could hardly see anything at all. Finally, the roar of the exploding fireworks settled to an occasional bang as yet another firecracker or rocket went off.

As folks began to walk back into the light afforded by the back porch light Dad had turned on, I saw Dan just standing alone by the side of the washhouse with a shocked look on his face. Right then, I felt really sorry for him. He had gone to so much trouble and expense just so others could have a good time and look what had happened. It just didn't seem fair to me.

Folks were standing around looking at the chaos. The back yard looked like a war zone. Parts of exploded fireworks were lying everywhere, some still smoldering and sending tendrils of smoke into the air. Overturned chairs and tables lay strewn around where people had flung them in their haste to get away from the exploding fireworks. A couple of Mom's tablecloths had holes burned in them as well and were lying in the grass by the tables.

Nobody was saying a word. When I looked back over at Dan, he looked like he was about to cry. That's when it happened. Someone started to clap their hands together slowly, then one by one, others joined in. Pretty soon, everyone was clapping and hollering and gathering around Dan. The shocked look on Dan's face began to be replaced with a grin. He took a bow from the waist like I'd seen done on some of the older classical movies.

"Best fireworks display I've ever seen," allowed Kenneth Bowling, a neighbor from up the street. "You couldn't have planned it any better." I'm not sure Mom felt the same way standing there looking at the ruined tablecloths and charred screen door.

It took a couple of hours the next morning to get it all gathered up and thrown into the big trash receptacle by the road. It took longer than that to put up a new screen door and wash the black smoke from the side of the house by the back door. Finally, all was as close to being back to normal as it was likely to get.

I won't ever forget that Independence Day in 1958 and the big fireworks display Dan put on. It will stand as a benchmark for all Independence Days to come. For pure unexpectedness and total chaos, I've never experienced one to match it and probably never will. I still marvel at Aunt Em's speed and agility that night. I'll never forget the look on Dan's face when the rocket went into the suitcase, one of total disbelief. You know, it worked out all right after all and in doing so, crafted a memory that I wouldn't otherwise have had. I don't remember all the Fourth of July celebrations we had when I was growing up, but I will always remember the one in 1958 when we all experienced "The Big Bang."

The End

Range Delivered

The term ***"range delivered"*** comes from a time when open range was common. Open range was land that belonged to the Government, and in most cases was available for homesteading. The big ranches would file for a quarter section of land around a source of water, usually a spring or fair sized lake that was known to provide water on a regular basis. Then they would have some of their cowboys file on adjacent parcels to enlarge the area they had under deed. If you controlled the water, you controlled the land. All the area around the deeded land would still be open range, and stock from several ranches would all use this "open range".

Cattle buyers would often come right out to the ranch to buy cattle. If a deal was struck, sometimes the rancher would deliver the cattle to a railhead or some other location named by the cattle buyer. But at other times, the cattle buyer would prefer to drive the cattle himself and would take delivery right where the cattle happened to be on the range. This was called ***"range delivered"***.

My only experience with range delivery was when my uncle Jasper bought six head of mamma cows from a fellar named Riley Fox down by Reagan USA. This fellar had gathered and sold all his stock except these six cows which, despite all he could do, couldn't be driven into the corral or cajoled into it with feed, or anything else that he had tried with the help of anybody he could find that was willing to try. Finally he just gave up on getting them to the sale, so he decided to try to unload them on somebody at a real bargain. That 'somebody' happened to be my Uncle Jasper. It wasn't until after Jasper bought the cows that he learned that two or three of them had what I'd call sour dispositions, and all the chasing and carousing trying to get them into the corral hadn't helped their dispositions one little bit. In fact, one fellar that was trying to help get them captured had been run up a tree and had to sit there in that tree for more than two hours with that old mad cow just a bawling and snorting and daring him to come down. When she finally left to go to the creek for a drink, he slithered down and was able to make it over the section line fence ahead of her, but just barely the way I heard it told.

Now Mr. Fox had leased his land to a man named Jarman and Mr. Jarman wanted those cows out of there so he could bring in his own stock. So who do you think Jasper came looking for to help him gather his 'bargain' cows? Yep, yours truly, along with Mike Peterson and Billy South. Put the three of us together, and we might just have been as ornery as them six cows Jasper needed gathered.

Let me tell you a little bit about these two saddle bums. Billy South was just a little bugger, stood about five foot six or seven, but knew cattle and could ride just about anything with hair on it. Kept a dip of Skoal between his lower lip and gum all the time. Looking back on it, it makes me wonder if he even took it out when he went to kiss a girl. He was a good hand with a rope, probably the best of the three of us, and had a good head on his shoulders when it came to stock and such.

Mike Peterson ran a little to the smallish side his self and was sort of what the old time cowboys would have called a 'Dandy'. Not saying it in a bad way, he just liked to look good no matter what he might happen to be doing or where he was. I've seen a couple of times when he would be gonna rope a cow out in the pasture and the cow would just plain run off and leave him. I wondered if the old jug headed horse he rode could even catch a cow. I finally figured out he was just afraid the wind would mess up his hair if he rode any faster. Wasn't afraid of nothing. Why he'd bust right in to the heaviest thicket you could imagine to roust out a renegade bull or an ornery old cow. Pretty good hand with a rope, and was as good a worker as I ever seen as long as you could ease him up to it before he recognized what it was.

Now that you can see what kind of fellars Jasper picked to help him round up them cows, I expect you can see that this job ain't gonna be no piece of cake. Oh, I forgot to mention a couple of other fellars that played a part in this little shindig, and one was Ortho Hibden. Now Ortho wasn't no cowboy, just a friend to my Uncle Jasper. I think he hung around Jasper just to see what kind of shenanigan he was gonna pull next. I'll get back to Ortho a little later in the story. The other was Jasper's young son, and he was just like a pet coon getting in the way every time a fellar would try to do something. He rode a little dapple Shetland pony and was a pretty fair hand on a horse to just be six or seven years old. We'll call him Rambo since he didn't figure anything could hurt him or keep him from doing whatever it was he had his mind set to do.

There's not really a good way that I've found to get cattle out of a thicket that they've taken a liking to. We knew there was no way that these cows were gonna let their selves be driven to the lot, so it meant that each and every one of the six cows were, more than likely, gonna have to be roped and dragged into the trailer.

Jasper had it figured out. A couple of us would haze the cows out of the thickets, and the other two would wait in a likely looking clearing and wait for one of the cows to bust out of the brush. Now you got to understand, when I say clearing, I'm talking about a little spot about twenty or thirty feet across with no big trees. Not much room to throw a rope, and not much time to do it. If you spent much time getting ready to throw, it was already too late. With that in mind, Jasper figured him and Mike would try to bust the cows out of the thicket while Billy and I waited to dab a loop on any that might try to cross one of the little clearings. Sure didn't want to take a chance on Mike trying to rope one of them wild ones. He was just as apt to be combing his hair or something when one of them busted out into the clearing, and Jasper's reflexes were too slow to nab one in the little time that he was likely to have if one hit the opening. Ortho would try to pull the truck and trailer as close as he could to where we had one roped so we wouldn't have to drag them any farther than we had to. That was the plan anyway. Ain't it amazing how plans don't always go just like you think they will?

We caught a break right off. There was a little neck of woods that ran out into the pasture just far enough to hide our view of the open field on the south side of the section. We unloaded the horses up by the barn and started down the timber line to where it ended just north of a small pond. When we turned the corner, the first thing we saw was a couple of the cows down by the pond. As soon as they saw us coming, they struck a bee line for the timber as fast as they could hoof it. Mike and Billy had been riding in front of me and Jasper, and they both took off at a high lope to try to beat them cows to the timber. Mike was shaking out a loop as he went, and just before the lead cow hit the timber, he dabbed the prettiest little loop you ever saw right around her horns. When she hit the end of the rope, all the fight went out of her. Mike dragged her back out into the opening a little ways while Ortho maneuvered the trailer up close. Billy was nowhere in sight though we could hear the brush popping just around the corner of the timber. Jasper got another loop on the cow and dragged her up into the trailer. One down and five to go. About then, Billy came around the corner of the timber with the second cow in tow. This was gonna be easy, looked like to me. We hadn't been there fifteen minutes and had already managed to catch two of the six cows. Wasn't long until I realized my celebration was just a little bit premature.

We eased on down the edge of the brush being as quiet as we could be. When we had ridden all the way down to the section line fence without seeing another cow, we knew we were gonna have to hit the brush. Jasper had figured out a way we could keep in touch with each other. Weren't no cell phones back then. If he or Mike happened to spot one of the cows and managed to get her on the run, they would holler to let me and Billy know where she was. With a little luck, we would be able to get ahead of her and be waiting in an opening when she busted out of the timber. If we were lucky enough to rope one, we would give the same holler. Sure enough, before long, I heard Jasper let out a whoop. Looked like Billy was a lot closer than I was, so he took off through the brush in the general direction he figured the cow was headed. Before long, I heard him holler and headed his way. He had a cow roped alright, but she was trying to fight his horse, and there didn't appear to be any way to get the truck and trailer through the brush to where he was. After about three tries, I managed to get a loop around a back foot and we were able to keep her between us that way.

When Jasper and Mike got there, they began to look for the best way to try to get her to a spot that Ortho could reach with the trailer. Jasper finally had to get the axe out of the truck and cut down a half dozen of the smaller trees to make a way for us to get her out to where Ortho was waiting with the trailer. By the time we got that one loaded, all four of us had a fair amount of hide missing where the brush had rubbed it off. Three down and three to go.

We managed to catch two more cows the same way and by mid-afternoon, had all but one old skinny brown and white cow in the trailer. We had seen her a few times during the day, but hadn't been able to get close to her. She was as wild as a March Hare. Jasper figured it was time for a break. The rest of us lay around in the shade while Ortho ran into Reagan to get us some hamburgers at Hazel Smith's Café.

"How you figure were gonna get that old heifer out of the brush?" Jasper asked. Well now, I had been giving some serious thought to that very thing while we sat there waiting on the hamburgers. Seemed to me like, if that old biddy wanted to stay in the timber so bad, then there might just be some way we could use that against her. I figured she would be watching for the horses, and would ease off in the other direction every time she spotted them coming. There was only about eighty acres or so of brush on the whole place, but it ran along the section line by the road for more than half a mile and was about four hundred yards wide.

"Why don't we try this," I said. "Why don't a couple of us head into the timber on this end on foot, while the other two ride all the way to the other end and start back through the timber toward us, on horseback. She's bound to try to stay in front of the horses and may not be paying much attention to where she's going. Might just walk right past one of the guys on foot if we play our cards right and stay hid as much as we can."

When nobody offered a better plan, Jasper figured we might as well give it a try. About then Ortho showed back up with the grub.

Walking through the brush, and trying to be quiet, wasn't as easy as it had sounded when I first mentioned it. A belly full of hamburgers and French fries didn't help much either. The loop I had ready in case I needed it seemed to catch on every rock and protruding limb I came to. I couldn't see Billy, but I knew he was off to my left somewhere. Really couldn't see very far in the thick brush anyway. Finally, I came to a fair sized opening and decided I would just hunker down behind a big red oak tree and rest a minute. Might be as good a place as any to just wait awhile anyway, I figured. I hadn't heard or seen a thing of Jasper or Mike, and as I sat there with my back to that big oak tree, I began to get sleepy. I would nod off for a second, and then jerk my head up and look around. Finally, the warm sun shining down through the leaves, and the belly full of hamburgers, got the best of me and I just fell asleep with my back to the tree and my chin on my chest.

I wouldn't have thought a thousand pound cow could get around in all that brush, with all the dead leaves on the ground without making enough racket to raise the dead, but when I opened my eyes, there she was, not ten feet from me, just looking me right in the eye. I think it must have took her by surprise when she saw me sitting there instead of on a horse, but by the time I had gotten my wits about me, she pawed the ground a time or two and headed right for me.

Holy Moses!! Looked like I was about to buy the farm!

I made it up off the ground and behind the tree just as her right horn brushed the right back pocket on my wranglers. Then around the tree we went, her a bawling, and slinging snot, and me trying to fight her off with the rope I had managed to hang on to when I started around the tree. To make matters worse, I had lost my glasses somehow in the scuffle, and with the sweat running into my eyes, I couldn't hardly see a thing. I had my left hand in the middle of her face trying to hold her off as we went around and around the tree, and the noose I had in my hand just naturally fell around her neck. When I realized I had her roped, I veered off and took a couple of wraps up short around a post oak tree that stood just a few feet from the big red oak we had been dancing around. Then I leaned back on the end of the rope to keep her yanked up close to the trunk of that post oak. My heart was beating so hard and fast, I thought it was gonna jump out of my mouth. I could hear something coming through the brush, and pretty soon Jasper and Mike both busted into the clearing. Billy wasn't far behind coming from the other direction.

It took a few minutes for me to catch my breath, and even longer to find my glasses under the churned up leaves. Luckily they weren't broken though it took a little straightening to get 'em to where they set right on my face again. My hat was a different story. Looked like that old cow had stepped right in the middle of it more than once, and the brim was hanging loose about three quarters of the way around. I put it on my head anyway because I didn't feel right without a hat.

By the time we snaked that old cow out of the brush to where Ortho was waiting with the trailer, it was getting on to late afternoon. As we unloaded her into a pen by herself back at Jasper's place, the sun was just going down behind a bank of clouds on the western horizon. We had unloaded all the horses in the lot that held a covered shed and all that was left after unsaddling and rubbing them down, was to get them fed. As Billy was lugging a bale of hay from the barn, I began to look around for the five gallon feed bucket we always kept hanging on a post just under the edge of the shed. Ortho and Mike were standing watching Billy with the hay, and Mike was filling the water trough with a garden hose at the same time. Looking around, I could see the feed bucket sitting almost in the exact center of the large pen where we unloaded the old rogue cow. Now how do you suppose the feed bucket got all the way out into the big pen? Wasn't no reason that I could see for it to be out there. I was just beginning to smell a rat when I heard Jasper holler at Ortho.

"Hey Ortho," he said. "Run out there and get that feed bucket sitting there in the big pen so we can feed these horses and get out of here."

Ortho never gave it a thought. He grabbed hold of the top rail and vaulted over into the big pen and started across the open area to get the feed bucket. He was almost to the bucket when he happened to glance toward the shed on the north side of the pen. That old cow had her head down, but her eyes had been following him as he moved across the pen. Ortho stopped dead still in his tracks. He looked at that old cow, and she looked back at him. Then he started to back step real slow like. He had forgotten all about the feed bucket he was supposed to get. Ortho would take a step backward, and the cow would take a step forward like there was an invisible line running between them. Finally, Ortho made up his mind to make a break for the fence. When he turned to run, that old rogue cow bawled and took out after him and she was gaining on him at every jump. I thought for a minute he was gonna make it and be able to vault back over the fence before she got him, but just as his feet left the ground, she caught him in the seat of the britches with her head and literally threw him over the fence. Ortho hit the ground and rolled, then came up with a mouth full of dirt.

Over by the water trough, Jasper was laughing and hee-hawing so hard he could hardly catch his breath. After I saw Ortho get up off the ground, apparently unhurt except for his pride, I couldn't help but join in on the fun. Ortho must have had a good sense of humor, because, in his place, I would have tried to get even with Jasper, but he just grinned that lop sided grin of his and started brushing the dirt off his clothes. Then something really strange happened. The cow had retreated back under the shed again by that time and was standing with her head high just looking at us. Billy climbed over the fence, walked out and got the bucket like he didn't have a care in the world, and all that time, that mean old cow just stood and watched him. As Billy headed off toward the feed room with the feed bucket, Ortho just stood there looking at him and shaking his head. I told you earlier that Billy knew cattle. For some reason, he knew that old cow had had all she wanted by that time and wasn't gonna do a thing when he went in after the bucket. Even so, I'll bet a brand new saddle that all four of us couldn't have gotten Ortho back into that pen with her.

Well, that ends the story of the ***"range delivered"*** cows. Both Ortho and my Uncle Jasper are chasing cows on the "Big Bosses" spread in the sky these days. Maybe all of us will be together up there in the sweet by and by. I can almost see that lop sided grin on Ortho's face as he tells everyone up there about the time the cow helped him over the fence. "I want to hear him tell the story myself one of these days."

The End

The Pup and the Pashofa

In the 1960's, right about where the Mill Creek Post Office is presently located, was just a vacant lot. To the east of the lot, beside the highway, was a building that had housed a variety of business ventures over the years. I remember at least two gas stations at that location, a café, a combination café and pool hall, and a beer joint. When Zebulon Colbert came to town, the building was empty and the vacant lot was overgrown with weeds.

Zeb set up camp in the vacant lot and commenced to shooing horses and breaking colts. Don't know where he came from or exactly when he got there. One day it was just a vacant lot, and the next day there was this old Dodge truck, a two horse trailer that had seen better days, a fair sized tent that looked to be Army surplus, and a menagerie of horses either in the round pen made of rope, or tied around to the various trees that grew around the perimeter of the lot. It never dawned on me at the time, but now I wonder how he got there with all those horses. I'm pretty sure they didn't all fit into that two horse trailer.

The first time I saw old Zeb, he was stirring a batch of pashofa in a big black pot over a wood fire next to the old, broken up sidewalk that ran down to Emory Sewell's Station. I know there are several variations of the pashofa recipe, but as best I can remember old Zeb used hominy corn and pork, either cut up pork chops or crumbled up bacon. Some folks also throw in a handful or two of pecans but I don't recall Zeb ever doing that. Nothing could fling a craving on Zeb like pashofa could. He was purely fond of it. That liking for pashofa played a big part in the story I'm fixin to tell.

I had taken to spending quite a bit of time down at Zeb's place, just watching him work with the young horses with his slow, patient way of moving. I learned a lot about horses from old Zeb in a pretty short span of time. I'd sit and watch him spend half a day in the round pen with a skittish colt, just following the colt around. Never got in a hurry. Never raised his voice. Just that slow walk and that constant low key monotone drawl. It took a while sometimes, but sooner or later, that colt would turn and walk right up to Zeb. As soon as it did, he would rub its ears a little, then get out of the pen. Before long, that colt would be following him around like a dog.

One day while we were just sitting in the shade talking, Zeb allowed as how he thought Mill Creek needed a trade day. Could have it right there on the street in front of his place. Doty's Café was right across the street on the northeast corner, but the rest of that side of the street was clear of buildings as well. A regular dog and mule trade was what it would be. Sounded good to me, but I hadn't really thought anymore about it until I saw the sign in the window of Rowe's Store and Gas Station at Ravia, Oklahoma a couple of weeks later. I was standing there drinking one of them tall sixteen ounce Mr. Colas when

Stud Suttles brought the notice to my attention. Here's how it read.

Dog Trade and Trade Day
Mill Creek, Oklahoma
Last Sunday every month
Just west of the stop light
You'all come.

By noon on the first Mill Creek Trade Day, both sides of the street running west from the stop light were filled with pickup trucks, dogs, mules, and kids. I don't believe any of the kids was for sale or trade, but about everything else was.

Doty's café was doing a landslide business, but both of the grocery stores on Main Street were closed it being Sunday afternoon. I'll bet old man Doty fried up more hamburgers in about six hours that Sunday afternoon then he had fried all week long. Zeb had a big pot of pashofa cooking out by the sidewalk and it was just about ready to move off the fire.

As I made my way down the street, it was quite a sight to see with whole families sitting around talking and laughing, dog and mule trading going full tilt, and kids running everywhere. They had to shut off both ends of the street to traffic to keep folks from getting run over. Friends and neighbors were using the trade day as an opportunity to get together and visit as well as do a little trading.

Down toward the end of the street, on the north side, I spotted Stud Suttles's old truck. He had a gun shy bird dog tied to the tailgate with a cotton rope and that there dog was going crazy. That thing would run and hit the end of that rope, then run under the truck, then up in the truck bed, then do it all over again. I couldn't figure what

Stud thought he was gonna trade a gun shy bird dog for anyway. Looked to me like he was gonna be lucky if the thing didn't kill itself before he could get it traded off.

I had started back up the other side of the street just stopping to shoot the bull with first one then the other, when somebody shot off a shotgun down by Emory Sewells Station. Not once, but three times. That's all it took. That bird dog hit the end of that cotton rope going ninety to nothing, and I could hear the snap all the way across the street when the rope broke. Up the street she went, Stud Suttles right behind her, dodging people and mules 'til she got almost up to Doty's Café, then she angled across the street toward Zeb's place. Just as she rounded an old blue truck parked at the curb, she ran right into a big spotted mule tied to a tree beside the sidewalk. That old mule was just as surprised as she was and commenced to bucking and snortin like all the buggers in Johnston County was after him. That bird dog was howling and jumping, trying to get out of the way of the flailing hooves, and landed right in that big pot of pashofa Zed had moved off the fire not ten minutes earlier.

If you have ever seen any pashofa, then you know that it has a consistency about like oatmeal, at least all I ever saw was that way. When that bird dog came barreling out of that big pot of pashofa, she had the stuff about an inch thick all over her. That scared the mule even more and it finally broke loose and headed up the street scattering kids and women with every jump. There was a man and woman with a passel of kids just loading up in a four door Ford car in front of the café. That bird dog went in the front driver's side window of that Ford, stringing pashofa all the way, then into the back seat with all the kids. All four doors flew open and kids commenced to come out of that thing with pashofa in their hair and ears and all over their clothes from top to bottom. The bird dog was right behind them and barely missed getting ran over by a truck that was coming down the highway. The last time I saw that bird dog, she was rounding the corner of the Post Office and was headed east as fast as she could run stringing pashofa at every jump.

Folks were busy picking up chairs and hunting up missing kids as I started over toward Zeb's place. I was looking around for Stud Suttles and finally spotted his old truck just rounding the corner down by Emory's Station. I expect he was trying to get out of Dodge before somebody remembered who owned the gun shy bird dog.

It was several months before I saw Stud at the dog trade again, and he didn't have a thing with him to trade. He did make it a point to put away several bowls of Zeb's pashofa though as best I can remember. The dog trade didn't last long after that. I happened by Zeb's place a few days later and I couldn't believe what I was seeing. Where just a few days earlier there was a rope corral, horses, trailers and trucks, there was just a vacant lot. The only reminder that Zeb had even been there was a large spot of bare ground where the rope corral had stood. I kicked the dead embers of the cooking fire where many a pot of pashofa had come to life. Funny how folks and events will come into your life and then vanish just as quickly. They make up a small part of what you are and what you will become.

I wonder what ever became of that bird dog. I smile every time that day comes to mind. And I wonder whatever happened to Zebulon Colbert. He had time to teach a young boy about horses and life. I will always remember him for that.

The End

Straight Eight and Crooked Roads

"Hey Pete! Come here a minute will you?"

It was Mr. Harkins hollering at me from the door to the shop building. As I crawled out from under the Ford "N" tractor where I had been loosening the plug to drain the oil, I wondered what was so all fired important it couldn't wait until I got the oil changed in that tractor. After all, it was the last of all the vehicles I had to change the oil in that day.

"I need you to run up to the barn on the hill and get the chain hoist hanging just inside the door," Mr. Harkins said as I walked up to the shop. "I want to raise this riding mower so I can change the blades."

I had gotten half way up the hill when I heard him holler again. Oh boy! What was it now? It was beginning to look like I wasn't gonna get through early like I had planned. I had a date with the future Miss America, and here I was getting jerked all over the place like a yo-yo evey time old man Harkins had a different idea about what he wanted me to do.

"You might need this key," he hollered. I had forgotten that the barn on the hill was always locked. I had never been in that particular barn, but had noticed it was locked a few months earlier when I had happened to venture by it on some errand or other. As I trudged back down the hill to retrieve the key, it seemed as if I could detect a slight grin on Mr. Harkins face. I figured he must be getting some kind of perverse pleasure out of keeping me working late with Miss America waiting for me back in town. As I walked back up the hill with the key, I realized there was no way he could know about my Saturday night plans and probably didn't even know my little future Miss America.

The old lock was rusty and it took some effort to get it to open. When it finally did, I swung the double doors open on squeaking hinges to reveal a dusty assortment of farm equipment, tools, old barrels full of this and that, and right in the middle of the alleyway, a large object covered with an old Army tarp. I spotted the chain hoist hanging just to the right of the door just like Mr. Harkins said I would. I took the hoist down but couldn't take my eyes off the big tarp covered object. It was like it was whispering to me. "Take a peek," it was saying. "Just take a small peek under the tarp to satisfy my curiosity."

I laid the hoist on the ground outside the door and walked over to the tarp. It was really nasty. Covered with dust, bird droppings, and spider webs, it looked like it had been there at least a hundred years. I finally picked up a corner of the tarp and started pulling it up and over the object exposing first a rounded fender and headlight, then a hood as long as a well rope. I couldn't believe what I was seeing. I couldn't determine the color of the vehicle in the gloom of the barn, but I could tell it was some kind of old car. I just stood and looked at the long sloping fender and hood for a couple of minutes and then pulled the tarp back down over the thing.

"Where's the chain hoist?" old man Harkins was asking. What chain hoist, I wondered. Then it hit me and the embarrassment started to set in. I had walked back down the hill, all the time with my mind full of what I had just seen under the tarp and forgot all about the chain hoist. As my face started to turn red, he began to chuckle.

"Let's go get it together," he said.

Sure enough, the chain hoist was lying right where I had left it when I started over to look under the tarp.

"What do you think?" he asked.

"I'll just take this hoist down to the shop and raise the mower for you," I said.

"No, I mean what do you think about the car?"

"You mean that car over there under that tarp?" I asked.

"Only car around here as far as I can see, "he said. "Let's have a look at it."

Well, we rolled that tarp off the car and I got my first good look at the big bad 1947 Buick.

"Go get the tractor and we'll see if we can get this thing out into the daylight", he said.

When we got it out of the barn with me on the tractor pulling and old man Harkins walking alongside the car keeping the steering wheel turned straight, I could see it was green. At least I believed it was green under all the dirt and dust that had managed to find its way under the tarp over the years.

"What is it?" I asked.

"It's a 1947 Buick, straight eight, hydrostatic transmission", he answered. "One problem though. Right front "A" frame is bent. Bent it when I ran off the road in it the last time I drove it. Must have been ten or eleven years ago. Never could find a replacement "A" frame for it, so I just drained the water out of it and parked it here in this barn. I thought I would eventually find a part for it, but it has just sat here all these years."

By then, I had walked all around the thing. Miss America was long gone out of my mind, replaced with what looked just like an Elliot Ness car to me. It was by far the biggest car I had ever seen. The long hood covering the straight eight motor made it look even longer than it was. Just about then, it began to dawn on me that there must be some reason old man Harkins had picked this particular day to pull the old car out of the barn.

"What you planning to do with this thing?" I asked.

"Well now, that presents a problem, don't it?" he answered. "I was thinking some enterprising young feller might figure out a way to get an "A" frame off something to work on this thing. I believe, with a little work, it could be put into running order. Make a kid a nice car was he of a mind to fix it up a little."

By then my mind was racing. I was that young feller he was talking about, I figured. The problem was, how much was he gonna want for this thing. I could work it out if it wasn't too much, but I didn't want to put everything I was likely to earn into it. After all, Miss America was still waiting on me. At least I hoped she was what with me already being late and all.

"How much you expect a young feller might have to have to get this car?" I asked. Old man Harkins just stood there rubbing his chin for what seemed like a full minute.

"Tell you what", he said. "I'll bet you've got a date tonight. I owe you for today and you're gonna work tomorrow. Let's see now. Eight hours today at seventy five cents an hour is six dollars. Another six dollars for tomorrow will make me owing you twelve bucks." He pulled out his wallet and handed me a $5 bill and a $1 bill.

"This is for today", he said. "You work another eight hours tomorrow and the car is yours. That suit you?" The grin on my face was all the answer he needed.

The next day after work my dad met me at the ranch and we started working on the Buick. First, we took the gas tank out from under the right back fender and poured the gas out of it on the ground. It looked like varnish. It took about three tries of pouring gas out of the five gallon can we brought with us into the tank and sloshing it around to get all the old gas out of the tank. When it was clean enough to suit Dad, we put it back on and poured a gallon or so of gas in the nozzle.

Dad had been taking spark plugs out while I was cleaning up the gas tank and had all but one of them lying on the front fender of the car. I took a little wire brush and started cleaning the carbon off the tips. The plugs looked pretty good when I got them all cleaned. Dad couldn't get the back plug out so without a choice in the matter, we left it there.

I took the breather off the carburetor and wiped what dust and grime I could out of the top of the thing. The Buick had an eight volt electrical system and Dad's truck was a six volt. I had never seen an eight volt battery and I knew the one in the Buick was dead as a door nail after sitting in the barn for all those years. Our only hope was that we could jump it off the six volt battery in Dad's truck.

We drained the old oil out of the crankcase and filled it back up with new oil 'til it showed full on the dipstick. After filling the radiator with clean water, there really wasn't much else left to do except to try it.

I opened the door and sat down in the driver's seat.

The hood looked as long as a gym floor sticking out there in front of me. I was looking for the starter when dad poked his head in the window.

"It's on the foot feed", he said. "When you get ready to try it, just push the foot feed all the way to the floorboard."

I got out of the Buick and hooked the jumper cables up and then started the truck and let it idle. I didn't figure it was gonna charge the old eight volt battery any at all, but I was sure hoping it had enough power to turn the straight eight over as long as it had been sitting there.

"I'm gonna pour a little gas in the carburetor," Dad said. "I'll let you know when to try it." When he hollered, I turned the key on and stepped on the gas pedal. That straight eight motor turned over real slow a couple of times and fired right off. It ran for just a few seconds then died.

"Hold on a minute," Dad said as he poured more gas into the carburetor.

"Now try her again."

I hit the foot feed again and the engine sputtered to life just like before. I kept pumping the foot feed and in just a few seconds she was running fine. I revved the motor a little and a big rat's nest came blowing out of the tailpipe. After that, it smoothed right out and started idling. I couldn't believe it had started after all the time sitting in the barn, but it did. While it sat there idling, I walked down to the shop and got the air compressor and pulled it back up to the barn. All the tires aired up just fine but they sure had a lot of weather cracking on the sidewalls.

"You better pour the rest of that gas in the tank before you head out," Dad said. "Take it real easy, that right front wheel is sitting at an angle because of that bent "A" frame."

I eased down the hill toward the shop building, then

down the drive to the county road. When I eased out onto the road and started picking up speed, I couldn't figure out how to change gears. The thing didn't have a clutch that I could see, but the gear shift looked like the one in Dad's truck. I eased off the gas and threw the gear shift up like I was shifting into second and she shifted just like a standard transmission. Same for third when I tried that. Pretty neat, I thought. I ran along about thirty miles an hour all the way to town and pulled into the circle drive at the house. I wanted to drive it more but I knew it had to have some better tires and an "A" frame before I could drive it much. Just the short drive from the ranch to town had just about worn all the tread off the right front tire with it sitting at an angle like it was.

The next week, I bought a set of good used tires from Doc down at the station and put them on the Buick. The next Saturday, dad and I drove around to several salvage yards trying to find an "A" frame. There was none to be found. Wendell Haynes said he doubted if we ever found one. I was sure we would be able to find one after all the years the Buicks had been on the road, but after stopping at all the salvage yards we knew of without any luck, I was fast losing hope.

The next Saturday, I took Dad's truck and drove to Wynnewood and Pauls Valley hunting an "A" frame. I tried all the shops and salvage yards I saw and started home all dejected around four o'clock. When I got to Pope's Salvage on the south side of the highway just west of Sulphur, I pulled in there thinking I'd get a cold bottle of pop. I knew there wasn't any chance Mr. Pope might have what I needed it being a really small salvage yard, so I didn't even ask. I got a bottle of pop out of the machine and took a seat out front on the wooden bench by the door. Mr. Pope was sitting in the old rocker like always. I bet he sat in that chair for at least ten hours a day six days a week.

"You huntin something or just visiting?" he asked.

"Well, I've been huntin something alright, but you ain't got it," I answered. I didn't see any need to waste his time with my story of needing an "A" frame for the Buick.

"Okay," he said, as he leaned back in the old rocker and closed his eyes.

"Never can tell though; I might have just what you need young fellar."

I took a long drink of that coke and leaned back against the building. What the heck, I thought. Might as well ask him about the "A" frame. Didn't look like he was gonna be satisfied until I did.

"I need an right side "A" frame for a 1947 Buick," I said. "I've looked all over and ain't nobody got one. You wouldn't happen to know where I might find one, do you?"

"I've got two out back there," he said. "You'll have to take it off the car yourself though, I'm here by myself today."

"What?" I shouted. "You've got an "A" frame for a 1947 Buick here? I didn't have any idea you'd have an old Buick back there."

"I don't have an old Buick back there," he said. "What I've got is two 1956 Oldsmobiles. If memory serves me correctly, it ought to be a perfect fit."

"Why didn't Mr. Harkins know that?" I asked. "Somebody should have told him an "A" frame off a 1956 Olds would work."

"Two problems with that thinking, son," Old man Pope said. "First off, 1956 Oldsmobiles hadn't even been made when he was hunting an "A" frame in 1949 or 1950. Secondly, how many other salvage yards have you been to that didn't even know it now?"

I could see his point. I finished my coke and walked around back and found a black and white 1956 Olds with the top and rear end caved in just sitting there by itself in the salvage yard. It took me a few minutes, but I finally got the old diesel fork lift started and I stuck the forks under the Olds and turned it over so I could get to the "A" frame. Then it hit me. I didn't even have a tool box with me. Luckily, Mr. Pope loaned me the tools and I took it off and put it in the back of the truck.

"What do I owe you, Mr. Pope?" I asked.

"Oh, I reckon three dollars ought to be about right," he answered.

I gladly paid him the three dollars and headed for Mill Creek USA. With Dad helping, I had that "A" frame on the Buick by bedtime that night. Mr. Pope was right, it fit right on like it was made for it. I could hardly wait to try it out the next day.

I worked on that old Buick every chance I got and before long she was looking almost like new. One day Ed Hensen and some of the guys were with me and we were driving the Buick out east of town. I still didn't have it running like I wanted it to run. We were going down Rawls Hill and I let the hammer down. That old Buick started to shudder and then the loudest bang you ever heard. Another big rat's nest came blowing out of the tailpipe and she smoothed out and went to running just the way she was supposed to run.

Finally, the time came to take her to the big town, so Ed Hensen, Davey, and I loaded up on a Saturday night and headed to Sulphur to the drive in movie. I had put a new six volt battery in it and it being an eight volt system, the lights were not as bright as they should be, but she started up every time. We got a lot of attention when we stopped at Doves Drive Inn for hamburgers before the show. There were also a lot of kids that stopped by where we were parked at the show and looked over the Buick.

When we got to the "Y" and headed south toward Mill Creek after the show, Davey allowed as how I ought to see how fast she would go. I got her up to about eighty and the front end started to shimmy so I slowed back down and we cruised the rest of the way home around fifty. Ed had left his car at my house, so we let Davey off at his house on the highway and then went on to my house. We turned into the drive leading to the house and when we got about half way around the circle drive, the right front wheel fell off the Buick and rolled over and bounced off the side of the house before coming to rest under the sycamore tree in the front yard. Ed and I looked over at each other.

"Holy crap," I said. What if that thing would have come off while we were doing about eighty?"

Ed just sat there. I'm not sure he could even talk at the moment. It was easy to see the problem when we got a flashlight shining on the front axle where the wheel was supposed to be. Those old Buicks didn't have lug nuts like on most cars, the entire lug bolt screwed into the hub. They were notorious for backing out and getting loose. We had lost all the bolts out of the thing. That's what was making it shimmy when we were doing eighty on the highway, I guess. One of the lug bolts was lying beside the hub and we found another one back up the circle drive a little way.

The next Monday, I went to Ravia and bought some lug bolts at the salvage yard and when I got them all tightened up as best I could, Dad spot welded all of them into place on every wheel. I could still bust the weld lose if I needed to get the wheels off, but at least they wouldn't come off on their own anymore.

I drove that old Buick around until 1966 when I graduated out of high school then I sold it to Charley

Goodman for $25.00. He wanted it, and I was leaving town and couldn't take it with me, so I let him have it dirt cheap. I don't know what he ever did with it.

Ed Hensen mentioned that old Buick the last time I talked to him in 2009. It is just a part of the memories I have of growing up, and apparently I am not the only one that remembers it. Those really were the good times. Good friends, old cars, and good memories.

The End

Don't Drive Through the Hay Knucklehead

Mr. Harkins was just about beside himself that spring of 1964. It had rained every few days, and we hadn't been able to get the ground broke up, much less planted for the Sudan hay crop that was needed for the next winters feed. What little land we had got broken up was coming up in clods and it took hour after hour with the harrow to get it in condition to plant. Just about the time the ground would get right, here would come another rain and put us out of business again. When the weather finally decided to clear, I plowed day and night for a week to get the fields ready for the seed drill. With us being a couple of weeks later than normal getting the crop in the ground, I figured we'd be lucky to make 75% of the previous year's crop. Sure enough, the Sudan came up weak looking and spotty in a couple of fields, though the big field north of the house looked about as good as I'd ever seen. The sparse growth in the west field though, was a disappointment and I knew we'd be lucky if we had enough hay to feed that coming winter without having to buy a little to supplement what we had. Mr. Harkins just really didn't ever want to have to buy any hay and knowing he might have to do just that is what put him in a foul mood that entire haying season.

It started on a Saturday morning. Bill Suggs and I had gotten an early start and by a little after sun-up I was down in the north field getting ready to start cutting hay. I had the sickle mower all hooked up on the back of the little Ford 9N tractor and was ready to go. Bill was up in the orchard with the other tractor and was discing around the fruit trees. Later, he would swap the disc for a hay rake and start win-rowing the hay for baling.

There was a little creek along the north side of the field I was planning to cut. It was just a little creek, about eight or ten feet wide at the top of the banks but it was about twelve feet deep in places and the sides just went down in sort of a "V" shape. The bottom of the creek was only a couple of feet wide. It was dry much of the time, but in the wet weather, there would be a trickle of water for a few days. The hay grew right up to the edge of the creek bank all the way down the north side of the field.

Now there is a right way to cut hay and a wrong way to cut hay. Then there was the Lloyd Harkins way. His way usually matched the right way, but not always. He was a stickler about how he wanted his hay cut. You had to cut the hay in a clockwise manner around the field. That way, the sickle was always in the hay and the tractor was running in the hay that was already cut, not the standing hay, if you catch my drift. He didn't believe in driving the tractor in the standing hay for any reason any time.

I knew we needed all that hay we could possibly get, so I decided to start on the side nearest the creek. I planned on making a starter cut down the edge of the creek bank, running counter clockwise with the sickle on the creek side. That way I figured, I could cut all the hay right up to the creek bank without wasting any. If I had started the other direction, I was going to waste all the hay for a tractor width along the creek bank. Besides that, I didn't really want to drive the tractor any closer to the bank of the creek bank than I had to for fear the bank would cave in. I could see a few spots along where the bank had started to cave in a little already. I figured I would make that starter cut, then turn around and cut the next swath in a clockwise direction. I hadn't gotten fifty feet up the creek when I heard the pickup horn honking. I looked up to see Mr. Harkins headed my way in the old black 1950 model Chevy truck. He was blowing the horn and had his head sticking out of the window and hollering for me to stop.

"Hold up there," he hollered. "You're going to wrong direction. I thought I told you to never cut hay in a counter clockwise direction."

I stopped the tractor as he came striding up to me. His face was as red as a beet, and his breath was coming in short gasps he was so mad.

"I was just gonna cut one swath this direction so I could get the hay next to the creek bank," I replied.

"There is no excuse to cut hay the wrong way," he said. "Get off that tractor and let me show you how to get that hay next to the creek."

I got down from the tractor and stepped out of the way as he backed all the way back to where I had started. Then he drove all the way around the field to the other end of the creek and started to cut back toward me. He was running along with the tractor wheels right on the edge of the creek bank to get as much of the hay as he could with the sickle. I started down toward him just as the bank gave way under his rear tire on the creek side. As I watched in horror, the tractor slid slowly, then faster as gravity took over, down into the creek, turning onto its back as it fell. I ran as hard as I could and baled off into the creek right in front of where the tractor lay on its top in the "V" made by the sloping sides of the creek banks. I could see an overall covered leg sticking out from under the tractor but that's all. I scurried up the bank and down into the creek again, this time behind the tractor. Now I could see his chest and upper body sticking out from under the tractor.

"You okay Mr. Harkins?" I asked. I could see he had his eyes open and his chest was moving like he was breathing.

"I can't get out from under this thing," he said. "It's got me trapped."

"Are you hurt bad?' I asked.

"Naw, I'm not hurt hardly at all," he said. "At least I'm not hurting anywhere. Just can't get out from under here. That oil is pretty hot though."

I looked down to where the oil from the tractor was dripping onto his other leg and gasoline was dripping onto his chest just about where his rib cage started.

I took off my shirt and put it under the oil drip. I didn't figure it would help much, but it was all I had.

"Just hold on," I said. "I'll be right back." I ran up to where he parked the pickup and headed for the orchard as fast as that old truck would go. I cut right across the hay field not caring how much hay I knocked down. Luckily, I spotted Bill Suggs just as I turned in the orchard gate.

I filled him in on what had happened as quickly as I could.

"You head down to the hay field," I said. "I'm going by the shop and get a chain."

By the time I got back down to the hay field, Bill had his tractor backed up to the creek bank and was down in the bottom of the creek with Mr. Harkins. I threw one end of the chain down to him and he hooked it onto the back axle of the tractor.

"I'm gonna try to lift it up off him enough so you can drag him out," I said. "Holler when you get him free." I hooked the other end of the chain into the draw bar of the tractor and pulled ahead until all the slack was out of the chain.

"Okay, easy does it," I said to myself. I eased out on the clutch as I pushed the throttle forward. I could feel the weight of the other tractor as I inched slowly forward. When the back wheels started to lose traction, I shut it down and stood on the brake.

"Can you get him out?' I hollered down to Bill.

"Got 'im," he hollered back. I hustled down the creek bank and helped him drag Mr. Harkins up out of the creek. We took him directly to the truck, and against his orders, I drove him to the emergency room at the Sulphur hospital. They bandaged up a cut on his right hand and put cream on the burns on his leg and chest and then wrapped his upper torso all the way around with gauze. He complained all the time that there wasn't anything wrong with him. Finally, they declared him well enough to go home, so I loaded him back in the truck and headed back down 177 highway. He never said a word all the way back to the ranch. When we got adjacent to the hay field, he looked over to where the pickup tracks were clearly visible all the way across the hay field. "

"Looks like some knucklehead drove right across the field through the hay," he said. I just shook my head and drove on up to the house and he got out of the truck. I started walking back down to the hay field to start cutting hay again. I hadn't gotten very far when he hollered at me.

"Might better cut that hay right next to the creek in a counter clockwise direction," he said. I could see a slight lifting at the corner of his mouth like he was trying to keep from smiling. I figured that was as close to a "thank you" as I was likely to get.

It took the rest of the morning to get the tractor out of the creek, new oil and gas in it and the fender straightened so it wouldn't drag on the back tire. After a short lunch break, I was back to cutting hay. Around 2:00 o'clock in the afternoon, I looked up to see the old black truck coming slowly around the field toward me. I stopped and waited while Mr. Harkins got gingerly out of the truck and walked over to where I was just sitting on the tractor waiting on him.

"I know its Saturday night and all," he said. "You probably got a date. We've sure wasted a lot of time today though. You better stay 'til you get this field cut, that way Bill can get started raking first thing tomorrow."

"Yes sir," I said.

He didn't say anything else, just got in the truck and drove off. It took me until well after 8:00 o'clock to get the field cut. Missed a Saturday night out and everything. He didn't have to come and tell me to stay 'til I got the field cut, I was going to anyway.

He never mentioned the incident to me after that day. He did make it a point to tell me the next day that I should never drive across standing hay. He couldn't quite keep the smile from showing that time though.

"Yes sir," I replied. I was grinning to as I went to hook up the baler. To this day though, it really does bother me to see where somebody drove through a hay field. Every time I see it, I wonder to myself; "now what knucklehead do you suppose did that?"

The End

and

California ~~or~~ Bust

The lazy, hazy, crazy days of summer were just around the corner. It was the last week of school 1963 and I was really looking forward to a break before hay hauling started. I was planning to just lie around and relax until Charlie McCause started hauling hay around the Mill Creek area. It was usually around the middle of June before the haying got started good, so I would have a couple of weeks to just lay around. I was just thirteen years old that summer, but was strong for my age. It would be my first year to haul hay with a regular crew.

I was just relaxing on the couch with a book in my lap dividing my attention between the book and a baseball game on the television. Mom and Dad were in the kitchen having a cup of coffee and talking. The word ***California*** caught my attention.

"What's that about California," I asked joining them in the kitchen.

"Well, hello 'Big Ears'," Mom said. "I thought you were watching the ballgame."

"I was 'til I heard you say something about California. "What were you talking about anyhow?'

"Well, your Uncle Gene has been transferred to Riverside California," Dad replied. Tinker Field is cutting down their workforce and some of the men are getting a chance to transfer to California. It's a choice of that or losing their jobs. Your uncle asked if I would pull a UHAUL trailer out there when they went. We were just thinking we might make a vacation out of it and all go."

"When we going?'

"Just keep your shirt on" Mom replied. "We haven't even decided if we are going yet. We'd all have to ride in the truck. Might not be too comfortable riding that way all the way to California."

"We could fix up some kind of a cover and us kids could ride in the back," I said.

"That might work if we don't have to haul things back there," Dad said. "I think I can borrow a camper top to put on it if we want to."

"Sounds like you guys have already decided we're going," Mom said. "I might just as well start packing."

It was the Saturday before Memorial Day and we were busy loading the Wheaton family possessions into the big UHAUL truck. In went the furniture, the clothing, mattresses, and all the many boxes of cooking utensils, and breakable items. The lawn mowers, bicycles, and outside stuff, along with the washing machine went into the trailer my dad was going to pull behind his pickup. The last thing that got loaded onto the trailer was my cousin Daniel's Harley Davidson motorcycle. When everything was loaded and secured, we all started down the street to the Dairy Queen for supper. With everything loaded either in the truck or on the trailer, there was no way to cook anything, so the Dairy Queen it was.

The downsizing at Tinker had touched a lot of folks and one of the ones it touched besides my uncle Gene was a neighbor just down the road and across the street. Unlike my uncle, he had decided to retire and move back east where his wife's folks lived. The short of it was, they were selling everything they didn't want to move and one of the things that was for sale was a motorcycle. And quite a motorcycle it was. I noticed it sitting there in the driveway with the "For Sale" sign on it when we were a block away. When we got even with the house, Daniel and I walked over to look it over. What a beaut! Black and silver with chrome everywhere. The silver badge on the side of the gas tank said "Zundapp." I had never heard of that brand of motorcycle, but it sure was a pretty thing.

We hurried to catch up with our folks at the Dairy Queen and all the time we were eating, I just couldn't get that motorcycle out of my mind. My dad had said he would help me buy a motorcycle that summer, but I don't think the big Zundapp was what he had in mind. Nevertheless, when everyone finished eating and we were headed back up the street, I just casually mentioned it to my dad. He agreed to stop and look at it on the way back to the house.

"Son, that motorcycle is just too big for you to handle," he said. "I'll bet he wants a pretty penny for it too."

My hopes were fast disappearing when the man came out of the house and walked out to where we were looking at the bike. "You boys interested in my bike?" he asked.

"Naw, guess not," my dad replied. "It's too big for the boy here. We've been looking for something for him and he wanted me to take a look at this bike, but it doesn't look to be something we could use."

"You might be surprised, "the man said. "By the way,

I'm Jack Anderson. That bike is balanced real well." He took a good look at me like he was sizing me up. "That boy looks to me to be plenty big enough for this bike. Here, just sit on her and see how she feels."

I looked over at Dad but he just shrugged his shoulders, so I threw a leg over the bike and pulled it up off the kickstand. It sat real good, easy to balance and all just like Mr. Anderson said.

"You rode a bike any son," he asked.

"Well, I've ridden a Cushman a lot," I said. "I've never ridden a motorcycle like this before."

"Why don't you give her a try just down the road a little ways," he said looking over at my dad. "I don't think you'll have a bit of trouble handling her."

"I'm not going to be responsible if he wrecks that thing," my dad said. "If you don't mind him riding it under those circumstances, I don't reckon I care."

Mr. Anderson showed me how to turn the gas on and how to choke it so it would start. He moved the shifter through all the gears so I could see how it worked as well. I gave it a couple of kicks and she started right up. After the engine slowed to an idle, I eased out on the clutch and rolled out of the driveway into the road. It took a couple of times for me to get used to how it shifted, but by the time I had ridden to the Dairy Queen and turned around, I was running through the gears like a pro. It didn't seem any harder to ride than the Cushman, though it was easy to see it had a lot more power. I pulled back into the driveway and shut the motor off. The grin on my face answered my dad's question before he had a chance to ask it.

"This is a nice bike," I said. "It's not hard to ride at all. What you asking for it Mr. Anderson?"

I knew in my heart that the asking price was going to be more than my dad was willing to pay, but I had to hear it anyway.

"Well, let's talk about that," Mr. Anderson said. "This bike is a 1958 Zundapp KS601. Real good German made bike. It's easy to ride and will go forever if you take care of it. You can see it hasn't been ridden hardly at all. I just don't want to have to haul it all the way to Pennsylvania. I'm leaving tomorrow and I don't want to have to find a way to haul the bike. I'd make you a real good deal on it today if you want it."

I looked over at my dad and waited for him to say something. When it became apparent that he wasn't going to, I decided I had better take the initiative here or we were going to stand there all day just looking at the bike.

"What you got to have for the bike Mr. Anderson?" I asked.

"Well, let me see now," he said. "That bike is worth $800 if it's worth a dime. I thought I might take as little as $500 for it much as I'd hate too."

I knew my dad wasn't gonna pay $500 for a motorcycle so when he said that was the lowest he was gonna take, I lost all hope of having that particular motorcycle.

"Thanks a lot for letting me ride the bike Mr. Anderson," I said. "It sure is a nice bike, but it's just a lot more bike than I ever intended to try to find. I'm just going to have to find something a little closer to what I can afford."

I knew I was gonna have to help pay for whatever motorcycle I ended up with and I didn't see any way I was gonna be able to come up with even half of $500. I turned to leave, not wanting to prolong the agony of looking at that bike knowing there was no way I was gonna have a bike like it. We got back up to the house and were kind of at a loss as to what to do. Everything was loaded as far as we could tell, and there was really not anywhere we could sleep or anything to sleep on. It was still a couple of hours 'til dark, so after talking about it awhile, my dad and Uncle Gene decided we might as well go ahead and get on the road. With two drivers in each vehicle, they could spell each other as they needed to.

We had just about all got loaded up when here came Mr. Anderson up the driveway to the house.

"Hold up," he hollered. "I just can't let you 'all get away without that motorcycle. I don't have any way of hauling the thing without renting a trailer, and I don't even have a trailer hookup on my car. I'm gonna let you have the bike for $300 just to save having to figure out a way of hauling it."

"Make it $250 and you've got a deal," my dad said. I thought Mr. Anderson was gonna choke, but finally he just nodded his head. I couldn't believe it. I was gonna be the owner of the best looking and best riding motorcycle I had ever seen! We started back down the hill to Mr. Anderson's house. Mom was writing out the check, but you could tell she wasn't too happy about it.

"I've got almost a hundred dollars at home," I said. I'll pay for the rest of it with my hay hauling money as soon as we get back from California. It won't take me much more than a month to make the other $150. It was going to be my first summer working on a hay crew with Charlie McCause. I had taken $20 out of my savings to spend on vacation and I had it tucked down deep in my billfold so I wouldn't lose it. The only other money I had on me was about eighty five cents in change in my left front pants pocket.

I'll give it to Mr. Anderson. After the shock of selling the bike so cheap wore off, he was all excited about showing me everything about it. How to check the oil and where to put in the gas. When he got the gas cap off he grabbed a gas can out of the back of his car and topped the tank off so I would have a full tank to start with. I looked back up toward the house and saw Daniel unloading his Harley off the trailer.

"Can we ride along behind 'til it gets dark?" I asked my dad. "Daniel already has his bike unloaded and everything."

Dad looked over at Gene and he nodded his head. "I reckon you can if you'll stay close behind and not get lost. There's not much traffic the way we're going to go, so just keep up. We'll stop and load the bikes before it gets dark."

We fell in behind them when they turned onto the street leading down to the highway. I gave Mr. Anderson a wave as we went by. I could see him standing there watching us until we went around a curve in the road. I knew he hated to let the bike go, but since he did, I was just glad it was me that got it.

Everything was going along fine and I was just enjoying the ride. After we had gone five or six miles, we had to make a detour because of a wreck. The policeman motioned us on through and pointed out the road we needed to take to get around the wreck. The problem was, we were now headed right into the rush hour traffic. We caught the first couple of lights green, but as luck would have it, the next light changed to red before we could follow the trucks through. By the time the light changed back to green and we could go, they were plumb out of sight in the traffic. We hurried as fast as we could through all the cars, but when we came to the next light, they were still not in sight. When we came to the main highway and needed to make a decision on which way to turn, I knew we'd lost them.

I figured to see the trucks waiting for us when we got to the highway, but they were nowhere in sight. We didn't know it at the time, but they had turned a mile or so back up the road and took the cut-a-cross to the highway. They were waiting for us alright, but they were two miles west of where we were sitting on the bikes wondering what to do. It was then that Daniel noticed the service station across the highway. We crossed the highway on the green light and pulled in to the station.

"What are we gonna do?" I asked. I was beginning to get a little panicked. I couldn't imagine them just running off and leaving us, but they sure weren't here waiting for us like I thought they'd be.

"We're gonna get us a map," Daniel replied. "We'll just head to California and we'll surely catch up with them sooner or later."

We walked into the service station and sure enough there was the little rack full of complimentary maps sitting in the window. We took an Oklahoma map and just for good luck, I grabbed a California map as well. Neither of us stopped to think that there would be other states like New Mexico and Arizona to cross before we got to California. I didn't figure to still be riding when we got out of Oklahoma anyway. We'd surely catch up to them in an hour or two, I figured.

Two miles west of our position at the service station, my mom was about to go berserk when she realized we weren't behind them. When they got to the highway, they waited fifteen minutes or so and then started backtracking to see if they could find us. It was all a matter of timing. If they had stayed where they were, we would have spotted them when we went by on the highway. We went right by where they had stopped to wait, but by that time they had already started backtracking looking for us. On the other hand, if we had stayed at the service station, they would have found us, since they decided that we must have missed the short cut turnoff. As it was, we missed each other by just a matter of a minute or two and we were now ahead of them and getting farther ahead with every passing minute.

My mom was all for just calling the cops and telling

them the whole story. Maybe they could find us, she figured. After a lengthy discussion, my dad and my Uncle Gene decided the best thing to do was just to keep going and hope we caught up. They would ease along and we'd catch up once we got on the right road. Daniel and I were thinking just the opposite. We figured they were already ahead of us and we were riding as fast as the speed limit would allow trying to catch up with them. It was just getting dusky dark when we left the lights of Oklahoma City behind us and headed west on highway 66 toward California.

We rode steadily until we got to El Reno and stopped to get gas. Right across the street from the gas station was the Squaw Drive In, so when we had gassed up, we drove across the highway and ordered hamburgers, fries and a big vanilla malt each. Money wasn't an issue for us right then and we never gave it a thought. I still had almost nineteen dollars after gassing up and paying for my part of the supper. I remember the gas being 19 cents a gallon and thought that was really high. We sat on a picnic table under a little awning and ate our supper. After we finished, we just sat there for a while not really knowing what to do next.

Looking at the clock on the wall inside the Squaw Drive In, it was just past ten o'clock. The drive in looked to be closing, so we finished up and walked back out to where we had left the bikes.

"What you figure we ought to do now," Daniel asked. "You want to keep on going or find a place to get a little sleep?"

"Why don't we ride for a while?" I said. "Maybe we'll find a good place pretty soon to stop and get a little sleep. We turned onto the highway and headed west. Full bellies and full tanks of gas, we were set to make some miles. We hadn't ridden more than ten miles or so before I began to get sleepy. It had been a long day. We had gotten up early and spent the whole day loading the truck and trailer and I was just plain tired.

We were almost past the little picnic spot before I noticed it in the dark. I slowed down and pulled over to the side of the road and Daniel turned around and rode back to where I was.

"What's wrong?" he asked.

"Nothing," I replied. "I saw a little park back down the road a ways. Might be a good place to get a little rest." We drove back to the picnic area and there were two cement picnic tables and a good place to park the bikes away from the road. We decided to give it a try. When I first stretched out on the top of the picnic table, I thought there would be no way I was ever gonna be able to go to sleep lying on the cement. I lay there just thinking about what kind of a pickle we had gotten ourselves into. I had no idea where my mom and dad were and they had to be worried sick about me, I knew. At least my mom would be. I wondered if she was lying awake somewhere wondering the same thing I was wondering.

Daniel shook me awake just as the sun was coming up. I couldn't believe I had slept over six hours. After a trip into the bushes behind the little park to take care of my morning business, I was ready for some breakfast. What I really wanted was a bath. The prospects of that were pretty poor for the foreseeable future I figured.

We started out just as the fog was lifting from the low places. We had already decided we would stop at the first place we came to that looked like it might have something to eat.

Two hundred fifty miles to the west, our families were sitting down to breakfast in a little diner at the side of the road in Amarillo, Texas. They had driven all night and had finally stopped to take a break. They had passed the little park where we were sleeping five hours earlier. In the dark, they had missed seeing the bikes parked next to the picnic table. The discussion centered around Daniel and me and where we were likely to be. They had come to the conclusion that we had decided to just go to Mill Creek since we surely wouldn't take out for California on our own. Mom was standing at the pay phone trying to get a call through to my Aunt Em back home.

"Hello," Em's voice on the phone was heavy with sleep. "Who is this?" She asked.

"This is your sister," Mom answered. "Have you seen Pete and Daniel? They may be over at the house. Would you check when you get up and see if they are? I'll call you back the next time we stop."

"Why would they be here anyway?" Em asked. I though you guys were headed for California."

Mom explained the whole thing to her and Em allowed as how she'd go right over and check. "What's the number there and I'll call you back in ten minutes," she said. Mom gave her the number from the pay phone and walked back to the table where everyone else was eating.

"She's gonna call back after she checks the house," she said. "I'll just wait by the phone 'til she calls."

"You sit right down here and eat," my dad said. "We can hear the phone from here when it rings." Mom sat down and picked at her food and when the phone rang, she was there and had it picked up on the second ring.

"What's that you say? They're not over there? Are you sure?"

"Of course I'm sure," Em replied. "I'll keep an eye out for them in case they show up. I expect they're all right though. I wouldn't worry too much about them two boys. They're big enough to take care of their selves."

Mom hung up the phone and walked slowly back to the table. Nobody said a word. They could see from her looks that we weren't in Mill Creek. Everybody finished up eating and in five minutes they were on the road again headed west. Before they even got out of town, they had the first bad luck of the trip. Someone had lost a two by four out of a truck and it was lying smack in the middle of the road just over the top of a hill. There was no avoiding it when Gene topped the hill in the UHAUL truck. The nail sticking up in the board was just in the perfect spot to penetrate the outside dual on the passenger side. A mile down the road, he pulled over to see what was causing the truck to pull to the right. The tire was almost flat by that time.

They could see a service station not a half mile down the highway, so they eased the truck along on the shoulder and pulled into the station. Luckily, there was a man on duty fixing flats and he said he's get right on it.

"You'll have to pull it around to the garage behind the station," he said. "I don't have a jack up here big enough to raise that truck up. Just pull inside the garage and I'll get right on it. Gene drove the truck into the garage and my dad pulled the pickup and trailer around behind the station as well to get them out of the driveway. That move caused me and Daniel to miss them again. We had been riding for several hours by that time, and we rode by the station just as the attendant was putting the wheel back on the truck. We never saw them as we rode by with the truck in the garage and the pickup and trailer parked behind the station. We would have one more chance just a few minutes later, but that chance would go by as well.

We stopped before we got out of Amarillo to grab a late lunch and gas up for the third time that day. By then, it was becoming apparent to me that we were gonna have to watch how we spent our money if we were gonna get all the way to California on what cash we had. After we filled up both tanks with gas, we took an inventory of our cash. I had seventeen dollars and two cents and Daniel had almost twelve dollars. Twenty-nine dollars to our name and still close to fifteen hundred miles to go. I walked back into the station and borrowed a pencil and a page out of a Big Chief tablet to do a little figuring.

"Let's see now," I said. "If we get forty miles to a gallon of gas for each bike, we'll use a gallon every twenty miles. That's five gallons every hundred miles. Fifteen hundred miles times five gallons is seventy-five gallons of gas we were likely to use. At 20 cents a gallon, we were gonna spend $15 of our $29 for gas, and that's if gas wasn't any higher as we went along. I was afraid it might be as we got closer to California. Looked like we might not have but ten bucks to eat on the rest of the way. Still, $10 would buy a lot of food if we were careful with it.

We found just what we were looking for about two miles down the road, a place selling six hamburgers for a dollar. It was a block off the highway and we were standing in line at the walk up window when our folks drove by on the main road a block away. It would be the last chance we had to hook back up with them 'til late the next day. By then we were both so sick, I doubt if we would have recognized them if we saw them.

"You reckon these hamburgers are still good?" I asked Daniel. We had just woke up from about a three hour nap on the side of the road by a little stream somewhere in New Mexico. We had eaten four of the six hamburgers we bought the day before and the other two had ridden in Daniel's saddlebag since.

"I don't see why not," Daniel replied. "I'm hungry enough to eat a bear." he handed me one of the hamburgers and we sat down at the little picnic table to eat. When we were finished, I walked down to the stream and, cupping my hand, drank three or four good handfuls of water. I still think that was what kept me from getting as sick as Daniel got from eating the rotten hamburgers.

We hadn't ridden more than three miles when my stomach begin to turn flip flops. I pulled off the road just in time to get down on my hands and knees and upchuck the hamburger and the water I had just finished not ten minutes earlier. When I finished, I felt a little better but I could tell I was getting a fever and the sweat was running off my chin and dripping onto the ground. Daniel didn't seem any the worse for wear, so I got back on my bike and we headed out again. Five minutes later, we were stopped on the side of the road again, but this time it was Daniel who was throwing up his shoelaces.

We stayed under the shade of a big cottonwood tree for about three hours before we both felt well enough to start out again. I figured if there was something good gonna come out of this thing, it was the fact that neither of us wanted to have anything to do with food. We were gonna save a lot of money not having to eat, I figured.

I craved a Coke. A big tall cold bottle of Coca Cola was what I wanted and needed. We pulled into a little wide spot in the road place called Glenrio, not very far east of Santa Rosa, New Mexico. The little store there didn't have much, but they had an old pop box and it was full of cold pops. I stuck the required fifteen cents in the slot and pulled out a big cold bottle of Coke. Man was that thing good. There was a Mexican running the little store and if he weighed an ounce, he weighed 350 pounds. Most of it hung over his belt and the dirty t-shirt he wore lacked about three inches covering all the bulge.

"Where you boys headed?" he asked in hesitant English.

"You all don't look like you been faring to good, appears like to me."

There was something about that guy that didn't sit well with me. I couldn't put my finger on anything out of the ordinary, but there was something not quite right here. I had seen him go into the back of the store right after we rode up. I didn't think too much about it at the time, but the longer we hung around the place, the more uneasy I became.

"Let's get out of here," I told Daniel the first chance I got where the big Mex couldn't hear what I was saying.

"What's the hurry?" he replied. "Let's rest up as little before we hit the road again."

"Let's go," I said again. I turned and walked out to where we had parked the bikes and kicked the big Zundapp off on the first try. By the time Daniel had gotten the Harley moving, the big Mexican was running toward us hollering at the top of his lungs. Just as we turned onto the highway, an old pickup truck without a muffler careened around the corner and slid into the parking lot of the little store. There were three Mexicans in the front seat and when they spotted us getting away, they spun the old truck around and took out after us. It was my first indication of how much get up and go was in the big engine I was astraddle of. Daniel blew by me with all the horses in that Harley 74 screaming for more distance. I let the hammer down and was steadily gaining on him. I chanced a look over my shoulder and I could see the old truck was falling back every second.

I caught him about a quarter of a mile farther down the road and we ran side by side for about three more miles with the white lines a blur under our wheels. When we pulled into Santa Rosa, my heart had just about gotten back down to where it ought to be in my chest instead of where it had been in my throat for the last few miles. We had been lucky. It was a set up all the way and them Mexicans figured to have easy pickings with a couple of dumb old kids. We were lucky we still had our money much less our skin all in one piece. I doubt they would have really hurt us much, but they would have sure enough taken all our money. I felt a shiver go through my body just thinking of what might have happened.

"How'd you know what they were up to?" Daniel asked.

"I don't know really," I answered. "Something just didn't feel right about that place."

No telling how many kids have lost all their money at that place in just that way. We had stopped in an empty parking lot to let our nerves settle a little and I felt the Coke coming up just in time to run to the edge of the concrete and fall down on my knees in the grass. Daniel was just a few feet away doing the same thing. There was a line of semi-trucks in the lane next to the parking lot and had our view of the highway blocked. The UHAUL truck and my dad's pickup and trailer passed by in the inside lane just as the light changed to green. They had passed by within 30 feet of us and never saw us there in the grass by the side of the road. If they had come by two minutes earlier, the trucks would not have been there blocking the view and the saga would have been over. It was not to be.

As we headed out of Santa Rosa, the setting sun was like a beacon showing the way to California. We rode toward it until it fell behind the mountain range west of Albuquerque. Not sleepy, and certainly not wanting anything to eat, we gassed up in Albuquerque and kept riding until we were both so tired we could barely keep the bikes upright. We stopped and filled up with gas at a little station just short of the Arizona state line. I walked down the road a ways to get the blood circulating in my legs again and when I got back to the bikes, Daniel was ready to go. We crossed over into Arizona around 11:00 o'clock and after riding another hour or so, we could see the lights of Holbrook That's when we caught the second piece of good luck we'd had since leaving Oklahoma City.

We pulled in to the little motel and stopped beside a cement block fence that ran almost back down to the highway. The sign on top of the motel flashed off and on and though a couple of bulbs were burned out, it was easy to see we had pulled into the parking lot of the Dewdrop Inn. I didn't see the old man sitting in the chair in front of the motel office until he struck a match to light a cigar. When he had the cigar going good, he got up and walked over to where we were just standing beside the bikes.

"You boys out a little late, ain't you," he said. It was more of a statement than a question. "You all live around here, do you?"

Now two run-ins with crooks was just a little too much for me I figured, so I wasn't about to volunteer any information I didn't have to. Turns out, I didn't have to worry about it 'cause Daniel was doing all the talking this time and he was saying a whole lot more than the old man needed to know as far as I was concerned.

"We're headed for California," he said. "Got separated from our folks, so we're going on by ourselves. Figure we ought to be there by day after tomorrow if everything goes right."

"You mean to tell me you two boys are riding motorcycles all the way from Oklahoma to California all by your selves," the old man said. "Why you boys can't be more than fifteen years old. How in the world did you get separated from your folks anyway?"

By the time Daniel had explained all that had happened, I felt myself beginning to nod off. It was all I could do to keep my eyes open.

"Mister," I said. "Do you mind if we lay down over here out of the way and sleep a few hours? We've gone about as far as we can go tonight. We won't get in the way or nothing. If somebody comes along and needs this spot, we'll move along."

"You boys are not gonna sleep out here in this parking lot tonight, the old man said. "By the way, my name is Cullin Webster. Most folks just call me Cully. I've got three or four empty rooms and you boys are welcome to one of them for the night. Might even rustle up a bite of something to eat if you ain't too particular."

"Thanks, just the same Mr. Webster," I said. "We ain't got the money to spend on a room. We'll be okay right here if that's okay with you."

"I ain't gonna hear no more about it," he said. "Now foller me up to the office and I'll get you a key. It's on me boys." With that , he turned and walked over to the office and came out with a key hanging from a brown shoestring. "Number 6 over there," he said. "Bring that key by the office when you leave in the morning."

I lay awake for quite a while just thinking. We were still a long way from California and no telling what might befall us before we got there. We were running short on cash and long on nerve the way I had it figured. We were gonna have to be mighty lucky if we made it to Riverside, California without something happening that would shut us down for good to my way of thinking.

We dropped the room key off at the office before daylight the next morning. There was nobody around so we didn't even get to thank Cully for the hospitality. After we filled both tanks at Holbrook and bought a bag of donuts at the little bakery across the street from the gas station, we had exactly $25 left in the little leather coin purse. I had taken to carrying the money since Daniel didn't trust himself with it and I doled out the money for the donuts reluctantly. I knew we had to eat, but gas for the motorcycles was gonna take precedent if it came right down to making a choice.

We made the short 33 mile run from Holbrook to Winslow in about 45 minutes. Not knowing where we might get another chance, we topped the gas tanks off. Another 72 cents down the drain. Just out of town about a mile, there was a sign on the side of the road that said, "Meteor Crater, 12 miles." We both wanted to see it in the worst way, but we didn't have the time or the money and we knew it. Right below the Meteor Crater sign was another sign that said, "Peach Springs 152 miles." I swallowed hard hoping we weren't going to have to ride all the way to Peach Springs before we found another gas station. That's when the wind hit us.

We rounded a curve and it was like riding into a wind tunnel. To make matters worse, it was a side-ways wind coming from our right and it was all we could do to keep the bikes upright. I could see Daniel ahead of me through the swirling dust, and his bike was leaning into the wind so far it looked weird. I knew I must look the same way. With no place to get out of the weather, we kept on riding. It was all we could do to average 30 miles per hour and stay on the road. Just about the time I thought I had gone as far as I could go, it just quit. One minute I was fighting to stay upright, and the next minute it was as calm as a summer morning. To make me feel even better, the sign on the side of the road read "Flagstaff 13 miles."

We pulled into the first service station we came to and I was shocked to see the price of gas was 38 cents a gallon. To make matters worse, we had to buy a quart of oil. The Zundapp was just a little low, but Daniel's Harley took almost half a quart to put it back on full. I squeezed the dime the man gave me back as change out of the two bucks I handed him. At this rate, we were gonna be shelling out way more cash than I had figured on. My stomach felt like it was attached to my backbone. It was getting up around the middle of the afternoon, and the donuts we had for breakfast had run out a while back. We headed into town and found a little diner that looked like it was a local favorite by the number of cars parked out front. We parked the bikes out of the way and went inside. The first thing I saw was an extra-large waitress headed our way and she had a look in her eye that meant business.

"You the boys what got separated from your folks?" She asked.

It took a few seconds for me to understand what she said. For some reason, it didn't even seem like we had gotten separated from them at all. It just sort of seemed like we had always been riding to California. Daniel finally answered her though before she had time to ask again.

"Reckon we are," he said. "We ain't lost though."

"Your folks were in here about two hours ago wanting to know if we had seen you," she said. "Seemed right worried about you. You boys might catch up with them if you hurry."

I wasn't about to hurry anywhere 'til I got some food of some kind into the vacuum that used to be my stomach. We sat down and ordered stew and cornbread and man was it good. That waitress must have felt sorry for us because she brought a big bowl of stew out and set it on the table just as we were finishing up the first round. I ate 'til I couldn't hold another bite. The sweet tea was just as good and I must have drunk a gallon. When I paid the $1.12 to get us out of there, we were down to $21.26 but at least we had full tanks of gas.

We were five miles out of Flagstaff when the Harley started to sputter. It would smooth out for a minute or two, then start sputtering again. About the time it quit altogether I spotted a building on the side of the road about a half mile ahead. Daniel was just standing there beside the bike looking like he lost his best friend.

"What we gonna do now?" he asked.

"Get on behind me and we'll ride up there and see what that building is," I said. "Might be somebody there that knows something about motorcycles." I didn't figure there was much chance of that but Daniel looked like he needed to think there might be.

"You ride on up there," he said. "I don't want to leave my bike sitting here on the side of the road."

When I was almost to the building, I could see the sign out front. "Tortilla Flats," it read. "Flats fixed and engine repair." There was an old decrepit gas pump out front that looked like it hadn't worked since Hector was a pup. I looked back down the road and I could see Daniel pushing the Harley along the shoulder of the highway. Didn't seem to be anyone around the place, the door was shut and there didn't appear to be a light on anywhere. I looked back down the road at Daniel, and when I turned back around, I almost fell off my bike.

I hadn't heard the door to the building open, but there, standing in the door was the tallest, skinniest man I had ever seen. He had a shock of red hair sticking out of one of those striped caps trainmen used to wear. The striped overalls lacked at least six inches reaching the tops of the old lace-up brogans he had on his feet. The brogans looked to be a size 18 or 20 and looked more like skis on his feet than shoes. His head was just under the top of the door opening, and it looked to be a seven foot door. When he spoke, his voice sounded like a girl's voice.

"You want something boy?" he asked. "Or are you just gonna stand there with your mouth open all day?"

I hadn't realized I had been staring 'til he started talking. I started to say something, but all that came out was a squeak. I could feel my face and neck getting red and the more I fumbled around for something to say, the redder they got. Finally, I managed to point back to where Daniel was just coming into the driveway pushing the Harley.

"Something's wrong with the Harley," I said. "It just started sputtering and quit about a half mile back down the road. Can you look at it and see if you can fix it?"

"You boys got any money?" he asked. "I don't work on anything for free."

"Well, we ain't got much money," I said. "How much you reckon it might cost to fix it?"

"Now how in the world am I supposed to know that?' he asked. "You thinking I'm one of them there psychotics or whatever they call them?"

Now my face was really getting red. Luckily, Daniel came walking up about that time and took charge. "You a mechanic?" he asked. He didn't even seem to notice the guy was seven feet tall and looked like a scarecrow.

"Reckon I am," Stringbean answered. "What's wrong with the Harley? By the way, you can call me Luther. Most folks just call me Luke, but you can call me Luther 'til I see the color of your money. "There was a smile on his face though that wasn't there earlier. When neither of us said anything, he started laughing.

"Just going on with you boys," he said. "Push the bike around back and I'll take a look at her."

I followed him around to the back and Daniel followed with the Harley. Luther took a light off the workbench and bent down to look at the engine. Pretty soon, he got up and started sorting through a pile of wrenches on the workbench. When he found the one he wanted, he got down on his knees beside the bike and went to work. I looked over at Daniel and he had the same concerned look on his face I knew I had on mine. It was just a minute later though that Luther stood up and pointed to the part he had in his hand.

"Here's the problem boys," he said. "Sparkplug burned out. The other one looks to be okay, but if it was me, I'd change both of them. The other one is bound to go bad pretty soon."

"What's this gonna cost us?" I asked. I figured we might have to get just the one plug. Might not even be able to do that, depending on how generous Luther was feeling.

Luther stood there and scratched his chin for a minute. "You got a bad sparkplug wire there too," he said. "I'll change both the plugs and put on a new wire for $5.00."

It sounded like highway robbery to me but I didn't see where we had much choice, so I told him to go ahead and change them. Ten minutes later, when Daniel kicked it off, the Harley sounded like new again. I handed Luther the money and we headed west again poorer by five bucks than we were when we stopped. Glancing at the sun, I knew it couldn't be over an hour 'til dark and we needed to find a place to eat and stop for the night.

Another hour of riding brought us to the little town of Bellemont Arizona, and we stopped at the Cities' Service gas station across from a place called "The Wooly Booger." There were Harleys parked all around the place, and as we stood there watching, three men in leather jackets came out and mounted three of the Harleys. They left out of there like they were headed to a fire with tires smoking and pipes blaring. I knew right then I didn't want anything to do with the Wooly Booger.

We filled up the bikes and I squeezed a little bit extra in my tank to make the pump end up on $2.26. When I paid for the gas with two dollar bills and the twenty six cents left from the Diner in Flagstaff, we had exactly $14 left and we still had to eat.

One thing I was beginning to notice, the farther west

we went, the more expensive things got. We were lucky to find gas under forty cents a gallon anywhere after we got past Holbrook, and there was no such thing as five or six hamburgers for a dollar. That became more apparent when we stopped at Jack's Burger Heaven just down the road from The Wooly Booger. Hamburgers were fifty cents and a medium drink was a quarter. When we added a large order of fries, the total came up to $2.00 even.

While we were sitting at a little picnic table eating the burgers, Daniel noticed a sign that read "Bellemont City Park, and had an arrow pointing north. When we finished eating, we headed down that way, and sure enough, just around the bend in the road was the prettiest little park you ever saw. There was a big open gazebo with tables under it and we headed that way. When we got off the bikes, I noticed a sign that said something about loitering being prohibited after dark, but I didn't pay much mind to it. After all, we weren't loitering, we were just gonna get a little sleep. What I really wanted was a bath. We hadn't had the opportunity to get a bath since we left the Dewdrop Inn. Another thing that kept bothering me was the fact that we had worn the same clothes since we left Oklahoma City. I wanted, in the worst way, to get a bath and a change of clothes, but the prospects of either one of them things happening were about as good as us finding a big wad of money.

To make matters worse, along about midnight, it started to rain. As long as the wind wasn't blowing, we were staying relatively dry under the roof of the gazebo, but our luck was not to last. Not only did the wind start blowing, it was coming up a regular storm. I could hear hail hitting the roof of the gazebo and the wind was blowing the rain in under the roof so hard we might as well have been standing out in the open. Just about the time I thought it couldn't get any worse, a car came down the road and stopped with the headlights shining right into the gazebo. I felt like the headlights had me pinned to the table top. When the man got out of the passenger side of the car and headed our way, I could see it was a cop. Now don't that put the icing on the cake? Laying on a picnic table nearly a thousand miles from home, rain running down my shirt collar and into my pants, nearly out of money and no prospect of getting any, and now a nosy cop was gonna arrest me for loitering.

"What you boys doing out here in this storm?" The policeman asked. "We don't allow no loitering in the park after dark. You boys get out of here and go home. I don't want to have to take you down to the station and call your parents, so just go on along home now you hear?"

"Yes sir," I said. "We were just leaving." I sure didn't want to go down to the station, especially since we didn't have any parents around anywhere close to call. We would have been just fine and on our way to California again if Daniel would have kept his mouth shut. Seems like sometimes a fellow just loses his good sense and says something so stupid that you wonder what he could have been thinking.

"We ain't from around here," he said. "You couldn't call our parents if you wanted to."

"You guys aren't from around here, you say?" the cop said. "Now what in the world would bring a couple of kids down here anyway? What you boys got in your mind to do? You fixin to rob somebody or pull a liquor store heist or something?"

"No sir!" I replied. We're just on a little vacation and stopped here to rest for a while. We'll just be on our way if you don't mind."

"I'll tell you what you're gonna do," he said. "Just you two follow us down to the station. We'll talk about it down there out of the rain. Now get them motorcycles started and follow us down to the station. It ain't but a mile or so." With that, he headed back to the cop car.

"What in the name of Sally were you thinking about?' I asked Daniel when the cop was out of hearing. "That's about as dumb a trick as I ever seen pulled."

"Just shut up and get your bike," he answered. "Maybe they'll let us take a bath and wash our clothes while we're down there."

We pulled out behind the cop car as he drove slowly back to the main drag. When he turned right and headed toward the center of town, I thought about going the other way for a minute, but I knew they would just catch us and then we would be in trouble. We had gotten back about even with The Wooly Booger when two motorcycles took out of there like they were headed for a free lunch somewhere. One of them hollered something at the cops when they went by us with pipes howling. The police car made a bat-turn and pulled up alongside of us.

"You boys make a right at the light," the cop that was driving hollered at us. "The station is just a block on your left. We'll be there soon as we catch those two no-accounts." With tires screaming, they took out after the two motorcycles. As soon as they were out of sight, I looked over at Daniel. You for getting out of here?" I asked. Without a word, he turned and started out in the direction of Route 66 westbound. With me keeping pace, he took the highway and wound out the Harley as fast as was safe to go in the drizzling rain. We kept up the pace for almost an hour. When the rain stopped, we stopped at a little pullover on the side of the road. I looked over at Daniel and he looked at me. All of a sudden we were laughing so hard it was all I could do to keep the bike from falling over.

"That's the dumbest stunt I ever pulled, Daniel said.

"I guess I was just mad cause they were making us leave. You think we got away clean?"

"Well, I don't think those two cops are going to waste much time worrying about a couple of kids. We didn't do anything for them to get excited about anyway. They've probably forgotten all about us by now. What we need is a dry place to catch a few hours of sleep."

We pulled back onto the highway and about five miles down the road, we came to an old abandoned gas station sitting at the corner of an intersection with a gravel road. There was an awning in front and a couple of old wooden benches sitting in front of the old station building. Looked like as good a place as any to try to catch a few winks, so we pulled in under the awning and got off. We each took a bench and the next thing I knew, the sun was shining and Daniel was shaking me awake.

"Let's go find some breakfast," he said. "I'm so hungry I could eat the south end of a north bound mule."

We pulled out of there just as the sun was starting to turn the wet highway into a steam bath. We hadn't gone more than a mile or two before the sun had done its job and we were running along on dry pavement. The next road sign we saw said it was 72 miles to Kingman, Arizona. We had to stop once for gas, but it was just past 10:00 o'clock when we pulled off the highway and stopped at Harvey's Café. The sign was what did it for us. "Breakfast served 24 hours" it read.

When I got off the bike, I could tell I smelled like a bear that had just got out of hibernation, but I didn't see how I was gonna do anything about it. The waitress turned up her nose at us after we took a seat in the only empty booth, but she took our order and that was all that mattered to us. The pancakes were soft and flaky and the hot maple syrup she brought in a little metal pitcher made them that much better. I had my heart set on about three or four fried eggs and some bacon, but the pancake special was just too good to pass up. All the pancakes you can eat for a dollar. With the drinks, the total came to $2.49 tax and all. I clutched the little coin purse tightly as we walked out of the café. There was a gas station across the way and we figured we might as well top them off before we headed out. After I paid the $1.45 the pump rang up, we had just seven dollars, a nickel, and a penny in the coin purse.

We left out of Kingman headed west toward Needles, California through the desert. As best we could figure, we had roughly 300 miles between us and Riverside. It was mighty hot and we were just taking our time running along around 50 miles per hour. We crossed over into California just after 2:00 o'clock and we had to stop a minute to savor the moment. We gassed up in Needles and headed out. We had been riding for almost two hours when I happened to look in my rear view mirror. What I saw made my heart jump up into my throat. It felt like my blood was all of a sudden too thick for my heart to pump through my body. I got Daniel's attention, and when he looked back, I could see his face turn a sickly looking white color. There were twenty or thirty Harleys coming up on us and from what I could see, they carried some mighty rough looking customers. You have to remember, this was 1963, and the Hells Angels were coming into their own in Arizona and California. There were several motorcycle gang movies out at the time and were the most popular movies that winter.

I figured the best thing we could do was to just slow down and let them pass. I didn't even mean to look at them or anything when they passed; just let them go their way. We had slowed to about 30 miles an hour and I kept looking for them to go around but to my horror, when the lead pair of cycles got even with us, they just slowed down and ran along between us. The lead cycle was a three wheeler and the guy on the front was a big guy with a red beard and had a couple of chains running from his shoulders in an "X" pattern on the outside of his leather jacket. He had the roughest looking woman sitting on the bench seat in the back that I had ever seen. When I glanced over at her, she smiled at me revealing a gap where one of her front teeth used to be. When she winked at me, I turned quickly back to where my eyes were fixed on the road ahead.

"What kind of a bike you got there son?" Red Beard asked. By that time, we had slowed down to not much over ten miles an hour. "I thought I'd seen them all but you got me on this one."

I tried a couple of times to say something but my tongue had forgotten how to talk. I sputtered around for a couple of seconds then managed to get out a squeaking answer. "It's a Zundapp," I finally said.

"Where you boys headed?" he asked.

"We're headed for Riverside California," I replied.

"Where'd you come from?"

"Oklahoma City," I said. "We've been on the road for three days."

"Holy crap!" he hollered. "You mean to tell me you two young'uns rode all the way from OKC by yourself? Ain't you all got no parents or nothing?

"It's a long story," I said. "We got separated from our folks."

"Bout two miles ahead, there's a Dairy Queen and a gas station on the right side of the road at the intersection," he said. "Pull in there."

"We ain't got time," I said. The last thing I wanted to do was stop at the Dairy Queen with them. Likely as not they'd kill us if they got half a chance. We'd be lucky if they just took our seven dollars and left us our bikes, I figured.

"I said pull in at the Dairy Queen," he said. I could tell by the way he said it that it wasn't open for further discussion. I looked over to the other side of the road at Daniel but he had his gaze fixed straight ahead. Two minutes later, the Dairy Queen came into view. We pulled in and stopped in front of the building surrounded by the motorcycle gang, and I got my first look at the back of the leather jackets. The patch was in a crescent shape and covered almost all the back of the jacket. "Brothers of the Blood" was stitched in red on the white background of the patch. At least they weren't the Hells Angels.

We followed them into the Dairy Queen and got a few puzzled looks from the patrons sitting in the booths on the right wall as we walked in. I expect they were just trying to figure out what a couple of kids were doing with that bunch of rough motorcycle guys and to tell you the truth, I was trying to figure it out myself.

"What you boys gonna have?" Red Beard asked.

"We don't want nothing," I managed to answer. "We just ate back at Kingman."

"That's been almost four hours ago," he said. "We saw you guys head out while we were gassing up. Kids like you have got to be hungry by now." He stood there looking at us and then it came to him. "You guys got any money on you?" he asked.

I knew it was bound to come sooner or later and it looked to be sooner. They were gonna take our seven dollars and leave us flat broke sure as shooting. I knew there just wasn't a thing we were gonna do about it either. What could we do, a couple of kids against twenty or thirty grown men and women. If I thought we were gonna get any help from the folks sitting in the booths I could think again. They all had gotten really interested in something on their plates all of a sudden.

"Give the boys here cheeseburgers, fries and vanilla

malts," Red Beard told the waitress. "I'll have the same thing. It's on me boys." He motioned us to an empty booth and we sat down on one side while he and the snaggle-toothed woman sat on the other. "Now tell me all about your ride from OKC to here," he said.

"We took turns telling about all the things that had happened since we first got separated from our folks in Oklahoma City. When we came to the part about the Mexicans in Glenrio, he got really mad and made a point of telling us he would take care of that little situation the next time they were by there. We sat there for over an hour. I had long since got over being scared of them and with a belly full of cheeseburgers and fries, we were ready to head out again.

"Pull them bikes over to the pumps," Red Beard said. I had already learned not to question what he said so we pulled in on one side of the pumps while the Harleys lined up on the other side. Red Beard filled both our bikes with gas and pushed a five dollar bill into my shirt pocket.

"Compliments of the Blood Brothers", he said. "Anybody gives you boys any trouble, tell them you're a friend of Red Makins." I locked eyes with him for just a second then he turned and walked away. We started our bikes and headed out. It was fifteen minutes and twelve miles later when Daniel pulled over to the side of the highway.

"Red Makins", he said. "I've heard of that guy. He's supposed to have whipped three guys from another gang all by his self not two weeks ago. Two of them were in the hospital last I heard. Why do you suppose he was so good to us?"

"Liked the way you looked in them tight jeans, I reckon," I quipped. I had to take off running to get out of the way of the rock he sent whistling my way.

"Take it easy," I said. "I was just joshing you a little." With that, we mounted up and headed west again. Always west. Seemed to me we had been going west long enough to fall off the edge of the earth. Or at least run into the Pacific Ocean. We passed through the little town of Essex without stopping, but by the time we got to Cadiz it was time to gas up and take a break.

After filling the tanks, I had $5.20 left in the coin purse plus the $5.00 Red gave me back at the Dairy Queen. We were feeling pretty prosperous by then so we opted for foot-long hot dogs and fries at Dan's Famous Dogs across from the gas station. To show my heart was in the right place, I ordered two large vanilla malts to boot. That set us back another $2.30, so we left out of there with a sum total of $7.90 stuck firmly in the front pocket of my jeans. Or at least I thought it was stuck firmly, that is.

We were just coasting along enjoying the view about ten miles west of Cadiz when something started nagging at me. I couldn't figure out what it was, but something was definitely not quite right. By habit, I reached down to feel the coin purse in my pocket and I darn near wrecked the bike. It wasn't there! It just wasn't there! I pulled over to the side of the road and Daniel stopped beside me.

"What's the matter now?" he asked. "We ain't never gonna get there if you keep stopping every few miles."

"I ain't got the money," I said.

"Say that again," Daniel said with a serious look on his face.

"I said I ain't got the money"

"What do you mean you ain't got the money," he shot back. "You got to have the money. We can't get to Riverside if you ain't got the money."

I didn't say anything, I just started the Zundapp and headed back the way we came. Daniel pulled alongside me after a minute or two.

"Where you going?" he asked.

"Just watch the road and see if you see the coin purse,"

I said. "It must have fallen out of my pocket while we were riding somewhere between here and Cadiz." We rode slowly back toward Cadiz with our eyes peeled to the road. If we didn't find that money, I knew we had run out our string of luck. We were almost back to Cadiz when I spotted two boys standing on the side of the highway and they had something they were mighty interested in. We pulled up right in front of them on our bikes and I could see the biggest boy had my coin purse in his hand.

"That's my money you got there," I said. "Must have fallen out of my pocket when we went by here a while ago. "I was hoping he was gonna see it my way and hand over the money. He looked to be around eighteen or nineteen years old and rather on the large side to boot.

"Now how do I know this is your money," he said. "Could be anybody's money. Right now, I reckon it's my money seeing's how I got it here in my hand."

Well, I didn't know how we were gonna go about it, but I knew we had to have that money. I was trying my best to figure a way to get the money and keep my skin mostly in one piece at the same time when Daniel had to put in his two cent's worth.

"How about we just take that money off you?" He said. "The way I see it, you can give us our money the easy way, or you can give it to us the hard way. Now how's it gonna be?"

I just about peed my pants when he said it, but I had to admire his gumption. After he said what he said next, I figured I'd admired him just a little prematurely.

"You see," he said. "We just left our buddies back up the road a piece and most of that money was given to us by them. Maybe you know 'em. "Brothers of the Blood" they're called, and Red Makins gave Pete here that money to buy gas with. You ain't fixin to take Red's money, are you?"

"Red Makins gave you that money?" the big guy asked. I could see the other boy's face getting a shade more pale as he digested what Daniel had said.

"Give him the money Bud," he said. "Give it to him right now!" Bud pitched the coin purse to me and I checked to see if all the money was in there and it was. Without another word, we turned our bikes and rode slowly out of there. When we were about fifty yards down the highway, I realized I had been holding my breath. I looked over at Daniel and he had the biggest grin on his face. "Catch me," he hollered, and out of there he went with all the horses screaming. I passed him a quarter of a mile farther down the road and slowed down for him to catch up.

"You're as crazy as a bed bug," I said. "What made you think you could get by with that back there?"

"Got by with it, didn't we?" he replied. "You hang around me a while and you'll learn a few things."

We stopped at Ludlow and filled up then headed on to Barstow. The coin purse now held Red's five dollar bill and ninety cents in change. We pulled into Barstow just as the sun was going down on day three. I figured we were less than a hundred miles from Riverside, and when I asked the man at the gas station, he confirmed it was only eighty miles. We talked it over and decided to ride on after getting a bite to eat and a tank of gas. We left out of there with two dollar bills and a dime in my pocket, but we had full bellies and full gas tanks.

A little over two hours later, we could see the lights of Riverside in the distance. I knew we were getting mighty low on fuel, so we stopped at the first gas station we came to and filled up. I put the forty cents we had left in the coin purse and made sure it was safely tucked away inside my front pants pocket. Daniel had the address of the new home on a little scrap of paper, and the lady at the station told us how to get there. It was only a couple of miles away. After a couple of wrong turns, we pulled into 945 Pullman Drive and the house was dark. Daniel checked the address again to be sure and we were right where we were supposed to be only there was no one there. Surely, after all the trouble we had and the delays and all, we hadn't beaten them to Riverside.

We checked all the doors and windows but they were all locked. Well, looked like we were gonna spend the night outside at least one more time. We sat up and talked for a while, then sacked out on the front porch. It must have been getting close to midnight by the time we decided to call it a day. Four hours later, we woke to lights shining in our faces and screams coming from the two vehicles that had just pulled into the driveway. We were soon surrounded by siblings all talking at once, wanting to know how we got there and where we had been.

Mom gave me a big hug and I could see tears in her eyes. Dad was there too and he had a wistful look in his eye. I got the feeling he was wishing he could have made the trip with us on the bikes.

"You boys have had us worried out of our minds," Mom said. "I haven't slept a wink for three days wondering where you were and if you were alright. How long have you been here waiting on us?"

"We just got here about four hours ago," I said. "We expected you guys to be here when we got here." By then the house was unlocked so we all went inside. There was no furniture anywhere in the house except there was a cook stove and an icebox in the kitchen.

"If somebody will go down to that store we saw about a mile down the road and get some eggs and bacon, I'll fix us all some breakfast," Aunt Dolly said. After a good breakfast, we all settled down for a few hours sleep. It was almost noon when I rolled out and looked out at a beautiful California day. It took the rest of the day to unload the truck and trailer, but by dark the house was beginning to look like a home.

We stayed three more days with my aunt and uncle and cousins, then it was time to head for Oklahoma and home. We were all standing in the yard saying our goodbyes when my dad noticed the Zundapp sitting in the driveway on its kickstand.

"You better get that motorcycle loaded up Pete," he said. "It's time we were on the road."

"Why don't I just ride along behind for a while," I said. "We can stop and load the bike when we get to Barstow."

"No you don't young man!" my mom hollered. "You get that bike on that trailer and that's where it's gonna stay 'til we get home."

Now what do you suppose brought on that kind of a reaction to a perfectly reasonable request? Sometimes parents just don't make no kind of sense at all.

The End

A Man Called Lige

It was just your normal run of the mill wire gate like goes into a thousand pastures across the state of Oklahoma. Nobody would dream the rutted, two-track road ended at a house, especially a house someone actually lived in. Come to think of it, most folks wouldn't think anyone lived in the old ramshackle house even after seeing it. The give-a-way was the fact that the hounds started bawling before you even got in sight of the place. And what a racket it was. There was no chance anyone was gonna sneak up on old Lige with that pack of hounds around.

I first met Lige at the dog trade Bill Bevins held monthly in the 1960s at Sulphur, Oklahoma. He was just sitting in the truck and never said a word. Charlie Backus had gone by and picked up Lige at his house and took him to Sulphur to get what few groceries he needed. Lige didn't buy much of anything at town, just what little he couldn't raise or kill. Things like flour and sugar mostly, and coffee. Lige purely liked his coffee. He would mix the store bought coffee with a mixture of his own making. I never asked what was in the mixture, I was afraid I didn't really want to know.

Charlie ran by the dog trade that day to pay Denver Sides for a load of cedar poles he had delivered the week before. He knew he would find Denver at the dog trade, he hadn't missed a trade day since Bill started having them some three years back.

They parked Charlie's old truck not far from where me and Louis Helms were sitting in the shade swapping coon hunting stories with a couple of guys from over around Brown's Valley. Lige was sitting in the truck looking straight ahead and I kind of got to watching him. He never moved. I began to think it wasn't a real person sitting in Charlie's truck, but maybe a mannequin or something. Sure was an ugly mannequin if that's what it was. Finally, my curiosity got the better of me and I got up and walked the short distance to the truck. As I got closer, I could see it was sure enough a real person sitting there. Then it hit me; the smell that is. Whew! What a smell! I stopped right where I was and would have gone back to the shade tree if Charlie hadn't come walking up about that time.

"Hey there Pete," he said. "Ain't seen you in a month of Sundays. Where you been keeping yourself these days?"

"Hey Charlie," I replied. "Somebody said you was dead. I heard that widow woman you was messing around with over at Berwyn wasn't a widow after all. Heard tell her husband came home and shot you in the south end as you was going out the bedroom window. Guess that explains it though; have to shoot you closer to your heart to kill you, I reckon."

Charlie just stood there and grinned. Everybody in that part of the country knew Charlie wasn't about to have anything to do with a woman. His mother made sure of that. Charlie was forty some odd years old and still lived with his mother. He just never broke the apron strings.

"Let me show you to Lige Biden here," he said. "Me and Lige do a lot of coon huntin together down on the river." Lige never acted like he heard a thing.

"Lige is a little bit bashful around folks he don't know," Charlie said. "He don't get to town much I reckon."

I hated to, but I held out my hand like I was going to shake hands with Lige. He still never looked around.

"Let's go Charlie," he finally said. His voice had a texture to it sorta like 80 grain sandpaper. It took me a little by surprise when he said it. I could see he wasn't going to shake my hand so I drew it back.

"Friendly cuss ain't he," I said as I turned and started back to the shade tree. Charlie just shook his head and got in the truck. I didn't figure to see old Lige again in my entire life, and if I didn't it would be too soon for me. Refusing to shake hands with me like he did. Why it was just plumb downright un-neighborly, that's what it was.

I had forgotten all about the encounter with Lige at the dog trade. It was several months later and I was at Wendell's Salvage Yard hunting a wheel to use as a spare for my horse trailer when I saw Lige come walking up out of the brush south of the salvage yard. He was carrying a piece of equipment of some kind and when he got closer I could see it was a short piece of shaft with a gear on it. I had already paid Wendell for the wheel and we was just standing around talking when old Lige walked up. I was thankful we had the wind on him.

"What you got there Lige?" Wendell asked.

"Key come out of this here gear," Lige volunteered. "I looked around a right smart but I couldn't find it. You reckon you can make me one to fit it?"

Wendell took the shaft from him and ran the gear up and down the length of it. He looked it over good before he said anything.

"Why don't I just spot weld that gear to the shaft?" he

said. "That way, you won't have to worry about losing the key again."

"Alright by me," Lige said. He walked over and sat down on a cement block and I walked back into the shop with Wendell.

"Where does that old man live?' I asked.

"Got him a place over across the river," Wendell replied. "I ain't never been over there, but it's just down the river a mile or so and then about a half mile on the other side from what I've been told. He comes over here every once in a while to get me to fix something or the other for him."

"You mean that old man walked all the way over here through that brush along the river," I said. "It must have took him two hours or more to walk all the way over here. Ain't he got a car or a truck or anything?"

"Naw, he's got an old mule he rides some, but I doubt he could get across the river on him. Hear tell he keeps an old flat bottom boat tied up down on the river to get across in."

I turned my head as he ran a bead about a half inch on each side of the gear to fasten it solidly to the shaft. When he was through welding, he shoved the shaft and gear down in a bucket of water to cool it down enough to handle. After inspecting the weld, he headed back out to where Lige was still sitting on the cement block.

"This ought to work," he said.

"What you got coming to you?" Lige asked.

"Oh, a dollar ought to be about right," Wendell replied.

Lige took an old worn out billfold out of his overalls pocket and turning so we couldn't see, opened it up and took out a one dollar bill and handed it to Wendell. "Much obliged," he said. He took the shaft Wendell held out to him and started toward the brush south of the yard. Whatever made me do it, I've wondered to this day. There was just something about that old man that caught my curiosity or something.

"Hold up Lige," I hollered. "I'm going around your way anyhow. You might as well let me give you a lift. Sure beat walking through that brush again."

The truth be known, I was really headed in the other direction, but I figured I had time to take old Lige by his place. I told myself I was just doing a good deed for an old man but I knew I really wanted to see where he lived and how he lived.

Lige stopped dead in his tracks when I hollered at him. He stood there for what seemed like a minute, then without a word, turned and walked to where my truck was parked in front of the shop and got in. I gave Wendell a questioning look, but he just shrugged his shoulders and walked back into the shop. When I got the truck turned around and headed out to the highway, I thought Lige would give me some indication of which way I should turn, but he just sat there looking straight ahead. I turned east and when I glanced over at him, he just nodded his head. I knew he lived across the river, so when I got to the "Y" in the road just west of Tishomingo, I took the right leg and headed toward Madill. About a mile after we went over the Washita River bridge, he finally spoke.

"You might want to take the gravel road to the right," he said. I turned down the county road and before long he spoke again. Well, now we were beginning to get somewhere. Two whole sentences in the space of five minutes.

"Turn in the gate just over the hill," he said. I slowed down going over the hill, and sure enough, there was a wire gate on the right and I could see a worn track headed off into the pasture toward the river. I turned in at the gate and stopped and waited for him to get out and open it. We sat there for a few seconds and it became apparent to me that he wasn't gonna open the gate so I got out and opened it. Sure was a strange old bird I thought. It was just plain courtesy for the passenger to get all the gates. Leastwise with all the folks I ran around with. It was beginning to be clear to me that Lige was not your ordinary folks.

I could hear the dogs when we were a quarter of a mile from the house. Hound dogs, by the sound of 'em. When we rounded the last curve and the house came into view, there they were lined up at the edge of the yard. Five of the best looking Black and Tan Hounds I had ever seen. I pulled the truck up to the end of the gravel and stopped. Lige never said a word, he just got out of the truck and headed off down to a little shed to the right and back of the house. I could see him puttering with something on a wooden table and it came to me that he was installing the shaft Wendell welded for him into some kind of a grinder looking machine.

I sat there in the truck for a minute not knowing what I ought to do. Finally, I opened the truck door and stepped down to the ground keeping my eye on those hounds the whole time. A man could never tell about dogs. These dogs didn't act like they were paying any mind to me but I wasn't about to take anything for granted.

They let me get far enough away from the truck that I couldn't get back and they came at me. One minute they were lying on the ground not paying me a bit of mind, and the next all five hounds were headed my way in full cry. There I was, hung out in no man's land. Too far to the truck and not another thing in sight I could get behind or up on. About the time I figured my goose was cooked and the dogs were no more than ten feet from me, he hollered.

"Moses," he hollered. It wasn't a loud holler, just loud enough for the dogs to hear. All five dogs stopped and dropped to the ground. It was like it never happened.

They were just lying there like they didn't have a care in the world. I eased one foot ahead of the other one and they all stood back up. I stopped, and they stopped.

"Come on now that you're started," Lige said. Them dogs won't bother you any. I walked on down to the shed and the dogs trailed behind. When I got to the shed, they all laid down about ten feet away.

"Hand me that there leather mallet," Lige said. I looked over to the workbench at the side of the shed and saw it lying there. After a few good sharp licks to the end of the shaft with the mallet, he seemed satisfied and gave the grinder handle a couple of experimental turns. He handed the mallet back to me and headed toward the house without a word.

I wasn't about to be left behind with them hounds so I took off after him. The hounds got up and followed along. Lige opened the back door to the house and went inside. After a minute's hesitation I opened the door and followed him in. My first impression upon seeing the inside of the house could only be described as shock. I don't know what I expected to see, but it wasn't what I saw. After the rundown condition of the outside of the house and the dilapidated appearance of the entire place, to see a well-kept, clean, orderly kitchen in front of me was just about more than I could fathom.

The linoleum on the floor was worn but was shiny clean. The kitchen table had a pretty lace tablecloth spread on it and there were two places set as if dinner was about to be served. There was not a dirty dish in the sink and the little side counter where the enamel coffee pot stood had a lace doily under a stack of clean coffee cups.

About that time, Lige came out of the door to the right of the kitchen. He didn't say a word, just started a pot of coffee going on the little one burner stove beside the sink. We stood there in silence until the pot had perked for a few minutes. When he was satisfied it was ready Lige took the pot off the stove and went out the back door with it. I took another look around at the clean kitchen then followed him out the door.

He was sitting in one of those old metal yard chairs under a shade tree and the coffee pot was sitting on the tree stump in front of him. There was another chair just like the one he was sitting in so I sat down across from him. He poured coffee into both the cups he brought from the house and picked one up and started sipping the hot liquid. After a second or two, I took the other cup.

All of a sudden he started to talk. It seemed so out of character for him that it took me a minute to realize what he was saying.

"You're wondering about the dogs ain't you'" he said.

Well, I was wondering more about the kitchen than I was the dogs, but it was a good place to start. I was still sort of shocked that he had started to talk at all.

"Yea, I reckon I am," I said. "I thought I heard you holler "Moses". Is that the name of one of the dogs?"

"Let me tell you about my dogs," he said. "Old Moses is the big stud dog, you see." He turned to where the dogs were lying in the shade of another tree just a few yards away. "That little dog on the south end there is "Joseph." The female dog there by Moses is "Delilah". The two big male dogs there together are "Sampson" and "David." Together, they are the best pack of coon hounds in this whole country.

"They all have Biblical names," I said. "What's the deal with that?"

"My Bertie named all them dogs," he said. "She was quite a church goer, she was. Thought all the dogs ought to have proper names. They are all used to them names or I'd change them. Figure they're all too old to learn new ones."

"Is there any reason for the particular names or did she just name them the first biblical names that came to mind?" I asked.

"Here's the way it was," he said. "My Bertie used to coon hunt with me before she died. I had raised Moses and Delilah from pups but I hadn't named them anything. They was the only two dogs I had and I knew them apart. I didn't see any reason to name 'em but she did. We was huntin one night down on the river and we had an ole he-coon from the tall timber going strong. Both dogs were right on his tail when all of a sudden they just stopped. I figured that old coon had hit the river and was swimming across to the other side. I was ready to call it a bad deal when all of a sudden old Moses opened up again and I could tell he was across the river.

"He's just like Moses when he parted the Red Sea," Bertie said. "He parted that river and went across after that coon." That name has stuck with him ever since. She named the female dog Delilah because she thought a dog with a name like Moses needed a mate with a fancy name. I pointed out to her later that Delilah was actually Sampson's girlfriend, so when Moses and Delilah had pups, she named one of the male pups Sampson. When David was just about a year old, he got into a fight with a big Redbone hound that wondered up one day. That dog was twice as big as David, but he put him on the run. His name was David by the end of the day.

"What's the story on Joseph?" I asked.

"Now that's the strangest thing," he replied. "When that pup was just a little runt, he'd howl all night. Bertie would get up and feed him and stay with him 'til he went back to sleep. It wouldn't be very long 'til he was at it again. One night we was sitting in the living room. I was looking at an old magazine I had picked up at the sale barn and Bertie was knitting a scarf. Real colorful scarf it was. Had stripes of every color in the rainbow. About that time, the pup went to howling. Bertie went off to see about him and when she had him calmed down and was back in the house, she realized she had left her knitting out with the pup. She just sat back down and figured she'd get it when she had to go out the next time.

That pup slept the rest of the night and when Bertie went out the next morning to look in on him, he was covered up with that striped scarf. She brought it back in the house and it wasn't ten minutes 'til that pup went to howling. She took the scarf back out there and covered him up with it and he calmed down. He never did cause any more trouble as long as he had that scarf out there with him. Bertie called it his 'coat of many colors' and named him Joseph. Now you know."

I visited with Lige for a couple of hours that day. I took to going by to see him every once in a while and we would sit out by the stump and drink coffee. I went coon hunting with him several times and we would cross the river back and forth in the little flat bottom boat. Moses and Delilah would swim the river after a coon, but Sampson and David would always wait to cross in the boat with us.

One night as we were sitting on a log above the river just drinking coffee and listening to the dogs, Lige told me about Bertie.

"She's buried there behind the house," he said. "She's been gone more than ten years now. Didn't figure to make it this long without her. We'd been together since she was sixteen years old and I was seventeen. We was raised in Tennessee and run off to get married. Her daddy was a Methodist preacher and he didn't want her having nothing to do with the likes of me. My daddy run a little moonshine, you see and her pa didn't think I was good enough for her. Funny thing about it was, he was right. Why she stayed with me all them years, I don't know. I never did give her any of the things she deserved. I tried, it just never did work out."

"Bertie always kept a clean house. You could eat off the floors. I try to keep it just like she would want it to be. At least on the inside. I told Charlie and I'll tell you too. I want to be buried beside my Bertie when I die. She ain't got no tombstone and I don't want one either. You see, this ain't my land, I'm just renting it. When I'm gone, they're likely to sell this place and I don't want anybody knowing where our graves are. Charlie knows what to do, long as he don't get drunk and forget it."

It was about as sad a story as I ever heard. I continued to coon hunt with Lige over the next year or so, but work and such soon began to demand more and more of my time and I found myself going by there less and less often. In the fall of 1971, I was in the Drug Store at Tishomingo one day and overheard a couple of old men talking about how old Lige had just come up missing. Seems Charlie had gone by one day to see him and he just wasn't there. Charlie had hung around for several hours waiting on him to come home, but he never did. He left all his coon dogs there and everything when he left. Nobody seemed to know where he went. It was a mystery, it surely was.

I saw Charlie at a steer roping not long after that and he told me what happened. He had gone by to get Lige to take him to get some groceries and found him dead in the chair by the tree stump. He hadn't been dead long, the coffee was still warm in the pot setting on the stump. He dressed him in his best clothes then dug a grave beside Bertie just like Lige asked him to do. He filled in the grave and smoothed it out as best he could so it wouldn't be easy to see. Then he spread dead leaves all over the two graves to further hide them.

"Did you say some words over him?" I asked.

Charlie looked a little uneasy and it took him a little

while to answer. "I took off my hat," he said. "The only words I could remember from what I heard my ma read from the Bible was something about doing to other folks the way you'd want them to do to you, so I just said that. Did I do good Pete?"

"You did just fine Charlie," I said. "Real Fine. Lige would be proud." Charlie just smiled.

The End

The Gypsy Girl

Do you remember the old sayings that were common to most folks during the time I was growing up in the fifties? Don't hear most of them these days, but they have stuck in my mind over the years. Here's a few of them that I heard a lot and some of you doubtless did as well.

> ***"If you don't shut up that crying, I'm gonna give you something to cry about."***
>
> ***"If you don't quit making those faces, your face is gonna freeze like that."***
>
> ***"If one of your friends jumped off a forty foot cliff, you'd have to do it too."***
>
> ***"Beauty may be skin deep, but if you're ugly, you are ugly to the bone."***
>
> ***"Don't spend all your money in one place."***

"Be home by midnight, ain't nothing good happens after midnight."

And my favorite, "If I give you an inch, you'll take a mile."

The last one, about taking a mile, is the basis of the story I'm fixin to tell about the Gypsy girl. My dad was particularly good at springing that one on me anytime he figured I had gone overboard doing whatever it was he had given me permission to do. I believe Leonard Williams and Roscoe Purdee did that very thing in the case of the gypsy girl and it almost got them into more hot water than they could get out of. Here's how it went down.

It was the fall of the year, along about the time the pecan trees started to shed their leaves and the persimmons were just about to start turning. It had been a nice autumn so far, with day after day of sunshine and warm temperatures. The nights were beginning to cool off to where a quilt was feeling good before morning rolled around. Indian summer, folks called it. It was on one of those sunny afternoons that Roscoe was just sitting on the bench outside of Doc's Station shootin the bull with whoever happened to come by.

Carl Bates had just sat down and commenced to carry on about the fact that it didn't look like he was gonna have any pecans on the big tree in his yard for the second year in a row. Without any pecans, there would be no pecan pies coming out of Mrs. Bates's oven and Carl purely loved her pecan pies.

"Guess I'm gonna have to buy some pecans again this year," he lamented. "Got to where a body can't count on nothing."

Roscoe grunted to make Carl think he was listening, but he was really listening to what was being said on the other side of the door to the station. Willy Reams and Bob McNally were having a conversation about girls and dates and such and Willy was going on about the fact that he just couldn't seem to get a date. Bob, being one of the more fortunate guys when it came around to girls, was having a little bit of trouble giving a darn about Willy's lack of success with the weaker sex. Roscoe, on the other hand, was beginning to form a plan in his mind to help Willy with his love life. When Bob got in his car and drove off, Roscoe took the opportunity to amble over to where Willy was sitting on the bench with a sour look on his face.

"What's that I heard you say about not having a date Willy?" he asked.

"Oh, it ain't nothing," Willy replied. "It ain't nothing different than always anyhow. Girls just don't seem to cotton to me for some reason or other.

Looking at Willy sitting there on the bench with his two day growth of whiskers and the head of drab brown hair that looked to have missed the last few chances to be cut, it was no mystery to Roscoe why members of the female gender were keeping their distance. The old Levis he had on looked like they needed an oil change as well. Roscoe figured it was his civic duty to help old Willy find a girl.

"If you're really serious about finding a girl Willy, I believe I may just be able to help you out."

"Huh, what's that you said about finding me a girl Roscoe?" Roscoe had gotten his attention real quick like when he said something about getting a girl for him.

Roscoe leaned down real close like he didn't want anybody else to hear what he was fixin to say. He looked first this way, then that, to make sure nobody was within earshot.

"There's this bunch of gypsies camped in a pasture a few miles out of town," he said. "There's a passel of them, but there is one girl looks to be around eighteen or nineteen that is 'shore-nuf' pretty with long blond hair and legs as long as a well rope. I'll bet a yearling colt she'd like for a strapping young fellar like you to pay her a midnight visit."

"You say she's pretty?"

"Pretty as a speckled pup under a red wagon."

After fixin it up with Willy to meet him at the station around 11:00 o'clock that night, Roscoe got in his truck and headed off to find a cohort in crime to help him pull off this Gypsy charade, and who do you think he made a bee line to? If you guessed Leonard Williams, you'd be right.

Now some folks will go to a lot of trouble to pull a joke on somebody, but the trouble these two jokesters went to just to pull off the Gypsy girl stunt almost defies logic. First, they hunted up the old white canvas tent they used when they went deer hunting and put it in the back of Roscoe's truck. Then they hunted up a gasoline lantern and got it to working. Finally, with Leonard's old twelve gauge shotgun standing in the floor board between them, they were ready to put their plan in motion.

Just about two hundred yards from the gravel road on the quarter section of land Leonard owned east of town was a clearing about an acre or so in size. It was in that clearing they set up the tent. They hung the lantern from the center support and by the time they were finished, the sun was going down over the old barn just to the west of the clearing. When they lit the lantern to try it out, it did just what they had hoped it would do. Roscoe got inside the tent and started to move around. The light from the lantern formed a perfect silhouette of his body on the white canvas wall of the tent. Now to find someone to play the gypsy girl. The logical suspect was Leonard's wife Bessie.

"I ain't gonna do it," Bessie hollered. "That's about the sorriest trick I ever heard of and I just ain't gonna do it."

It was coming on to 11:00 o'clock and they still hadn't talked Bessie into playing the part of the gypsy girl. I don't know if they finally just wore her down or if they promised her something to do it, but the short of it was that Bessie rode with Leonard down to the tent while Roscoe drove down to the station to meet up with Willy.

Willy had just about given up on Roscoe when he saw him pull his old truck up beside the gas pump.

"You ready to go see that gypsy girl Willy?" he asked when Willy came walking up out of the darkness.

"You sure this gal is gonna want to see me Roscoe?"

"Course she is. I've already told her you were coming. She's gonna be in the first tent, and she's gonna have a light burning. It'll be the only tent with a light. Just ease down through the woods until you can see the tent with the light on. Be real careful though, her pa is gonna be sleeping in the old barn off to the right of her tent a ways. Shore don't to wake that old man up, he might come up a shootin."

Roscoe turned off his headlights when they were still a quarter of a mile from the gate going into the pasture. "Don't want anyone to see us coming," he told Willy. When they finally coasted to a stop even with the gate, he killed the motor and went over the instructions with Willy one last time.

"Now remember, be as quite as you can getting down there. When you come out of the timber into the clearing, you can see the tent with the light on. That light means she's waiting for you. You ought to be able to see her inside the tent. Ease up pretty close to the tent and call her name. She'll turn the light off and you can go on into the tent when she does. Remember now, be quiet, 'cause her old man is sleeping not far away.

Willy opened the door and eased over the bob wire fence. Roscoe sat in the truck trying to keep from laughing as he watched him disappear into the darkness. He was just about to start out after him so he could see the fun, when Willy came walking back out of the darkness and stopped at the fence.

"Roscoe," he whispered. "Roscoe, you still there?"

"Yea, I'm still here. What is it?"

"What's her name? You forgot to tell me her name."

"Why it's Ramona," Roscoe answered thinking fast. "Her name's Ramona."

He gave Willy time to be about a hundred feet ahead of him then got out of the truck and eased over the fence. This was gonna be too good to miss. He could see Willy sneaking along a good ways ahead of him after his eyes became accustomed to the darkness. He stayed close enough to see him as he made his way through the woods toward the tent.

When Willy got to the far edge of the woods, the tent was clearly visible sitting in the middle of the clearing. As he stopped to build up his nerve, he could see the silhouette of a girl moving around inside the tent. His heart skipped a beat as he watched her move around. It was clearly a girl, and he could hardly wait to see what she looked like. He peered into the darkness to the west of the tent but try as he might, he couldn't make out the old barn where the girls pa was supposed to be sleeping.

Across the clearing, just south of the old barn, Leonard was lying on the ground beside a hackberry bush with the shotgun lying on the ground beside him. He was watching Willy as he stood just inside the woods with his eyes on the tent. Inside the tent, Bessie was moving seductively back and forth across the floor so the lantern would silhouette her form perfectly on the tent wall.

Roscoe watched from hiding as Willy finally got up the

nerve to ease across the clearing. When he was just a few feet from the tent, he stopped and called softly.

"Romona, it's me, Willy. Can I come in?"

Immediately, the lantern went out inside the tent and Leonard jumped up off the ground with the barrel of the shotgun pointed straight up into the air. The first shot sounded like it was right beside the tent and Bessie screamed like she had been shot. As the second shot from the shotgun rattled the limbs over his head, all the color drained out of Willy's face and he took off running as fast as he could go back toward the road where the truck was parked. In his haste, he missed the trail he had come in on and was just rushing headlong through the brush and trees making a way as he went. He was losing a lot of hide as he barreled through the brush, but he wasn't slowing down one little bit. Roscoe hollered at him as he went by, but he didn't act like he heard him at all.

Willy cleared the timber about fifty yards east of where the truck was parked and at that particular spot, the fence was only a few feet from the woods. He hit that barb wire fence at full gallop and Roscoe could hear the wire singing from his position a hundred yards south of the road. He could hear Willy screaming and took off at a high lope to where the sound was coming from. He had a flashlight with him and when the beam settled on the spot where the screaming was coming from, he almost lost his supper. There was Willy, all tangled in the barb wire and blood was running from a dozen places on him and pooling on the ground.

Bessie and Leonard had finally gotten through the brush and came running up just as Roscoe was getting Willy untangled from the wire. Bessie went to screaming and fell to her knees and commenced to wringing her hands. Willy had quit hollering and was just standing there with blood running from the numerous wire cuts on his body. He looked to be in shock. Leonard and Roscoe carried him down to the truck and took off as fast as the old truck would run, headed to Sulphur and the emergency room at the Delay Hospital. Bessie walked back down to the clearing and got Leonard's truck from where it was hidden and drove slowly back to town, sobbing softly all the way.

Two hours and sixty-seven stitches later, a very sober looking pair of would be jokesters loaded Willy back into Roscoe's old truck and started back to Mill Creek. They offered to take him home and explain what happened but Willy insisted they let him off at the station so he could get his car. The apologies they gave as he got out of the truck sounded hollow even to them. Willy didn't say anything, he just got into his car and drove slowly out of town.

There never was really anything much said about what happened with the gypsy girl debacle as best I can recall. I know Roscoe and Leonard split the emergency room bill and paid it off. It was quite a burden to them, but served them right for doing what they did to Willy. Oh, I know there was never any intention for anyone to get hurt or for anything bad to happen for that matter, but you just never know what might happen in circumstances such as that.

I thought about it a long time before I decided to include the story of "The Gypsy Girl" in this book. It is a story though, that was part of my growing up and seemed to be begging to be told. I sincerely hope no one takes offense at anything said in this story. The story is not meant to speak badly about either of the jokesters or anyone else mentioned in the telling. It was something that happened in a different time, a time when folks did things differently and a time when there just weren't a lot of things to do for fun, so they manufactured their own brand of fun. Sometimes, things didn't turn out the way they were intended to turn out and that is sadly unfortunate in the case of "The Gypsy Girl."

I think the reality of what happened that night, really slowed down the practical joking where Roscoe and Leonard were concerned. As far as I know, Willy's injuries healed up nicely over time and he had no lasting problems associated with "The Gypsy Girl" incident. I'm glad he didn't, and I imagine a couple of other fellows were as well.

Aside from the bad ending, the drama that was played out that night would have been hilarious. I can't help but smile when I try to picture the look on Willy's face when that shotgun went off and the light went out in the tent.

The End

Haunted Memories

We talked about it for most of a month before we gathered the nerve to do it. At least we thought we had the nerve to do it. I had walked by it on the street in the daylight a hundred times or more and it always gave me a creepy feeling. I couldn't image what the feeling would be like inside the old two story house in the dark of night, but that was just what I had agreed to do.

"Double dog dare you." That's the exact words that came out of Jerry's mouth and nobody I knew was gonna pass on a double dog dare. At least not and still have any respect from the regular guys I ran around with. Not that Jerry was what I'd call a role model or anything like that, but he was with us when we talked about doing it, so that made him part of the club for that day at least, so to speak.

"Who's going with me?" I asked. "I sure ain't going in that old house by myself."

"I ain't going," Davey admitted. "You couldn't run me

in there with a stick with a rusty nail in the end of it. I'll wait out by the road and stand guard."

"Stand guard over what?" Leon chortled. "You afraid somebody's gonna come along and arrest us for trespassing or something? I'll go if you're too much of a fraidy-cat."

"Okay, then it's me, Petey, and Leon," Jerry said. "Let's all meet at Leon's house about 10:00 o'clock tonight. Ought to be good and dark by then."

I couldn't eat a bite of supper, and something had to be awfully wrong for me to not eat a big supper.

"What's wrong with you tonight?" Mom asked. "You haven't eaten a bite of your supper. I hope you're not coming down with something." She held the back of her hand against my forehead to check for fever. I never could figure why she always used the back of her hand to check for fever, most folks used the inside of their wrist. She was about as reliable as a fever thermometer though, so I guess she knew what she was doing.

"I just ain't hungry tonight," I said. "I think I'll turn in early and get a good night's sleep. I might just lay down and read for a while 'til I get sleepy." With that, I got up out of my chair and headed down the hall to my room. I had it in my mind to just kind of lay low 'til it got time to sneak out of the window and head over to Leon's house. I picked up the paperback western I had been reading and settled down on the bed to read a few minutes. I must have been sleepier than I thought, because the next thing I knew, I was waking up and when I looked at the clock it showed to be ten minutes short of 10:00 o'clock.

As I eased out of the west bedroom window, I could see there was a bank of clouds almost obscuring the moon. As I hurried along to Leon's house, the night got spookier and spookier. The clouds drifting across the moon gave an eerie feel to the night. Before I reached the sidewalk in front of Leon's house, the wind had sprung up and was howling through the trees and around the corner of the house as I stepped up onto the front porch.

"Who goes there?" The suddenness of the voice shocked me and almost made me pee my pants. I was about to make myself scarce when Jerry and Leon stepped around the corner of the house.

"Scared you, didn't we?" Jerry chuckled. "I thought for a minute you was gonna take out running or something."

"Something's right," I replied. "You were about this close to getting a knuckle sandwich." Before I could finish what I was saying, Davey came walking up out of the darkness and was the only one of us smart enough to bring a light. Before I could compliment him on his forward thinking, the light went out.

"What kind of a light you got there Davey?"

"It's a carbide light, that's what it is. Wind keeps blowing the dang thing out."

"Alright, let's go," Leon whispered. "If we wake my folks up, that's gonna be the end of me for tonight."

We eased out of there and headed across town to where the old two story house stood waiting like a silent sentinel in the night. As we got close enough to make out the shape of the house, I thought I saw a light in one of the upstairs windows. Not what you would call a real bright light, just a flicker like a candle was being snuffed out or something. I could feel the blood run cold in my cheeks.

"You guys see that light!" I whispered. It was more of a command than a question. I was sure hoping I wasn't the only one who had seen the quick flicker of light.

"What light?" Davey whispered back. "I didn't see no light."

"There ain't no light," Jerry said. "Petey's just trying to back out of going into the old house is all."

"Ain't neither," I shot back at him. "You just wait 'til we get in there and you'll see."

Davey had finally got the old carbide light to working again. From the look on his face though, it was apparent he wasn't about to part with it. He did walk up to the front of the house with us so we could see to open the massive front door. When Jerry turned the knob and pushed, the door began to creak open ever so slowly. About that time, the moon went behind the clouds again.

"Bring that light over here a minute Davey," Leon whispered. "I think I see a lantern hanging on the wall over there."

Sure enough, when Davey held the carbide light up over his head, it was clear there was one of those old kerosene lanterns hanging on a nail about head high just inside the door. Leon reached up to take it off the nail and jumped back so suddenly he about knocked me and Jerry both back out the door.

"Now what's the matter?' I asked.

"That there lantern is still warm," Leon whispered back. "It's like somebody just blew it out and hung it up there on that nail."

"Let me get that lantern," Jerry smirked. "I never seen so many fraidy cats in one place in all my born life." he reached up and took the lantern off the nail. I could see he was shocked to see it really was still warm from being used, but he had already popped off too much to let it show. "Follow me," he whispered as he turned to face the staircase on the far side of the room.

One by one we made our way across the room toward the staircase. I could feel my heart in my throat and it was getting harder and harder to swallow. It was like a slow waltz, one foot forward, hesitate, and then the other foot following. When he reached the bottom of the stairs Jerry stopped and looked back at us. I could barely make out his face by the pale moonlight finding its way into the front door we had left open.

"You want to go first Petey?"

So there it was. When it came time to put up or shut up, he had lost his nerve. Jerry, the one who had been the macho man through the entire thing. The one who kept making fun of the rest of us for being just a little bit scared. Right there at the bottom of the stairs, he had lost his nerve. Might have known it. Right then, I felt a surge of adrenaline and all my fears just went away.

"Sure I'll go first." I felt my way around Leon and took the still unlit lantern from Jerry. I felt in my pocket for the little penny box of matches that I knew was still there from the firecracker popping episode earlier that day. It took three matches to get it going, but soon the kerosene lantern was lighting up the entire room, staircase and all. With a little more confidence than I felt, I raised my foot and stepped up onto the bottom step.

SCREEECH!! The sound was like an omen of doom in the still air of the room. When my heart settled back down into my chest, I took another step, and then another. The stairway was one of the kind I always called 'split level' staircases. It went up for ten or twelve steps, then took a ninety degree turn to the left and went up five or six more steps into the upstairs hallway. Screechy step after screechy step, we made our slow way up to the first level. I didn't realize I had been holding my breath until I felt it expel out of my lungs once I was safe on the first landing.

When Leon had caught up to my position with Jerry following closely behind, I turned and took the first step up the second flight of stairs. I could feel a pretty good draft of air coming from the hallway just above my head and I remember figuring at least one of the upstairs windows must be broken out to let so much air into the hallway like that.

It happened so suddenly, I still can't to this day recall

the exact series of events that led to what happened. I do recall that I had been looking back at Leon and Jerry when I got high enough onto the second set of stairs to see clearly down the upstairs hallway. At least as clearly as the flickering flame from the kerosene lantern would allow me to see. And what I saw turned my blood to ice! There coming down the hallway toward me was a genuine ghost with the white sheet look and everything. Just as a strong puff of wind blew the lantern out, that ghost let loose with the most blood-curdling scream I had ever heard or have ever heard since.

"WHOOOOO!!, it screamed, then again, WHOOOO!!. I remember slinging the now useless lantern in the general direction of the apparition just before I ran over both Leon and Jerry as I rushed headlong down the stairs. One problem!! I had forgotten the stairs made a turn to the right and I kept right on going straight ahead and crashed through the side rail. I could feel myself falling through the air but my legs kept right on pumping, just waiting for something solid for my feet to touch.

When my feet hit the floor, the momentum propelled me forward toward the door and I knocked both Jerry and Leon off their feet a second time in as many seconds. We all scrambled back to our feet and out the door we went just in time to see a second ghost, an exact replica of the first, come around the corner of the house with white fabric flapping in the wind.

"OOOOOOH!!, this one screamed. Looking ahead down the road, I could see the carbide light Davey was carrying bobbing up and down as he ran for dear life trying to get away from the ghosts. I always figured I could run faster than just about anybody around our neck of the woods, but Jerry passed me like I was still in first gear. Way back behind us, in the neighborhood of the old two story house, I could hear a steady stream of whimpering cries.

"Hold up," I hollered. "Something's got leon. "We got to go back and help him." Before anybody could answer, we could see Leon coming down the street as fast as he could run. We fell in with him when he got even with us and we ran all the way to Main Street where we finally stopped in the light of one of the few street lights that graced the wide street.

"What happened?"

"Something grabbed me just as I ran out the yard gate," Leon replied. Looked like a ghost, but I'm pretty sure I smelled shaving lotion. You reckon ghosts wear after shave lotion Petey?"

"I don't figure a ghost even shaves, I answered shakily. "At least I never heard of one that had a beard."

"I seen one on Casper one time that had a beard, Davey volunteered. "Never did see him shave it though best I can recollect."

"We've been took," I said. "Somebody found out about our little episode tonight and thought they'd teach us a lesson.

"What's wrong with your leg Petey"? Davey asked.

Looking down at my right leg, I could see my jeans were torn just above the knee and blood had soaked through the material and down my leg into my shoe. When I rolled the pants leg up, there was a pretty deep gash about two inches long running across the muscle just above the kneecap.

"Better get that thing sewed up," Leon said. "You're gonna have to go to the hospital and get some stitches in that."

"No I'm not," I shot back. "I'm gonna go home and clean it up and put some band aids on it. Better not any of you say anything to your folks about it either."

It took about three weeks before it was completely well, and I'll wear the scar the rest of my life, but anything was better than owning up to being a fraidy cat and getting hurt, I figured.

We tried really hard, but I was never sure who the after shave wearing ghosts were that night. I'm pretty sure one of them was Jimmy Cox because I believe I recognized his voice. The other one, I'm not so sure of. It may have been my brother Dan, but if it was, he never owned up to it. If you are reading this story and if you know who it was, let me know. Even if it was you. I would never try to get even, you know.

The End

The Old Barber Shop

I will never forget the old barber shops. They served as a place for the old men to gather and swap stories and catch up on the latest news. All the daily newspapers would be lying around on the benches and chairs and would supply endless subjects for discussion and at times, some heated debates. The smell of bay rum and talcum powder mixed with the smell of wood burning in the stove, and the inevitable spittoons beside the stove and between the chairs.

The sound the clippers made as they cut through the hair was a little scary to a five year old boy the first time I sat and waited for my turn to get a haircut at Benny Reynolds's Barber Shop. My hand clutched the quarter Mom had given me to pay for the haircut as I waited in the chair farthest from where the action was taking place. I remember thinking if I took the seat way down at the end, someone might come in and get in line ahead of me thus postponing my turn at the chair. With a little luck, it might even get to be closing time before it came my turn if enough people got ahead of me. I might not even be able to get a haircut at all.

A high school guy was getting his hair cut when I went in and took a seat. I believe it was one of the Settles boys, but I can't recall which one. I know he had a Cushman Scooter though because I had stopped to admire it on the sidewalk out in front of the Barber Shop before I came in. He was getting a 'flat top' haircut and I figured to get me a flat top when I got a little older. Right now, I didn't want a haircut of any description, and wasn't gonna get one if I could help it.

Two old men were sitting in the comfortable chairs up toward the front of the shop and stopped talking to look at me when I came in. I didn't figure they were in there to get a haircut, just shooting the bull and killing time most likely. Mom had walked me to the door of the shop, and after giving me instructions to get a haircut, then wait in the Barber Shop until she came back for me, she headed up the street to the grocery store.

I was sitting and looking at all the tall glass bottles full of after shave lotion and hair oil and such on the shelf above the mirror and it took me by surprise when Benny called my name.

"You're up next young fellar," he said. "Petey, ain't it? Here, let me get this here booster for you to sit on." He placed a little wooden chair in the seat of the big barber chair then motioned for me to climb up and take a seat.

"I ain't here to get a haircut," I said. I'm just waiting on my mom to get back from the grocery store."

"Is that a fact?" he said. "What you got that quarter for if you ain't here to get a haircut? He glanced over at the two old men and I could see him wink at them when he thought I wasn't looking.

Well, he had me there. Before I could think of something to say to that, he took a little white towel and wrapped around my neck and then he took a pair of scissors off the shelf under the mirror.

"This won't take but a minute," he said. He didn't even ask me if I wanted a flat top, he just started in with the scissors. He had his big old hand on top of my head, and every once in a while, he'd turn my head this way or that to get a better angle for the scissors. Before long, he jerked the towel off my neck and with a powdered brush, he brushed most of the hair from off my shirt and from around my collar. He took a bottle of some red looking liquid off the shelf, shook some out in his hands and ran his hands through my hair 'til it was coated with the stuff. A few swishes with the comb and I was ready to go. He picked me up and set me down on the floor beside the chair. I put the quarter in the hand he held out to me.

Well now, this haircut business wasn't as bad as I had it figured to be. As I turned to look out the plate glass window in the front of the Barber Shop, I could see my mom coming down the sidewalk with two big bags of groceries.

"How'd it go?" she asked.

"Ain't nothing to it," I replied. "I was just getting a haircut. What's so special about getting a haircut anyway?" Now that it was over, I could afford to be the big shot.

I got a lot of haircuts at Benny's Barber Shop over the years. I got regular haircuts, burr haircuts, and yes, a flat top or two and I've come to this conclusion. Boys now-a-days that don't have the opportunity to go to one of the old time barber shops are missing out on a really unique American experience. Barber shops, for many years, were the center of communication around small town America. Elections were won and lost and baseball championships were decided inside the walls of the local barber shop.

When I first started getting my hair cut at Benny's, regular haircuts and burr haircuts were 25 cents. Flat tops were 50 cents. I believe those were the only choices. Contrary to common belief among us kids, I never saw a bowl being used in Benny's Barber Shop. Barbering tools haven't changed a lot over the years. They still use the clippers and shears just like they did in the 1950s. The one thing you see now that you never saw back then in an old time barber shop is the hair dryer. Men were too macho to use such a feminine thing as a hair dryer.

I'd like to have the opportunity, just one more time, to sit in the old barber chair at Benny's and listen to the old men talk while he cut my hair. I'd like to smell the powder and hair tonic again mixed with the smell of the wood burning in the cast iron stove. Even more than that, I'd like to pay 25 cents for a haircut instead of the $10 or more that it costs now. I don't figure there's much chance of that happening!

The End

Hay Hauling on Old Blue

Hauling hay is hard work anyway you want to slice it. The pay is terrible as well, or at least it was when I was a teenager. I hauled hay for Charlie McCuase, Weldon Jarman, a little for my uncle Jasper and others, but the summer I hauled for Bob Callen was by far the hardest work and the most fun at the same time.

Mr. Callen was a teacher at school and had a couple of hay trucks. In the summer, he would haul hay to make extra money. He was from down around the Blue River area of southeast Johnston County and that was where we did most of our hay hauling. He had a camp set up by the river and we would stay there for three or four days at a time just hauling hay up and down the river bottom for first one then the other. We slept in tents, cooked out on a campfire when we cooked at all, and swam in the river to keep clean. We must have hauled more than a hundred thousand bales of hay out of the river bottom that summer.

We had two crews working most of the time and when

you get that many guys together for any length of time there are bound to be a few things happen that might not be good to take home and tell your folks about. Like the night we all decided we would go over to the Blue River Bar and get a little beer. It was a Friday night and we had been on the river since the preceding Sunday night. Mr. Callen had gone to Mill Creek to pick up a few things we needed and was gonna stop by the grocery store on the way back. We had just about run out of anything to eat at the camp after we finished supper that night. He gave us all strict orders to be back in camp by midnight if we went anywhere since we had an early start the next morning.

We had all had a swim and was just sitting around the camp talking when Ed Hensen said he thought he would drive over to Tishomingo for a while. Ed had a girl at Tish he had been seeing a little and thought he might catch her in town. I was a good mind to go with him and would have if Johnny Nelson hadn't said something about the Blue River Bar. It was only a few miles over to the Bar and Johnny thought we could just run over there and get some beer and bring it back to camp. Sounded like a good idea to me, so along with Leroy Bishop and James Bell we headed out toward where the cars were parked. That beer must have started to sound good to Bobby McCloud as well because we hadn't gotten ten feet when he allowed as how he'd just go with us. When Robert Hously decided he'd go as well, we knew we were gonna have to take two cars.

"Why don't we just drive one of the hay trucks over there"? Johnny asked. "We can just ride on the back. Be more fun anyway."

With Ed driving, we all jumped on the back of the truck and headed out to the road. There were eight or nine of us guys riding on the back of the truck and Paul Simms was in the cab with Ed.

If we would have just bought the beer and headed back to camp like we planned to do, everything would have been alright. But that's not what we did. Wasn't our fault, what was a bunch of guys supposed to do when challenged to a game of pool? Especially when we really didn't have a chance to turn down the challenge.

There were three or four pretty rough looking guys sitting around in the bar and two more guys playing pool when we walked in. None of us were old enough to buy beer, but we figured way out in the boonies like we were, they'd probably sell it to us anyway. We had taken up a collection before we went in and Johnny had the money in his pocket when he walked up and ordered a case of beer.

"You old enough to buy beer?" the fat man behind the bar asked.

"My money's the same color as them guys," Johnny replied. He pulled the wad of bills out of his pocket and showed it to the bartender. Trouble was, the two guys playing pool saw it too.

"How'd you like to try to double that money kid?" the tall Indian guy asked. "Me and Jack here will play you and somebody for a dollar a game. You pick the somebody."

"I don't think so," Johnny said. "We just came in here to get some beer. We got to get back down to the river."

The other guy walked around the table and stopped right in front of Johnny. "Maybe you didn't hear what Frank said," he said. "Pick you a partner and let's play pool. Lay your dollar on the bar there and get a stick. You can break."

Now this was quite a fix we had gotten ourselves into. There were more of us than there was of them, but they looked to me like they had seen a lot of barroom fighting and were all grown men to boot. The guys at the bar were all looking to see what Johnny was gonna do and if it didn't go well, I knew they would all be in on whatever happened.

What they didn't know, was that Johnny was about as good a pool player as there was around and Leroy was almost as good. I was doing some quick thinking here and it didn't look to me like there was a chance this was gonna turn out well. As it turned out, it went about as badly as it could have.

Leroy had his stick picked out and was chalking it up. He was going to break the rack. Johnny had laid a dollar on the bar and the tall Indian put another one on top of it. Leroy made a stripe and two solids on the break and took the solids since they looked to be laid out real good. He made a couple of balls, then missed a bank shot to the corner giving up the table to Jack and Frank. Frank made three balls in a row and I began to think he was gonna run the table when the twelve ball hung in the side pocket and just sat there on the table not a half inch from falling in. It would be the last shot they would get. Johnny ran the last of the solids one by one and then called the eight ball in the corner pocket. When it went in, he walked over and picked up both dollars off the bar.

"Give us another shot," Jack said. I looked over at Johnny and shook my head in the negative. I figured we might have a chance to get out of there if we left right then. If we stayed any longer, things were likely to get ugly and I knew it. By then though, Johnny had figured he might as well oblige them and take their money if they were so set on giving it away, so he laid another dollar on the bar.

"Why not play for five bucks this time?" Frank asked.

"Suits me," Johnny replied, and laid another four dollars on the bar. Frank covered it with a five spot and the game was on. Johnny broke and made a solid on the break. Then he commenced to methodically make one ball after the other until he had only the eight ball left to make.

Problem was, it was hidden behind a stripe ball way down at the far end of the table. He studied it for at least two or three minutes.

"What's the matter Hot Shot?" Frank asked. "Thought you were gonna run the table, didn't you?" Johnny didn't say a word. With one last look, he lined up for a two-bank shot that I figured would lose the game for him. If he hit another ball before he hit the eight ball, he would lose the game. The stroke was so slow that I didn't think it was gonna be hard enough to knock the ball into the pocket even if it got there. I guess that's why Johnny was playing and I was watching. The cue ball came off the second bank and just kissed the eight ball ever so slightly as it went by; just enough to send it rolling slowly into the corner pocket. Silence for what seemed like a minute though it couldn't have been over a couple of seconds.

If Leroy hadn't started laughing, we might have gotten out of there even after Johnny picked up the ten bucks and started for the door. I could see the blood coming up into Jack's face and I knew he was fixin to blow up. We all headed for the door just as Jack started around the pool table with blood in his eyes. Leroy still had the pool stick in his hand and he reached up with it and busted the light bulb over the pool table, then headed for the door. Ed hit the light switch by the door as he went out plunging the entire barroom into total darkness. He had the hay truck running as we all jumped on. Somebody grabbed James's hand and helped him onto the truck. He had been the last one out the door and was running to try to catch the truck. Ed pulled off the road into a hay field about two miles down the road and we sat there on the truck until we saw a car go by on the road at a high rate of speed.

"Ought to be safe to go now," Robert said, so we headed back to camp. When we were almost back to camp it came to me. We never got any beer. It was a good thing 'cause when we pulled up to the camp, Mr. Callen was unloading groceries from his car and he would have thrown a shoe if we came back to camp with beer.

"Where you boys been?" he asked.

We all just looked at each other and started laughing. "We just thought we'd go for a little ride, that's all," Ed replied. "Hard to stay hooked up in camp on a Friday night."

We stayed at that camp and hauled hay the better part of the summer. We'd go home every few nights and get our clothes washed and then head back the next morning. We developed a camaraderie while working together every day. Oh, there were some disagreements like there will be when a bunch of guys get together, and even a skirmish or two. But I'll guarantee you if one of us was to get into something we couldn't handle, the others would jump in to help in a heartbeat.

It was only a few miles to the little town of Milburn, Oklahoma from where we were camped, and we went through there on a regular basis going from one hay field to another or from one barn to another. There was an old store there where we would stop and buy pops and such and the old man that ran the store had a daughter that worked behind the counter. I can't, for the life of me, remember what her name was, so I'll just call her Betty. She wasn't what you would call a beauty queen, but Leroy took a liking to her and one day when we stopped there, he talked her into meeting him out in front of her house later that night.

When we finished supper that evening, Leroy, Bobby, and James all piled up in James's pickup and headed over to Milburn. I didn't go with them, so the story I'm about to tell is second hand and is James's version of what happened. Leroy never did tell his side of the story and since I could tell he didn't want to talk about it, I never mentioned it to him.

It was good and dark by the time they eased up and stopped about a half a block north of the house. Bobby and James were going to wait in the truck while Leroy went on up to the yard to meet Betty. It was about as good a plan as any I guess, but it didn't work out worth a hoot.

Leroy eased up the street until he was even with the front porch of the house and stopped behind a bush to gather his nerve. He figured to wait right there behind the bush until he saw her come out of the house. After waiting for a few minutes, he could hear a noise in the bushes about half way between his position and the front porch. As he stood there, it came to him that Betty was probably doing the same thing he was doing. She was waiting in the bushes for him, and he was waiting in the bushes for her. The noise he kept hearing had to be her.

He stood there a few more minutes building his nerve and then he whispered just loud enough for her to hear him if it was her hiding in the bushes there between him and the house.

"Betty," he whispered. When he didn't get a reply, he whispered a little louder. "Betty, is that you Betty?" As he said it the second time, he stepped out from behind the bush. The bushes up ahead started moving and out she stepped into the faint moonlight. Only it wasn't Betty, it was her old man and as soon as he saw Leroy, he let loose with the double-barreled shotgun he had in his hands. Leroy just had time to dive back into the bushes as the bird shot sailed over his head. Out of the far side of the bushes he ran and was making for the pickup as fast as his legs could carry him.

Back up the street, James and Bobby had heard the shot and had the motor running when Leroy dove into the bed of the truck. The second barrel went off as they made a bat-turn and headed north out of town with the tires squealing. Bobby said he thought he could hear the shot hitting the truck as they went out of sight around the corner. Sure enough, the next morning, we could see the little spots of missing paint where the bird shot hit on the right front fender of the pickup.

A couple of days later, we stopped at the store to get something to drink, but Leroy wouldn't go in. Betty was behind the counter as usual and she was looking around trying to see if Leroy was with us. Her old man looked us over pretty good as well, but he didn't say anything about the episode with the shotgun.

Several years after that incident, I went to work for the tire plant at Ardmore. I had been working there for a few months and had gone into the break area to eat lunch one afternoon and you'll never guess who was sitting there drinking a coke. Yea, it was Betty. She looked at me, and I looked at her. I'm sure she recognized me, but she never said a word and I didn't either. She didn't work there very long and I didn't see her but one or two more times after that.

I'd hate to think I had to haul hay now-a-days. I just couldn't do it. Back in the 1960s we didn't think anything about hauling hay twelve to fourteen hours a day. It was hard work, but we sure had a lot of good times doing it. The best ones were the days camping out on Blue River the summer of 1964. I grew up a lot that summer, but not too much to realize that those days were almost over and we'd soon all go our own way. The memories, though, will always be there if we will just take the time to reflect on them. I wonder if Leroy ever got to where he could see the humor in the shotgun episode?

The End

The Old Grey Mare

In 1957, my Uncle Jasper and Aunt Em moved into a log house in the country about half way between Mill Creek Oklahoma and Reagan Oklahoma. I spent a lot of time at that old log house for a couple of years and had some of the most enjoyable times of my childhood there.

It was just a four room log house. It had a "front room," as they called them back then, two bedrooms and a kitchen. There was no bathroom in the house, but there was two-holer outhouse out back. I remember the bucket of corncobs that always sat in the corner by the door of that outhouse and the big Sears and Roebuck catalog that lay between the thrones. The catalog had a lot of missing pages, of course, but I would sit and look at the toy section, especially the bicycles, baseball gloves and such. I suppose some folks used the corncobs, but I never was tough enough. Didn't take but one try for me to figure out the pages from the catalog was a whole lot better deal.

I would ride the school bus to their place on Friday

afternoon when school let out and spend the weekend. Some of the time, Mom would drive out and get me on Sunday night, and other times, I would just ride the bus to school on Monday morning. Being a town kid at the time, I thought it was quite a big deal getting to ride the school bus.

There was a well in the back yard that had one of them long skinny buckets with a handle on the top you pulled to let the water out. I always had chores to do when I stayed with Jasper and Em, and one of them was filling the water bucket. There was a two gallon galvanized bucket that sat on the kitchen counter with a dipper in it. Em used the water in the bucket to cook with as well, so it had to be filled several times a day. When it was really cold outside, filling the water bucket was quite a chore.

The old house didn't have any kind of heat except a wood stove, and it was in the front room. The bedrooms were on the north side, one off the front room and one off the kitchen. When I stayed there, I stayed in the bedroom off the front room. Aunt Em would pile three or four homemade quilts on my bed and I would snuggle in. It was the best sleeping I've ever done in my life.

In the spring and fall, Jasper would break the garden spot and put in a big garden. Em would can vegetables in glass jars and put them in the cellar so they wouldn't freeze. Jasper and I would pick the vegetables and wash them real good. Em had a big canner that sat on a one-burner propane stove hooked to a ten gallon propane tank. Jasper would have to take the propane tank to town and get it filled up a time or two before all the canning was done.

Jasper broke the garden with an old grey mare and a walk-behind plow. Don't see that done anymore. I'd follow along behind and pick up the red worms that got turned up with the dirt. I'd have a can full by the time the garden was all plowed, and we'd all go fishing down at the pond. There would be fried fish for supper that night.

That old mare and I spent a lot of time together. She would let me climb all over her and I rode many a mile around that part of the country on that old mare. We had a ritual every weekend. When I would get there on Friday afternoon, I would head off to the pasture to catch the old grey mare. I would stop by the feed house and put twenty or thirty cattle cubes in a bucket. It was the only way I could ever catch her. When I would find her in the pasture, I would lay down a cube on the ground and she'd come and eat it. She would never let me catch her though. I'd head back to the barn dropping a cattle cube every fifty or sixty feet and she'd follow along eating the cubes. Finally, we'd end up in the lot and I was always able to catch her then. She had to know what was going on; I think she just did it as a way to get the cattle cubes.

Jasper made it a point to caution me about riding the old mare too hard. "She's getting pretty old," he'd say. "She might just fall with you if you get her to going too fast." 'Course nine year old boys are so much smarter than grown men, so I didn't pay too much attention to Jasper's going on about the old mare. I knew enough not to over work a horse anyway.

One Saturday morning in November, I was riding the mare about a mile west of Jasper's and Em's place. It was a brisk, cool fall morning with just a touch of frost on the ground. The trees had mostly lost their leaves by that time, and I could see a fair distance through the woods in front of me. A time or two, I thought I had spotted something moving through the trees ahead of me, but could never really make out what it was. It was a lazy day as the sun climbed higher in the sky. I had watched a covey of quail take to wing about a hundred yards ahead of me, but it didn't occur to me to wonder what spooked them enough to make them fly.

What had my attention was a grove of persimmon trees right in a little clearing, and the ripe fruit was hanging so heavily on the limbs it looked like they were about to break. I knew I wanted me some of those persimmons, and had in mind to gather a hat full to take back to Em. I figured she might make me a persimmon pie which was just about my favorite kind of pie.

As I rode up to the persimmon trees, I thought I caught a glimpse of something ducking back into the timber off to the right where the ground began to fall off into six mile creek bottom. By that time, I was beginning to get a little spooked about whatever it was that seemed to be watching me. I soon forgot all about the unknown creature as I began to stuff the ripe persimmons into my mouth. Not much of anything is as good as ripe persimmons, in my opinion, though they don't seem to taste nearly as good now as they did back then. Something must have happened to change the taste of persimmons over the years, I figure.

I had tied the old mare to a limb of a persimmon tree and she was going after the persimmons as well. When I had my fill, I began to fill my cap with the ripe fruit. When I had a cap full, it didn't look like enough persimmons to make a pie, so I took off my shirt and filled it with persimmons as well. After pulling the shirt tails together and tying them in a knot, I had a nice little bundle of goodies ready to take to Aunt Em. Problem was, how was I gonna manage to get on my horse with a cap full of persimmons in one hand and a shirt full of persimmons in the other. I finally led the mare over to a spot where a tree had fallen and got hung up with a bigger tree on the way down. The leaning tree trunk was just right for me to stand on and jump to the mare's bare back.

By that time, all thought of the thing in the woods had left my mind. Nine year old boys don't always have a very long attention span, and as for me, I sort of figured I was invincible anyway. I had gotten about half way back through the woods to the open pasture west of the cabin when it happened. I was just riding along, not a care in the world, with my mind on that persimmon pie, when something flung itself out of a tree directly in front of me with the loudest scream I ever heard. That thing looked for all the world like a big hairy ape and the old grey mare must have thought so as well because she took out of there like all the demons ever made were after her. I barely managed to hang on, what with both hands being full of persimmons. As she ducked and dodged her way through the trees as fast as she could run, I was just hoping that mare could stay on her feet.

Meanwhile, back behind me, the screams and howls had turned to laughter. It was taking all my attention just to stay on the back of the hard running mare and it took a few seconds for it to dawn on me that it was laughter I was hearing from back behind me. I turned and looked back for just a second to see if I could spot the critter that was now laughing and when I turned around again it was just in time for a big limb hanging over the trail to catch me right across the forehead. Off the back of the horse I went to land heavily on my back in the trail. The mare kept on running toward the cabin as fast as she could run. I struggled to catch the breath that had been knocked out of me by the fall. My eyes were open, but things were sort of spinning around. I blinked a couple of times and things began to settle down enough that my eyes could get a grip on them.

Just as I thought I might try to sit up, something grabbed me by the shoulders and picked me up. I just knew the critter had me until Jasper started talking.

"You okay Pete?" he asked with a quiver in his voice. "Can you stand up?"

As my vision began to clear, I could see it was Jasper standing there, but he had on some kind of big furry coat that hung from his shoulders almost down to his feet. He had that thing girted around him with a piece of rope, and with the furry cap he had on his head, looked for all the world like some kind of prehistoric animal.

We started back to the cabin walking slowly down the trail. As we walked out of the woods into the pasture west of the cabin, I could see Em running across the pasture toward us. She had spotted the mare running into the corral and knew something had happened. She stopped when she saw us coming her way and stood there with a worried look on her face.

"What in the world happened to you?" she asked as we came walking up. "Where did you get that skinned spot on your forehead?"

"I guess I fell off my horse," I answered.

"And what did you have to do with this?" Em asked looking right at Jasper. "What is that contraption you've got on anyway?"

Jasper just stood there with a sheepish look on his face. Wasn't much he could say. He was just gonna have a little fun and scare me with an old bearskin that had been hanging in the smokehouse since my Uncle Ervie had brought it to him from New Mexico the previous summer. He didn't intend for things to go the way they did, and he was feeling mighty sorry about the whole episode by that time.

"What's that you've got in your hand there Pete?" Em asked. I looked down to see I was still clutching the shirt full of persimmons. Problem was, they had gotten mashed pretty good in the fall and persimmon juice was dripping from the bundle down to form a puddle on the ground. I had no idea where my cap had gotten off to.

"I thought you might make a persimmon pie," I said looking at Em. "Looks like all the persimmons are ruined though."

"That's just what I'm gonna do," she replied. "Just as soon as Jasper gets his ornery hide back over there and picks some more persimmons." The look on her face didn't leave any room for argument, so Jasper just turned and started walking back toward the persimmon patch.

A couple of hours later, after the old mare had been taken care of and the pie was out of the oven, we all sat down at the kitchen table to rest and enjoy some of the pie. Jasper and Em had steaming hot cups of coffee and I had a tall glass of milk fresh from the morning milking. All was good and right with the world again.

Jasper would rather pull a practical joke on somebody as to sit down to a steak dinner. It's one of the things I will always remember about him. The bear skin caper was one I was wishing he hadn't pulled that day though. I had a headache for most of a week. I'm sure now that I had a concussion, but we didn't know about things like that back then.

Jasper and Em didn't live in the log cabin but a couple of years but it is one of the spots that holds a special place in the memories of my childhood. I learned to milk a cow and plow a straight furrow on that place. I spent many a Saturday afternoon exploring the countryside on the old grey mare. Good times, quiet times. Perfect for a young mind to begin to learn the lessons of life and appreciate just being allowed to be a kid. A far cry from what a lot of kids do today with all the time spent with video games, cell phones, and television. It is my desire that this story will inspire a kid to want to get out into the woods and fill up on ripe persimmons. Maybe even fill his cap with persimmons to take home for a persimmon pie. If it does, and that kid spots something in the woods, it might just be Uncle Jasper in a bear skin waiting to pounce out of a tree with a squall and a growl. He might want to watch out for that low hanging limb, it packs quite a wallop.

The End

Short Takes

This section contains s few shorter stories that I thought might be of interest to readers. These are all true mini-stories that have stuck in my memory over the years. I wanted to include them, so here they are in the form of "Short takes." Hope you enjoy them.

A Case of Mistaken Identity

It was on a Saturday night in late January 1967. I had me a 1963 Ford with a 390 Police interceptor motor and a special Highway Patrol transmission. It was just a plain Ford Custom, but what it lacked in looks, it made up for in pure dee get up and go. On this particular night, however, it was playing a more mundane role. Hank Graham and I had been out coon hunting down on Pennington Creek near the town of Reagan USA and had started back home to Mill Creek. It was about 2:00 o'clock in the morning as best I can remember. We had the trunk of that Ford full of coon dogs and the rear end of the thing was sitting perceptibly lower than normal.

We was just cruising along on the highway south of town, talking and not paying much attention to anything else, when I happened to notice headlights coming up on us pretty fast from behind. I had just brought that fact to Hank's attention when all of a sudden the red lights came on and the siren started blaring.

"Now what in the world can this be about?" Hank asked. "We couldn't have been speeding, we weren't running over fifty miles an hour if that, don't you think Petey?"

"We sure enough weren't speeding," I replied as I pulled the Ford into the entrance to Indian Springs. "Probably got a tail light out or something. I brought the Ford to a stop and opened the door to get out.

"Hold it right there," a voice hollered. "Put them hands up over your head and don't make any funny moves."

Well, as soon as I heard the voice, I knew who it was; Kenneth Rueben, Sheriff of Johnston County Oklahoma. It wasn't like Kenneth didn't know us, or us him for that matter, and the more I thought about him stopping us and pulling a gun on us, the madder I got.

"Kenneth," I said. "What in the world has got into you throwing a gun on me and Hank like this?"

"That you Pete?" he answered.

"Well, of course it's me," I said. "Me and Hank. What are you doing out stopping folks at this time of the night anyway?"

I could tell I might be taking things a little too far, so I shut up and just stood there with my hands up. Meanwhile, Hank had gotten out of the car and was standing beside the open door. He didn't know whether to stick his hands up or not.

"What you boys got in the trunk of that car?" Kenneth

wanted to know. "And you can take your hands down now too."

"Coon dogs."

"What?"

"You asked what we had in the trunk of the car and I just told you. Coon dogs."

"What if I said I didn't believe you?"

"Now why would me and Hank lie to you about it?" I said. "All you got to do is look for yourself."

"And that's just what I'm gonna do. Open the trunk."

I looked over at Hank and he was grinning from ear to ear. I knew right off what he had in mind.

"Why are you in such an all fired hurry to look in that trunk anyway?" Hank wanted to know. "What you reckon we got in there anyway.?"

"Well, some guys stole a bunch of copper wire down at the Rock Wool Plant a couple of hours ago. Eye witness described a car that fits the description of this car right here. I'd say it's a pretty good bet that I'm fixin to find that copper wire right in that there trunk."

"Why don't you just let us go Kenneth?" Hank pleaded. "You don't really want to look in that trunk , do you?"

By that time, Hank really had Kenneth convinced the copper wire was in the trunk. Every time he opened his mouth, the more convinced Kenneth became that he had found the culprits.

"Might as well let him look Pete," Hank finally said. "Looks like he's got us fair and square. Now for the last time Kenneth, are you sure you gotta look in that trunk?"

"Open that trunk Pete," Kenneth said as he walked up right behind the car. As I reached into my pocket for the trunk key, he pulled his flashlight out of the leather holster on his belt and leaned down close to the trunk to get a good look when the trunk opened. I fumbled with the key, trying to get it into the lock, and the more I fumbled, the closer Kenneth got his face to the trunk. Finally, I turned the key and threw the trunk open right in his face.

Glory Be!!! Them coon dogs came pouring out of that trunk like they were headed to the Last Supper for coon dogs. In a matter of seconds, Kenneth had coon dogs in his face, on top of his head, and everywhere in between. As he staggered backward, one of the dogs ran between his legs and down he went onto the damp ground. Hank was laughing as hard as he could laugh and I was too 'til I saw the look on Kenneth's face when he came lunging up off the ground.

"I ought to take you both down to the County Jail," he hollered.

"What for?" I asked.

He stuttered around for a few seconds and finally made up his mind what he was gonna do. "You boys get them dogs gathered up and get home. If I catch you back out again tonight, I am gonna take you and lock you up."

"Yes sir!" we both said in unison. We were both trying hard to keep a straight face. We gathered the dogs all up but it took a while. By that time, they were all scattered out looking for more coons. As we drove on into town, we finally got to laugh about how funny Kenneth looked when the dogs came pouring out of the trunk on top of him. He was so sure we had the copper wire; he didn't stop to think that we might really have been coon hunting.

He should have known we wouldn't do anything like stealing a bunch of copper wire anyway. Why, we was as pure as the driven snow. I'll bet mothers all over the county were telling their sons. "You ought to be more like Pete and Hank. Now there is a couple of boys to model yourself after. We do what we can to help, you know. It ain't easy being a role model, but we tried.

A Profound Statement

Every town back in the 1950s and 1960s had spit and whittle benches. I would sit and listen to the old men tell their stories about how much wilder and uncivilized the country had been when they were youngsters. They'd talk about moonshine whisky and brush arbor revivals like they were subjects that went together like apple pie and ice cream. They'd talk about women and cars, politics and fighting, favorite foods and fast horses. And they'd talk about the wars, both WW1 and WW2.

It was on one of those occasions that I happened to be sitting there listening to them talk when I noticed a jet airplane high in the sky. That plane was leaving a vapor trail and it stretched almost from one horizon to the other. I wasn't the only one who noticed it either. Willard McCartney looked over at Frank Holley with a grin on his face.

"How'd you like to be up there in that there jet airplane with that old boy Frank?"

Frank cocked his head to one side so he could look up at the plane that was now almost directly overhead. He kept that position for what seemed like two or three minutes. Finally, he spoke.

"I'd a whole lot druther be up there with him than up there without him," he finally replied. I'd say that was one profound statement.

The Neighborly Thing to Do

You remember the story in "Black Cotton" where I talked about my paper route and how I used it to pay off a new bicycle that my dad had already paid for? You do! Well, then you remember that when the bike was finally paid for, I turned the paper route over to my friend Davey. Now Davey had a similar problem to the one I had. He didn't have a decent bike to deliver papers on. I don't recall exactly how it happened, but he got a new bike right after he started delivering the papers. Seems like his dad got it for him and he was supposed to use some of his paper money to pay for part of it or something.

Be that as it may, the day he brought the new bike home, he and I were just riding around letting him get the feel of it when we ran up behind a road grader moving at the slow pace road graders move at. We followed along for a while, like kids will do, just riding slowly and talking. The grader was headed out of town to the west and was just about to cross the railroad tracks down by Emory Sewell's Station. In the 1950s the road from Main Street to the railroad tracks was blacktop except for the last fifty feet or so nearest the tracks. The road going west that is now called Old Mill Creek Road was gravel all the way to the highway that ran south out of Sulphur. It was that last fifty feet the grader operator was attempting to smooth up.

We should have been paying more attention than we were, but you know how boys can be when they get all wrapped up in talking about girls or what have you. At any rate, when the grader stopped and started to back up, it caught us totally by surprise. I managed to get stopped and turned around headed back east, but Davey hit the gravel strewn over the end of the blacktop apron and down he went, new bicycle and all. As he rolled out of the path of the grader and onto the shoulder of the road, all I could do was stand and watch the grader smash Davey's new bicycle to pieces under its giant tires.

The grader operator must have heard or felt the grader wheels hit the bicycle because he came to a complete stop.

By the time he had dismounted from the tall grader cab and walked around behind to see what he had hit, both Davey and I were just standing there shell-shocked looking at the ruined bike.

"You boys alright?" he asked.

Davey had tears running down his cheeks as he stood and looked at the bike. I just didn't know what to say. Finally, I nodded my head when the grader operator asked the same question again.

I walked along as Davey pushed the ruined bike home. It was pretty much of a chore to do because both wheels were smashed and rubbed against the frame in two or three places as it rolled along. I left him standing there in his yard as his dad walked out to look at the bike. My heart went out to him.

It was the next day before I saw Davey again. I did what I thought was the only thing I could do to help. I offered to let him use my bike to deliver the papers, but he refused.

"I don't deserve a bike," he said. "Not 'til I learn to take care of one. That's what my daddy said."

I know he walked that paper route just like I had done for at least a week. Then one day, just as we were sitting down for supper, I heard Davey outside in my front yard hollering his head off. The first thing I saw when I went to the door was Davey standing there with a big old grin on his face. He was standing astride a brand new bike exactly like the one the road grader ran over.

"Where did you get it?" I asked.

Mr. Hudgens brought it to me just a while ago," he said. ***(Bob Hudgens was County Commissioner at the time)*** "He thought the neighborly thing to do would be for the County to pay for the ruined bike and so he brought it up at the monthly meeting. To make a long story short, here is my new bike."

It was about a week later and we were just riding along slowly, following a road grader and talking. "What," you say!! "Following a road grader after what happened to Davey's bike while following a grader?"

"Yep," that is just exactly what we were doing. Boys have been following road graders on bicycles ever since road graders were invented. Who were we to break that tradition? I'll tell you one thing though; we didn't get close enough for anything to happen like happened before with Davey's new bike. After all, we might not be so lucky next time. I remember my dad saying we needed to use what happened as a learning experience. I had heard that before. I was just ready to learn something just one time, without having to pay a big price for the lesson.

I've learned though as I've grown older, the lessons learned that cost the most stick with you the longest. I began to think for a while that I wasn't gonna have a spare place for another lesson to stick to if I didn't slow down with my learning. Fortunately, by the time I got into my teens, I knew everything there was to know, so I really didn't have to worry about it anyway. You know what I mean?

The Blue Jean Jacket

Fashions come and go every year or so now-a-days and kids today wouldn't be caught dead in last year's fashions if they can help it. As a result, parents spend an exorbitant amount of money trying to make sure their kids keep up with what all the so called "popular" kids are wearing. $200 tennis shoes are fairly common for kids today as are $300 jackets. Heaven forbid for a kid to go to school in shoes that don't sport the logo of one of the high fashion brands. I believe, a lot of the time, while we are trying so hard to keep up with the Joneses, the Joneses are just wishing we would slow down so they wouldn't have to try so hard to stay ahead of us. That's really not what this story is about though, not sure why I got off on that rant.

One of the things that has stood the test of time and seems to stay in fashion year after year is the blue jean jacket, sometimes called denim jackets now-a-days. When I was a kid, one thing a guy had to have when school started each year was a blue jean jacket. That very thing is the basis for this story.

It was September 1957, the year the most beautiful car ever to be produced graced the showrooms of America, the 1957 Chevrolet, 2 door hardtop. It was also the year that, just four days before school was to start, and I still didn't have a blue jean jacket. Oh, I had the one from the previous year, but it was too small and I certainly wasn't about to wear it out in public, you know what I mean? It was my own fault, I guess. When Mom had taken the girls shopping for school clothes a couple of weeks back, I had been too busy fishing to go. Since I wasn't there to try it on, Mom didn't buy me a blue jean jacket.

"I'm not about to buy you a jacket and not have it fit," I remember her saying. "If you want a jacket, you better be ready to go when we go shopping." As it turned out, I was at Lake Texoma with Jasper and Em trying to catch a mess of catfish when the shopping day rolled around.

"You reckon Frank would have a jacket to fit him?" Dad asked. "He carries blue jean jackets, you know."

"I doubt it," Mom replied. "But it wouldn't hurt to look. I hate to make another trip to Ardmore when we don't need anything else."

I felt to make sure I still had the ten dollar bill Mom had given me when Dad and I walked out of the house. "Yea", there it was, still snuggled deep down in the pocket of my jeans right where I had put it. The little bell above the door jingled as we walked in. Frank had put the bell there to make sure he heard folks when they entered the store. He was from Syria and was of the Jewish persuasion. I've heard folks say he would squeeze a penny so hard you could hear Old Abe squeal.

Let me tell you a little about Frank's store. It was a rock building like all the buildings on Main Street in Mill Creek, Oklahoma at the time. It had hardwood floors and a twenty foot high ceiling. There was the obligatory wood stove sitting in the middle of the floor toward the back of the store and it was surrounded by chairs for folks to sit in and warm up. Spittoons were stationed around at likely spots as well. Frank ran a unique business; he carried everything from groceries to sewing goods and everything in between. He would sell one 22 rifle shell out of a box if that was all a customer wanted. Of course, he put a hefty price on that one shell compared to the box price. Still, for a kid, that was usually a good deal since I seldom had the price of a full box of anything.

"What can I help you fellows with?" Frank asked as we made our way into the store.

"Boy needs a blue jean jacket," Dad replied. "You reckon you got a blue jean jacket that will fit him?"

Old Frank looked me over real good and then proclaimed as how he thought a size small in a man's jacket would do the trick. We walked back to where a circular rack of jackets was standing just to the west of the wood stove. Taking a jacket from the rack, Frank held it out for me to try on for size. I could tell the jacket was way too big before I even put my arms into the sleeves. Sure enough, when I had it on, the arms hung at least six inches past my hands, the shoulders were a couple of inches down the sides of my arms, and the bottom hem was about an inch above my knees.

"I believe that jacket is too big for the boy," Dad said.

"Naw, Naw," Frank answered. Just what he needs. Need to buy a jacket a little too big for a boy his age. That way he can wear it for two or three years."

"I don't know," Dad replied. "Sure looks way too big to me."

"Naw, it's just right for him," Frank said again. He wasn't about to miss a sale if he could help it.

It was then that my dad looked over at me and winked. He had something up his sleeve, but it took me a little while to catch on. I knew one thing, I wasn't about to leave the store with that jacket. I'd be the laughing stock of the whole school with that thing on.

Everybody in town knew that Frank did not do any business on credit. If you bought something from Frank, you paid cash for it. Knowing this, my dad decided to have a little fun out of Frank. He wasn't about to buy the jacket, and he knew I had the ten dollar bill in my pocket to pay for a jacket if we found one.

"Well, tell you what." he said. "If you think that jacket is what the boy needs I guess we'll take it. One thing though, I plumb forgot my billfold when we left the house. You'll have to charge it to me and I'll try to get down here and pay you for it in a few days." Another wink at me when Frank wasn't looking.

You'd have thought my dad slapped him by the look on Frank's face. He started stuttering and his face turned a sickly pale color. He grabbed me by the arm and started turning me around and around.

"Little big on him," he squeaked. "More I look at that jacket the more it looks too big for him," he said. "Yea, too big for him, just too big for him." With that, he jerked the jacket off of me and quickly hung it back on the rack.

"Anything else I can do for you boys?" he asked, but he was already headed back to the back of the store where he was busy putting price stickers on some newly arrived merchandise. We had interrupted that chore when we came into the store.

Dad laughed all the way out of the store. He got a kick out of Frank's reaction to the suggestion he sell the jacket on credit. I wonder what dad would have done if Frank had taken him up on it. No need to wonder though, 'cause that just wasn't gonna happen.

That same afternoon, we drove to Sulphur and I got a blue jean jacket that fit at Green's Department Store. It wasn't nearly as much fun as shopping at Frank's though. I spent a lot of time in Frank's store when I was a kid. Frugal as he was, I believe he had a soft spot for kids. I've bought two or three 22 shells at a time and a couple of shotgun shells when it was all I could afford. Couldn't do that many places. Wonder what the folks at Wal-Mart would think of Frank's store. It's almost unbelievable that we've come so far related to stores and shopping in such a relatively short time. I know we have a lot more convenient shopping today, and you can find most anything you could possibly need or want very easily, but I still miss the old time general stores. They've gone the way of the drive in movies and the local cafés. One thing is still certain though in my mind; the 1957 Chevy 2 door hardtop with a 283 V8 motor is still the hottest car ever made. What do you think?

Barefoot Days

The last day of school always signaled the start of barefoot days. From the middle of May 'til the beginning of September, my buddies and I probably didn't have on a pair of shoes of any kind more than once or twice, and then probably just an old pair of tennis shoes. Sitting on the cement dam on Three Mile Creek, just west of the railroad depot, with bare feet dangling, a fishing pole in one hand and a Mr. Cola in the other was one of the most relaxing ways to spend a summer afternoon. I've sat there for hours, watching the red and white bobber bouncing in the swirling water ten feet below.

Goggle-eye perch as big as your hand, sunfish with the telltale yellow underbelly, and an occasional catfish of the smaller variety, kept the attention of a couple of ten year old boys for hours on end. Lazy days with not a care in the world. A tin can full of worms or a pop bottle full of grasshoppers was all it took to keep us occupied. Fried fish for supper was the reward for all the fun of catching them in the first place.

Feet so tough from traipsing through the gravel and grass that a grass burr or goat-head sticker could hardly penetrate them. We walked or rode bikes to all our favorite fishing and swimming holes as well as the shaded groves of pecan trees that were known to yield a squirrel or two to satisfy a growing boy's hunger. We had little parental supervision because we didn't need it. We carried 22 rifles at nine and ten years of age and knew how to carry and use them safely.

Good friends. I mean really good friends to wile away the hours with. Davey Robbins and Hank Graham were that kind of friends. We spent a lot of time together and I only remember getting crosswise with either of them on one occasion and that was over a girl so was to be expected.

By the time school took up in the fall, we were so used to running around barefoot and free that it was a grueling ordeal to have to put on a pair of shoes. Mom always said that running around all summer barefoot made my feet so wide she could hardly find shoes to fit me in the fall.

The infamous stub-toe was the worst thing about running around with no shoes all the time. During the course of the summer, I would stub the skin off the end of my big toe at least three or four times. Remember that?

Some smaller kids still go barefoot a lot, but by the time kids reach eight or nine years old these days, the barefoot days are largely over for the most part. Not many tough feet around these days!

I'll wager that most kids around Mill Creek don't even know there is a dam on Three Mile Creek by the softball facility in the old park. It looks to be so overgrown that it might not even be accessible. I wonder if water is even flowing there now. I think I'll walk over there and look next time I'm by there.

The Persimmon Wars

Ever get hit with a green persimmon coming at you at around 100 miles per hour? I can tell you from experience, that it is not a good feeling. The persimmon wars started when I was about eleven or twelve years old and continued for a number of years. They were cavalry style wars and took place in the early fall before the persimmons ripened and mostly on Preacher John's place just west of the railroad tracks. Here's how the wars were conducted.

There were usually four of us but sometimes as many as six. In the open pasture south of Preacher John's house were two persimmon thickets separated by a couple hundred yards of open ground. Jamey Brockton, ***(Jamey was Preacher John's son)***, Leon Doughty, Bill Suggs, and myself were the regular combatants and on occasion, Dale Clementine and Jim Peterson would join in as well. The rules were real simple. Rule #1---There ain't no rules.

All you needed was a willow throwing stick about four feet long and about as big around as your finger. Sharpen the small end to a point. Sick a green persimmon on the point of the throwing stick and get ready for battle. A flexible willow limb would allow a person to throw a persimmon about four times as far as you could throw one by hand. Oh yea, one other thing. You had to have a horse.

The teams would get ready, one at each persimmon thicket. Each combatant would have a sack full of green persimmons on his saddle so as to be ready to reload quickly. It took a little practice, but in short order, you could become fairly accurate with the little green messengers of pain. The war would usually begin by a series of taunting maneuvers. One man from each team would ride helter-skelter toward the middle of the open area. But these were just decoy moves with the real intention being to get the attention of the opponent so the other man on your side could get a clear shot at him. The whizzing sound the persimmons made as they sailed through the air would cause goose bumps to come up on my arms when one got really close.

One fine, sunny fall afternoon as all six of us were having the persimmon war of the decade, Bill Suggs and I happened to be on the same team and were doing a number on the opposing team of Jamey Brockton, Dale Clementine, and Leon Doughty. Leon was out of the game as was Jim who was on our team. We had both Jamey and Dale hidden back in the persimmon thicket on their side of the pasture. We had stopped to give our horses a blow when I saw movement in the thicket across the field from us.

"They're up to something," I said. "They're liable to come flying out of there any second now."

"You take Dale and I'll take Jamey," Bill said. "We'll

charge right down the middle when they come out of the thicket."

We were lined up about thirty feet apart just facing the thicket. Our horses were prancing around so much we could hardly keep them facing the right direction. They knew what was coming and were as ready as we were.

"Here they come!!" Bill yelled as they broke out of the thicket and headed our way at a dead run.

I finally got my rearing horse under control, and together we rode to meet them. It was like the charge of the light brigade, whooping and hollering and willow limbs whirling in the air. The sound of iron clad hooves beating the ground as we raced toward each other. At around 150 feet, I let fly my first projectile. Dale dodged that one as it flew by his head but he couldn't get out of the way of my following shot and it caught him on the right shoulder putting him out of the game.

My charge had taken me past Jamey as he went by me so fast all I could see was a blur. I whirled to get back into the fight, but there was no fight to get into. What I saw instead was Jamey lying flat on his back on the ground and Bill jogging back toward him on his horse. Dale came riding up, and together we knelt beside Jamey. His face was as white as a sheet except for the red knot directly in the center of his forehead.

"Jamey," I said as I patted his pale cheeks with the palms of my hands. Nothing!

"Go get some water," Leon hollered. Then taking his own advice, jumped on his horse and tore out for the house as fast as he could ride. Meanwhile, Jamey lay there not making a sound. His chest was rising and falling, so I could see he was breathing. Looking toward the house, we could see Leon headed back across the pasture with Preacher John in hot pursuit. In all his haste, Leon had forgotten his horse and was running back with water splashing out of the bucket he was carrying at every step.

Bill had taken off his shirt, and as Leon sat the bucket down, he dipped it in the water and commenced to wash Jamey's face with the cold water. Almost immediately, Jamey began to move his head from side to side. About as quickly, his eyes fluttered open and he looked from one of us to the other. I could tell it wasn't registering in his mind.

"Let him lay there for a few minutes," Preacher John said. "Maybe he'll come to his self."

Jamey lay there just looking from one to another. Finally he looked at Preacher John and I could see the recognition come into his eyes.

"Daddy," he said.

"Yea son," Preacher John replied. "You gonna be alright? You took a pretty good lick on the noggin, looks like."

Jamey grinned and looked at Bill. "You got me fair and square Bill," he said. I knew right then he was gonna be alright.

We played persimmon wars for a few more years until we got too big to enjoy it anymore. As we got into high school and other things occupied our time, the persimmon wars were all but forgotten. Occasionally, through high school, somebody would mention the good times we had slinging persimmons, but we never really got serious enough about it to go and do it again.

Many years later, with children of my own, I was riding a young horse in the pasture behind our house one fall and came upon a persimmon thicket with the still green fruit hanging in clusters. Not far away, near the edge of a pond, there was a willow tree growing. I couldn't help myself. I tied the horse to a dead snag and took out my pocket knife. The long slender limb I chose from the willow tree was just like I remembered using all those many years ago. I sharpened the small end with the knife until it was just the way I liked it. With a wistful smile on my face, I stuck a green persimmon onto the pointed end of the limber switch.

Walking away from the pond a little way, I spotted a dead tree standing in a low spot all of a hundred yards across the field. The dead trunk stood stately and white like a sentinel in the field of browning grass. I took a couple of tentative swings around my head with the limb, and then with more confidence, three or four fast swings. With the limb whirling, I took a forward stride releasing the persimmon with a snap of the wrist in the direction of the dead tree.

I followed the flight of the persimmon through the air with my eyes. SMACK!! The white of the tree trunk was disturbed by a green smear as the persimmon exploded into a hundred pieces. A feeling of satisfaction came over me as I pitched the willow limb into a brush pile. Feeling a little sheepish, I looked around to see if there was anyone close enough to see my little display. There was not. As I mounted the colt, I couldn't keep the smile from coming back. Pretty good shot, even if I do have to say so myself. Not as good as the one Bill made on Jamey at a full gallop that day, but a pretty good shot nevertheless.

I've told my kids and others about the persimmon wars we had as kids. As far as I know, none of them ever tried throwing a green persimmon with a willow switch. Well, it's not too late. There are seven little grandsons just waiting to learn to do it. If their dads don't teach them, maybe I will. Then again, maybe not. The memory of Jamey lying there all still on the ground is still as fresh as it was that day in 1960. I'm too old to have a persimmon war now. Perhaps I'll dream about it. Safer that way.

Ugly Goats and Pretty Girls

I'm not real sure how it got started. Ain't that a strange thing? You'd think a body would be able to recollect something as important as that, but I just can't seem to get my memory wrapped around the why and when of it. Oh, I remember it being in 1973 when we got started, but what I can't seem to recall is why we did it in the first place.

The Roundup Club had built an arena at the north end of the park right beside the tracks in Mill Creek. If my memory serves me correctly, I believe it sat in precisely the same spot as the Mill Creek High School football field when they used to play football back in the 1930s.

A few of us were doing quite a bit of steer roping at the arena in Tishomingo at the time, but what we really wanted to do was rope calves. We got to driving all the way to Seminole to enter some calf ropings and were wishing all the time we had someplace closer to go. We even talked about buying some roping calves ourselves, but that proposition proved to be too expensive for a couple of redneck cowboys like me and Billy South. What we finally ended up deciding to do was invest in about twenty or so roping goats.

We started hitting all the sales and such around the area but were having one heck of a time finding good roping goats. Finally, we decided we would just take out driving and when we spotted goats we would stop and try to buy them. It was over in the eastern part of the state where we had the most luck. After spending the better part of three weekends in this manner, we had twelve or fifteen pretty good goats. The goat ropings started the very next Sunday afternoon.

I met Billy at his place and we loaded the goats and

horses up in my 32 foot trailer and headed to the park. It was just after lunch time that first Sunday. We didn't really know what to expect, so when we pulled into the park, I was surprised to see eight or ten pickups and horse trailers already there waiting on us. That first Sunday, we had Jamey Brockton, Jim Hooker, Blister Reed, Mike Peterson, Dalton Hooker, Walton Brighton, Jasper Johnston, Rambo Johnston, and a couple of others not including myself and Billy. We saw right quick we were gonna have to come up with more goats somewhere and quickly.

After that first week, the goat roping just grew and grew. Billy and I picked up several more goats and by the third or fourth week, had close to 30 goats to run through the chutes. We had the darndest variety you ever seen. Tall rangy goats that would run like a deer, short stocky goats, and everything in between. We had a couple of little black goats a fellow brought in from Mississippi that were as hard to rope as jackrabbits. We called them "Mississippi Rambler", and "Biloxi Belle." They would come out of the chute like they were shot out of a cannon and run with their head at an angle looking back at the horse and rider. Just when a roper would throw his loop, they would duck out of the way and the loop would fall harmlessly onto the floor of the arena. I know several ropers re-named both those goats several times 'cause I would hear them talking about their parentage as they rode out of the arena after a miss like that.

Pretty soon, the talk about the weekly goat ropings was all over the country and there were more and more folks showing up just to watch and enjoy the show. I knew we had a good thing going, but I didn't realize how much attention we were getting 'til I got the call from the Ada Evening News.

"Are you the fellow that holds the goat roping every Sunday?" The man asked when I picked up the phone.

He didn't even give me time to say "hello", "how-de-do," or "go to the dickens," he just commenced to carrying on about how he wanted to come to the goat roping and write an article about it for the paper.

"Just come on over any time," I told him. "We rope every Sunday afternoon starting about 1:00 o'clock."

"I'll be there this next Sunday," he said.

I hung up the phone and hadn't gotten twenty feet when it began to ring again.

"This is the Ada Evening News again," he said when I answered the phone. "I plumb forgot to tell you that Channel 10, KTEN, wants to come down and shoot an piece for their Local Interest Show they carry on Sunday afternoons. Is that okay by you?"

"Bring 'em on," I replied.

Nobody could believe we were gonna be on television and the more I thought about it, the more I figured they wouldn't show up the next week. Oh, I figured the guys from the newspaper would be there, but the television guys were another thing all together. Both Billy and I figured the odds of them showing up were less than fifty percent.

We rolled in to the park the next Sunday at exactly 12:45. By the time we had the goats unloaded and things ready to go, I looked up to see a white van coming across the double culverts at the entrance to the park. When it turned to pull into a parking space just west of the arena, I could clearly see the writing on the side of the van in big, bold, black letters**. "Ada Evening News".**

As I stood and watched the guys unload cameras and tripods out of the back of the van, Billy tapped me on the shoulder and pointed down toward the entrance to the park. Another van was just turning into the park and it was a much bigger van than the Ada Evening News van. When they crossed the low spot and turned to find a parking space, the big red lettering was visible on the side of the van. **"KTEN Channel 10 *Your News Source*."**

I looked over at Billy and he was grinning like a possum eating ripe persimmons. It took about fifteen minutes for them to get set up then the roping started. They got a lot of good pictures and video and talked to all the ropers present that day. The result was a fifteen minute video that aired at least three or four different times on KTEN, and a page and a half section in the Ada Evening News.

I drove to Ada a week or so later and the man at the newspaper office gave me three or four papers with the article in them, and the folks at KTEN gave me a video tape like the one they were showing on Sunday afternoons. I don't have either now and I sure would like to see them again for old time's sake.

As much fun as we had roping goats and especially getting in the paper and on television, the best thing about the goat ropings for me had nothing to do with newspapers, television, or even roping goats for that matter. The best thing about those Sunday afternoons was the pretty, blond, young lady who volunteered to run the chute gate each week. She would sit on the top of the chute and work the head gate when ropers would nod for the goat to be released. I got acquainted with her and we started dating some shortly after the goat ropings started. That young lady has been my wife for almost 37 years now. I believe that makes me the all-time winner of the goat ropings.

We roped goats at Mill Creek for a couple of years, then folks began to tire of it and ventured off to other things. I haven't been to a goat roping since. I doubt I could find one to go to if I was of a mind to try. But for a time, a lot of folks got a lot of entertainment out of the weekly goat ropings. I have a lot of good memories of those Sunday afternoons.

If anyone reading this story has a copy of either the newspaper article or a copy of the KTEN video, I would like to see them. Just call it nostalgia for an old goat roper. I missed a lot of throws in that arena on many a Sunday afternoon, but the catch I made when I threw my loop on the pretty girl running the head gate has defined my life and made me a very happy man. We have a passel of grandkids running around the place now-a-days and not a goat roper among them. Go figure!

The End

The Old Time Toys

As I watch my grandkids playing with the toys of today; the computer games, the transformers, dolls that talk and walk and have boyfriends, Wii games on the TV set, I marvel at the way things have changed in just a relatively few years. When I was a kid growing up, maybe the age of my oldest grandson, we played mostly with toys we made. A couple of reasons for that. Outside of BB guns, toy soldiers and cowboys, cap pistols and the like, there just wasn't much else available. We played marbles and spun tops, but mostly we played with homemade toys, they were just more fun. The fact that money was a little scarce played a part in that as well.

I've talked to my kids about the toys we played with way back then and have explained how to make them and use them just hoping they might take a hint and follow that path themselves as they were growing up, but sadly, to no avail. They did like to play with a cardboard box more than most of their store bought toys, however.

Some of my favorite toys were just things I made

and played with. I'll name a few and describe how they were made and used. There was, of course, the old time favorite of kids, especially boys, for many years during the 1920s and up into the 1960s, the stick horse. The best stick horses were persimmon poles about an inch and a half in diameter and eight feet long or so. With the branches all trimmed off and a string bridle, you were ready to go after the bad guys. It helped if you had a cap pistol strapped around your waist of course. Me and my buddies rode those things 'til they were too short to use just from dragging on the ground.

The next best toy we all played with was a wheel and trough. It was made by bending a lard bucket lid into a "V" shape and nailing it to the end of a "1 by 2" board about three feet long. It was held with the "V" facing forward in front of your body. A wheel, usually from a wagon or other toy, was inserted into the "V" made by the lard bucket lid. As you walked along, the wheel would roll down the road along in front or beside you. Lots of kids would walk all over town rolling a wheel in this manner. My dad showed me how to make them and he called them "Rolly Trollies."

My uncle Lloyd, "Sot" McDonald showed me how to make what he called "Chicken Airplanes." Takes a fresh corn cob and three large chicken or turkey feathers. Chicken feathers have a natural curl to them and were perfect for the "Chicken Airplanes." Turkey feathers worked well also, but you needed a longer corn cob for them. Here's how to make a "Chicken Airplane."

Push the hard end of a feather into the end of the corn cob about an inch or so. Then a second being sure to position it so the curl was facing at right angles to the first feather. The third feather completes the circle and the chicken airplane is ready to fly. I sometimes colored the corn cob to make it look like an airplane.

Grasp the cob with the thumb and first two fingers on your throwing hand and let her fly. The curved feathers would naturally force the airplane to rotate as it flew through the air, making a whirring sound clearly audible from several feet away. They would fly as far as a hundred feet after you got the hang of how to throw them.

We played washers and horseshoes, even the adults. I've seen grown men play washers for hours in the shade of the horseapple tree in our back yard. They would get mighty serious about their washers, and I've seen tempers flare on a few occasions when a measurement was in dispute.

I never see kids spin tops these days. I bought one of the old time wooden tops at a market in San Antonio a few years ago with the intention of teaching the grandkids how to spin it, but when I got around to it, the thing had disappeared. For a lot of years, us boys would spin tops on the school cellar. It had a rather large cement top that was just perfect for spinning tops. Most everybody had several tops, at least one good "killer' top and a few smaller fast spinning tops. Here's how it was played.

Draw a circle about five feet in diameter with a piece of chalk. Draw lots to determine the order of play. The first guy would throw a spinning top and let it spin. The next guy could either throw a spinner or try to knock the first guy out with a killer top. If he hit the spinner and knocked it out of the circle, it belonged to him. If he missed it, his killer was a prime target for the next guy in line. Most guys would keep their "killer"until several tops were out there spinning. Sometimes, the killer top would split a spinner right in half if it was hit correctly. It then belonged to the guy who threw the killer, though it wasn't of much use in two pieces.

When all players had a spinner out in the circle, the first guy would throw his "killer." If he hit a spinner and either knocked it out of the circle or stopped it from spinning, it belonged to him. Then the next guy and so on until one guy was left with a spinner and a "killer." The guy whose spinner was the last one spinning was the winner.

We had contests to see who could make a top spin the longest time. Several guys would throw spinners at the same time, and the one left spinning after the others stopped, was the winner. I've seen tops spin for as long as five or six minutes before finally slowing and falling over. Some guys could do amazing things with a spinner. I've seen guys spin a top on top of their head, on the back of their hands, and even on the lid of a fruit jar. I was always pretty good, but the best I ever saw, I believe was Jimbo Pitmon. I know he was the best with a "killer" I ever saw.

The girls spent a lot of time playing "jacks" and would compete for space on top of the cellar. I could never see the point in jacks, probably because I didn't have the hand and eye coordination it took to be good at it. My sisters played it religiously for several years.

Jump ropes were always popular and most kids that had one had a homemade one. The hula hoop about put the jump ropes out of business when they came along.

Homemade stilts were a common thing around Mill Creek for a lot of years. I'll never forget the time Davey slipped while stepping up onto the school cellar on a pair of stilts. His foot slipped out of the stirrup on one side and the top of the stilt pole caught him right under the chin as he went down. He bit his tongue almost all the way off. He had it sewed back on at the emergency room in Sulphur and had to stay a few days in the hospital. It was sort of ironic though, the hospital being full, they put his bed in the hall and the only other patient in the hall was the high school superintendent, Mr. Harden. Davey said later that it wasn't even like he got to miss school having to spend all that time with Mr. Harden.

After I got to the age of nine or ten, hunting and fishing dominated my life and I outgrew the tops and rolly trollies. 22 caliber rifles and fishing poles took the place of stick horses and chicken airplanes. I remember the many hours spent with those old time toys and the friendships that grew out of that playtime together. Kids really miss out on a lot of that these days, I believe.

From the time I was about five years old, my brother Dan and I hunted squirrels with a slingshot. A green forked stick about six or eight inches in length made the best slingshots. Rubber bands made from inner tubes were fastened to each fork and the tongue out of an old pair of shoes sufficed for the rock holder. I recall vividly the day I got into a lot of trouble because of a slingshot.

It was the summer before my fifth birthday. Dan and I were squirrel hunting on a little branch east of the house where we lived in the country east of Mill Creek. Dan had killed a couple of squirrels and I hadn't even gotten a shot. All of a sudden, a squirrel ran down the trunk of a tree ahead of us and just stopped right there in plain sight on the trunk of the tree. I hurriedly retrieved a good smooth rock from the pocket of my overalls and was just pulling the slingshot back when I heard Dan's slingshot snap back as he put a rock dead center on that squirrel's head. Down from the tree he fell; my squirrel. He had shot my squirrel. I was just about to shoot that squirrel and he knew I was. He went ahead and shot it anyway. It made me so mad that I just sort of lost all my common sense there for a second or two. During that second or two, I turned and let the rock fly right toward Dan's head.

I'll never forget the horror I felt as I watched that rock plow a bloody furrow down the side of his head right above his ear. I stood and watched as he ran screaming to the house. I remember thinking I ought to just start running the other direction and keep on running. I knew my bacon was cooked when Dad saw Dan's head. Sure enough, after it became apparent that Dan would actually survive, I got a good switching with a willow switch. I also was grounded from using a slingshot for some period of time, I don't recall how long.

Over the next couple of years, I got really good with a slingshot. I could hit a running rabbit most every time and have shot squirrels from the highest trees. When I got about nine years old, I graduated to a 22 rifle and the slingshot days were over for the most part.

Maybe some kid will read this story and feel the urge to make a chicken airplane or a rolly trollie. Maybe even a slingshot or a pair of stilts. I hope to find a place that sells the old time wooden tops. I'd like to see if I can still spin one. Even better, I'd like to teach my grandkids to do it. I know they would have as much fun as I did back in the days of the old time toys.

The End

The Dry Summer of 1956

1956 was one of the driest years on record in southern Oklahoma. You remember it, don't you? By the middle of July, the pastures looked like they normally do in the middle of winter; the grass all dry and brown and sort of crispy when you walk on it. A lot of folks in town were afraid their water wells might dry up and they'd be left without any water. It was before the city water system was installed, and everybody had a well out behind the house.

The gardens were just burned up. Nobody was brave enough to use well water to keep the gardens alive, so they just shriveled up and died. They say there is always a silver lining around every cloud, and if there was one in the summer of 1956, it was that I didn't have to mow the lawn. Mowed it once in the spring, and it didn't need it again all summer. The swimming hole on Mill Creek got so shallow all you could do was just wade around in it. Before the summer was over, it became too slimy and nasty to swim in at all.

One thing that was good about the drought for an eight year old kid, was how good the fishing was until the ponds started to dry up. I probably caught more fish that summer than the next two or three summers combined. I had eaten so many fish that year that I didn't care if I ever ate another one. It got to the point I would about as soon have a big mess of turnips and I didn't like turnips at all.

July 4th came along, but it was so dry that most folks were afraid to shoot off any fireworks. It was the dullest Fourth of July holiday I can remember. No watermelons, no fireworks, no fun at all. Mom did make a big freezer of homemade ice cream, and we sat out in the yard and wished we were watching a fireworks display. The fourth was on a Wednesday that year, and the following Saturday, my Uncle Jasper came by and wanted to know if we'd like to go down to Oil Creek fishing. My brother Dan and I piled into the back of Jasper's old Dodge truck and Dad took the front seat.

Back in those days, the road through Rock Prairie had about four or five gates you had to open. There were no cattle guards. It was a county road, but the Daube Ranch ran for miles on both sides of the road and the pastures were separated by barbed wire fences and every fence had a gate on the county road. Of course the job of opening and closing the gates fell to either me or Dan. The worst thing about it, Uncle Jasper's truck didn't have any brakes, so he would slow down pretty slow as we approached a gate. Dan or I would jump out and run and open the gate before the truck got there. Then we would have to close the gate and run to catch up with the truck again. By the time we got to Oil Creek, we were both worn out from running.

We rounded the last curve on the road and saw Oil Creek in the distance. What was left of Oil Creek, I should have said. What used to be a deep running creek full of fresh water was now a smattering of water holes in the deepest parts of the creek. I would say a good two thirds of the creek bed was dry as a bone.

We parked the old truck on an incline so we could push it if it wouldn't start. Jasper wasn't known for having the best kind of truck, you know. As we got closer to the creek, I could see the water in one of the deeper holes was working alive with something. It was soon apparent that every water hole on the creek was full of fish. They had moved into the deeper holes as the creek dried up and now the scattered pools of water held every fish that had been in the entire creek.

As we moved farther down the creek, in one of the deeper holes, we could see a couple of flathead catfish that looked like they might weigh over twenty five or thirty pounds. "I want you to look at them fish," Jasper said. "What are we gonna do with all them fish?"

"I'll tell you what we're gonna do," my dad said. "Let's go back home and get some 55 gallon barrels. We'll fill 'em up with fish and haul 'em down to my place and dump 'em in the ponds. We'll keep the bigger fish and have us a big fish fry."

We all jumped back in the old truck and headed back to town. We loaded both Jasper's and Dad's trucks down with 55 gallon barrels and hustled back to Oil Creek. We had brought along a seine and as soon as we got back to the creek, we started seining the deeper holes. The smaller fish, we would put in the barrels along with some water from the creek, but the larger catfish we would put in five gallon buckets to clean later.

It was mighty hard work, hauling fish and water up the creek bank in five gallon buckets, trip after trip and pouring them into the barrels in the back of the trucks. By late that afternoon, we had eight barrels full of fish and we started home. When we had finally dumped all the barrels in the big pond on our farm, we could see a few fish floating on top of the water. Looked like we saved most of them though, couldn't have been more than a couple dozen that didn't make it. It took a couple more hours to clean all the fish in the buckets we had put back. There was one catfish that was as long as my little sister Virginia was tall. Dad figured it would weigh around thirty pounds. Lots more in the five to ten pound range.

Mom drug the old cast iron pot out of the washhouse and we built a big fire in the back yard. When the grease was hot, in went the fish all covered with cornmeal. Mom dropped a couple of fairly good sized onions into the grease. She allowed as how that helped the flavor somewhat. Along with fried potatoes and pork and beans, we had as fine a supper as you could imagine. Jasper and Aunt Em were there along with various other aunts and uncles and some of the closer neighbors. I ate so much fish, I was miserable the rest of the night.

The next day after Sunday school, I took my 22 rifle and walked off into the woods behind the house hoping I might see a squirrel. I had walked most of the way up the branch and had a couple of squirrels on a stick slung over my shoulder when I came upon the pond where the timber started to thin out. There was usually a squirrel or two around the pond, it being the only source of water for quite some distance. I eased up alongside a big pecan tree and was standing there looking the area over. I could hear a strange noise just over the pond dam, but for the life of me, I couldn't figure out just what was making the sound or exactly where it was coming from. After a few minutes, I got down on my hands and knees and crawled up to where I could see over the pond dam. It didn't take me but a second to see what was making the noise. The water in the pond had shrunk to less than a third of its normal area and depth, and the remaining water was just alive with fairly large channel catfish. I had hunted around that pond for years, but thinking it had no fish in it, had never fished there. It was apparent, someone, at some time, had stocked that pond with channel cats.

I ran all the way back to the house and burst into the living room where Dad was taking a Sunday afternoon nap on the couch. I must have been making a fair amount of noise, because I hadn't no more than got into the room good, when up from the couch he came.

"I'll swear Pete," he said. "A man can't even get in a little nap with you making so much racket. What in the world is it that couldn't wait 'til I woke up?"

"You gotta come look," I hollered. "There must be two truckloads of channel catfish about to die in the pond at the end of the branch."

About that time, Dan came running into the room from the kitchen. "Did you say channel cats," he asked. "In the pond up by the road?"

"Yeah," I answered. "They're all gonna die if we don't get them out of there pretty quick. There ain't much water left in that pond."

"Call your Uncle Jasper and tell him to get over here," Dad said. "We'll seine the pond and put the fish in the back of the truck."

"Hold it a minute," Dan said. "There ain't any fish in that old pond. I've been around that pond for years and there ain't ever been any fish in it. It went plumb dry about ten years ago." I used to fish in it until it went dry. Never was much of anything in it but crawdads. Petey's just pulling your leg because we got all them fish yesterday."

"I ain't pulling nobody's leg," I shot back. "You just stay here if you don't believe me." With that, I started out the door.

"Hold up Pete," Dad hollered. "Call Jasper and tell him to get over here. I'll walk over to the pond and see for myself how many fish are in there." Wasn't long 'til he was back with a big grin on his face. "Don't know if there are two truckloads of catfish in that pond," he said. "But I'll bet there is a pickup load."

"What?" Dan hollered. "You mean there really are catfish in that pond?"

"Told you so, Smart Alec," I said as I went out the door to meet Jasper's old truck that was just pulling into the yard.

"Where's them fish Petey?" he asked. "Heard tell there was two truckloads of catfish in a pond 'bout to go dry."

"Well, maybe not two truckloads," I admitted. "But Dad said there was at least a pickup load."

"Let's go get 'em then," he replied.

We all loaded up in Dad's 1950 Chevy pickup and headed into the pasture through the gate Dan was holding open. Sure enough, when we got to the pond, all you could see was fins sticking up out of the shallow water in the pond. It took us more than three hours to seine all the fish out of the pond, and when we were through, the fish came to within six inches of the top of the bed of Dad's truck. Granted, it was a short narrow bed like what was common at the time, but that's still a lot of catfish.

"What are we gonna do with all these fish?" Jasper wanted to know. "I cleaned fish yesterday 'til I was sick of 'em."

"Let's just drive around town and give a bunch of 'em away," Dad answered. "Ought to be a lot of folks that would like a good mess of catfish." So that's what we did. After we had given away as many as we could, there was still maybe a hundred pounds of fish left in the truck. We all pitched in and got them cleaned in short order. Mom walked out of the house as we were finishing up.

"What's for supper Mom," I asked?

"Well, I figured we might as well have catfish with all these fish cleaned and ready to cook," she replied.

"You got to be kidding," I shot back. "I've swallowed so many fish I'm about to start growing gills. You ain't got a good mess of turnips you could fix, have you?"

I've seen some dry years since 1956, but I don't think I've seen one as dry. The old timers say they come in cycles and maybe they do. I got over the feeling of never wanting to eat another catfish in short order. They are still one of my favorite things to eat. I've even come to like turnips. At times, when we are enjoying catfish at home or at one of the fine catfish restaurants around, the memories of that summer in 1956 and all the catfish we ate come back to me. They are good memories of a good time in my life.

The End

The Old Gym

For those of you who don't remember, and those who never attended a small rural school, the significant role the school gymnasium played in the lives of folks in the surrounding community will be under appreciated. As was the case in all the small schools in Johnston County Oklahoma in the 1940s, 1950s and early 1960s, the school gymnasium at Mill Creek served many purposes. It was the only building in the area large enough to host many functions, such as Halloween carnivals, donkey basketball games, school dances, (yes we had school dances back then), and an occasional funeral or wedding. I have fond memories of the old gym at Mill Creek before the new gym was built in the early 1960s.

There were really only a couple of varieties of gyms around the small schools when I was growing up. There were the ones constructed of native rock, built in most cases by the WPA (Works Progress Administration) during the depression, and the classic wooden barn-like structures like we had at Mill Creek. It was a place of enchantment for me as I grew up almost in its shadow, and a time of sadness as I watched the demolition crew from Madill tear it down in 1964.

Many of the old time gyms had a stage at one end and served as the auditorium for the school as well as a gym. I remember the old gym at Troy Oklahoma had a stage at the west end. We had a lot of exciting grade school basketball tournaments inside that old gym. I need to get my terminology correct, I suppose. There are no more "grade schools," they are all now "elementary schools."

The old gym at Mill Creek had four tiny dressing rooms at the east end and they had no heat or water in them as I recall. The main gym was heated (sort of) by two huge coal fired cast iron stoves, one on each end of the building on the north wall. When I was just a little tyke, one of my chores was getting the coal stoves going in the gym on nights when there was a home basketball game. The stoves would get cherry red when fully fired and would put out a lot of heat. I am amazed, looking back, that nobody ever ran into one of these stoves during a basketball game. There was no barrier of any kind separating the stoves from the gym floor. Men would crowd around the stoves and stand to watch the game. As the stoves got hotter, they would move farther away, and would finally have to find a seat in the stands if any were available.

There were always two or three old coal buckets about half full of ashes sitting around the stoves and these served as spittoons for the snuff dippers and tobacco chewers which were common at the time.

There was a big pile of coal just outside the door at the northeast corner of the gym. I would take a couple of coal buckets and a shovel out there and fill up the buckets. There had to be full buckets sitting inside in case the stoves needed to be replenished.

The gym floor was made of one by four planks and had

a lot of dead spots. You could be dribbling the ball down the court and all of a sudden, the ball would hit a dead spot in the floor and bounce only about half as high as a normal bounce. You had to be ready when that happened, or you were likely to double dribble or walk with the ball. There I go again with the terminology thing. There is no longer such a thing as "walking with the ball" it is now known as "traveling." I did a lot of "traveling" when I was playing and didn't even realize what I was doing.

One needed to be careful when driving for a lay-up in the old gym. The wall was only about three feet behind the basket, and crashing into that wall was never a good thing. A lot of gyms had mattresses attached to the walls behind the goals to minimize the shock when you crashed.

One memory of the old gym at Mill Creek was also one of the most embarrassing moments of my life. I was in the seventh grade and we were all standing outside the entrance to the gym waiting for someone to come unlock the door so we could get in to practice. There was an entryway going into the gym and it was about twenty feet long and ten feet wide. On the north side were the restrooms and on the south wall of the entryway was a pop machine. One of the old type where you had to pull the bottles down the row to the end and then out the trap door that was released when you put the money in. Some of the high school boys got in trouble for robbing that pop machine. They brought a bottle opener and some straws to school one day and they just opened all the bottles of pop with the bottle opener and sucked them all dry with the straws. There was nothing left in the machine except empty bottles.

On the north wall was one of the white porcelain drinking fountains that were common at the time. When the door was unlocked, about twenty boys were trying to get through at the same time. I was one of the first ones through, and when I started running down the hallway, I tripped on someone's feet and smashed headlong into that porcelain drinking fountain. It busted all to pieces and fell to the floor. Water was going everywhere. The impact knocked me silly for a few minutes, but luckily, I didn't get a single cut from the broken porcelain. Just goes to show how hard headed I was back then. Fortunately, I grew out of that as I got older.

I remember playing at the old gym in Vamoosa, Oklahoma when I was a freshman point guard. I didn't realize I was a point guard at the time, we just called that position "the man who brought the ball down the court."

Anyway, the gym at Vamoosa was one of the old-time gyms and the brackets for the goals were bolted to the walls at each end of the court, leaving only a couple of feet between the out of bounds line and the wall. By the way, the backboards were all solid metal back then, no glass backboards were in use anywhere.

The same space limitations were true for the sidelines. The bleachers, (what we called the seating area), were raised from the floor about four or five feet. If you were standing on the sideline to throw the ball in, your head was about even with the feet of the fans sitting in the first row. There was a board wall separating the fans from the players and it was about head high to someone standing on the sideline.

As I recall, we were leading by just a couple of points late in the game and the fans were going wild. At least the Vamoosa fans were. They were undefeated at the time and thought the refs were giving them the short end of the stick the entire game. There had been a couple of fans escorted out of the gym already on the home side.

The ball was out of bounds to us on the home sideline and Coach called time out with just over a minute to go in the game. "You throw the ball in Pete," he said. "We can't stand a turnover, so if you can't get it in clean, call another timeout." The Vamoosa fans were screaming as we ran back out onto the floor. I took the ball the ref handed me, and when the whistle blew for play to resume, I could see Gary Reeves breaking free down the court. As I turned to throw the ball to him, suddenly a cascade of cold liquid hit my head, ran down my face and into my eyes. I couldn't see a thing. The referee was blowing his whistle as loud as he could. I had managed to hang onto the ball, and was desperately trying to claw the liquid out of my eyes. Someone threw me a towel, and I was finally able to wipe enough of the stuff out of my eyes to see what was going on.

A fat lady from Vamoosa was sitting in the front row just behind and above me, and she had just lost her cool and poured a full cup of coke and ice on my head as I was getting ready to throw the ball in. She had seen Gary running open down the court, and before she realized what she was doing, she poured the 32 ounce cup of coke and ice she had just purchased at the concession stand on my head to keep me from throwing the ball to him.

It took a little while to get me cleaned up and all the coke and ice mopped up before play could resume. Someone ushered the fat lady from the gym. She looked back at me just before she went out the door, and I could tell by the look on her face that she was sorry she had done it. We went on to win the game by 2 points.

I got to play two seasons in the new gym at Mill Creek before I graduated. It was nice to play in a gym with a good floor, glass backboards, heat and water in the dressing rooms, and room between the backboards and the walls. For some reason though, my fondest memories are of the old gyms with the fans sitting right up against the floor, the cramped cold dressing rooms, the coal stoves glowing red in the corners, and the sound the ball made when it hit the metal backboards.

How many of you remember the donkey basketball games we used to have in the 1950's in the old gym at Mill Creek USA? For those of you that have never seen a donkey basketball game, or even heard of one for that matter, here's how it went.

There were several companies that traveled around over the country in the fall and winter and put on donkey basketball games. They would schedule the games a month or more in advance so everybody around was sure to hear about it. The school would get a cut of the cost of admission and the owner of the donkeys would get the rest. There would be two teams of guys chosen to play against one another, usually local high school boys. It was just like regular basketball, with five guys on each team, except they had to ride the donkeys on offense and defense.

These donkeys were specially trained to be as ornery and cantankerous as they could be. Just about the time you would get going good, dribbling the ball alongside the donkey, it would go to bucking or kicking, or anything else to get you off its back.

I remember one particular year when I was about 10 years old that a donkey basketball game was scheduled to be played on a Friday night. It was before the regular basketball season was set to begin. The owner of the donkeys arrived about mid-afternoon and unloaded all the donkeys just south of the old gym where there was a grove of Bois 'de Arc trees. He had a line stretched between the trees and had tied all the donkeys to the line. After making sure they had feed and water, he and his helpers all piled into one of the trucks and headed downtown to Doty's café to get some supper before the game.

Me and a friend ***(I won't give his name here, but his***

initials were Jerry Swain) ventured down to look at the donkeys. They seemed really gentle, not like the ones we had seen during a donkey basketball game. We petted around on all of them for a while, then one of us decided we would just sit on one of the donkeys for a minute. Just a minute, mind you. Before long, we were both sitting on donkeys and they just kept on feeding on the hay that was spread on the ground in front of them.

All of a sudden, the truck carrying the donkey handlers came around the corner of the gym and pulled up right behind the donkeys. They had finished their supper and returned to get the donkeys ready for the game. When they saw us sitting on the donkeys, you would have thought we had stolen them or something by the fuss they put on. They started screaming for us to get off the donkeys, which we did as quickly as we could. I just knew they were going to have us arrested or fined or something else just about as bad when one of them started smiling.

"Sorry to scare you boys like that," he said. "You see, if anybody saw you sitting on the donkeys like that, then they might think they wouldn't buck or anything and wouldn't come to the game. These donkeys are trained to buck and put up a fuss only when they are in the gym. I can ride them all over the place and they won't buck or anything. We just don't want anybody else to know that. Tell you what, you guys be back down here just before the game starts and we'll let you help us lead the donkeys to the gym. That way you can get in free. How's that sound?"

"Gosh, thanks mister," I replied. Jerry had a big grin on his face as well.

I haven't been to or even heard of a donkey basketball game in years. The annual donkey basketball game was a highlight of my year every year when I was growing up. It's a shame they stopped having them. I know my grandkids would get a big kick of them.

These are memories of a time in my life when I thought I was invincible and would live forever. Memories of a seemingly more innocent time as well. Though kids today have so much more and so many more opportunities than we did, I wonder if they really appreciate the simple everyday things that are a part of growing up. The meaning and reality of the word "family" has changed so much since I was a kid that many young people grow into adulthood without ever getting to experience the true family environment as we did back then. I wish I could take my grown children back in time for just a day to see and experience the old gyms that were so much a part of community life in the early and middle parts of the 20th century. I realize they will most likely have similar remembrances of how things were as they were growing up. It is just a part of life and living. We can't go back, nor would I want to. It is good to have the memories though. I hope yours are as special to you as mine are to me.

The End

Unemployed

As I've gotten older, and experienced most everything life has to offer, there have been many times when decisions I made were impacted, as least to some degree, by things that happened in my life experience; mostly things that happened as I was in my prime learning years. Old enough to act like a grown man, but not old enough to think like one. By and large, these life experiences involved folks that I worked for, or had dealings with around Mill Creek, Oklahoma as I was growing up. I have come to understand over the years, that the way we believe, and the way we react to circumstances, is a direct reflection of the way we were raised and the life experiences with which we have dealt. That is why we all have a slightly different perspective about things, though folks that have like childhood experiences tend to think alike in a general sense.

For example, the State of Oklahoma has been a conservative voting state for several years. When it comes to politics, most Oklahomans generally think alike. In marriage, couples that had similar childhood upbringing, and thus similar values, tend to have a better chance of making it work than folks with drastically different moral values and experiences. But that is getting way over my head. Don't know how I got to that sort of thing when I started out to tell a story about a life experience that has stood me in good stead most of my adult years.

I had been working for Mr. Harkins off and on for the better part of my high school years. You know, all the things it takes to put in a hay crop every year like plowing, harrowing, planting, raking, and baling. Then in the winter, feeding the cows every afternoon after school, and various other tasks that are common around a farm. I started working for Mr. Harkins in 1962 for seventy-five cents an hour, and three years later was still earning seventy-five cents an hour. Don't hardly seem right, does it? Sure didn't to me. To make matters worse, Hank Graham had started to work just a few months earlier and was making the same as I was, seventy-five cents an hour. We had put in a hay crop that spring of about sixty acres, and it being mid-summer, was now ready to bale. We had cut and raked about twenty acres on a Friday, and I was gonna start baling on Sunday morning after the hay had time to cure a little. Hank was gonna start cutting on another field if the weather looked like it was gonna hold. Anyway, here's how it went down.

"I don't know about you Hank," I said. "But I'm tired of working my butt off for seventy-five cents an hour. Everybody ought to get a raise every now and then. At least once in every three years, don't you think?"

"You ain't gonna quit are you Pete?" Hank asked. "I sure don't aim to bale and haul all this hay by myself!"

"Naw, I ain't gonna quit," I said. "Just trying to figure out a way to get me a raise, that's all. Takes about all I make on a Saturday just to have a decent date on Saturday night. What with having to buy gas, hamburgers, french fries, and drinks at Doves Drive In, and the cost to get in the drive-in movie, a guy can spend around four or five bucks. That doesn't even count the snacks at the show. Know what I mean?"

"What you got in mind?" Hank wanted to know.

"Well," I said as I rubbed my chin like I had seen folks do when they was thinking real hard like. "Looks to me like we got the old man over a barrel."

"What you mean, over a barrel?" Hank wasn't sure what I had in mind, and he wasn't following along with my thinking either.

"Look at all this hay just raked up and laying here on the ground," I replied. "Lots of hay here that needs baling. Supposed to rain Monday or Tuesday. If this hay ain't baled and in the barn before the rain starts, sure gonna be lots of hay go to ruin don't you think? "I could see the light bulb come on in his head.

"The way I see it," I continued. "We tell the old man that we gotta have a raise before we bale and haul this here hay. He ain't got a choice to my way of thinking. Can't afford to just let this hay lay here and ruin. He couldn't ever get it all baled before it starts to rain all by his self, and he sure can't haul it to the barn and unload it. Especially with all the trouble we had been having with the old hay baler."

It was one of the last of the old balers that made the little round bales. About the same size as the square bales, only round. Why Mr. Harkins didn't break down and buy a good square bale baler, I'd never know. We generally wasted more time working on the baler than we did baling hay.

"How we gonna go about it?" Hank asked.

"Well," I said. "We'll just show up here Sunday morning

like we was gonna start to work, 'cept we'll tell Mr. Harkins we ain't gonna start work until we get a raise."

"How much of a raise we gonna ask for?" Hank wanted to know.

"Might as well ask for a dollar an hour while we're at it," I said. "That's a quarter an hour raise. We ought to be worth a dollar an hour."

"Works for me," Hank said.

We was feeling pretty proud of ourselves all day Saturday. I was figuring up all the stuff I was gonna be able to buy with that extra two bits an hour. Let's see now. Twenty-five cents an hour for eight hours a day was gonna be, yep, two whole bucks a day extra. Can't beat a deal like that with a stick.

When we pulled into the gate by the barn Sunday morning in my old 1954 Chevy, I could see old man Harkins down in the hay field piddling with the baler.

"Well, here we go," I said.

I had sort of a funny feeling in the pit of my stomach that somehow this wasn't gonna go right, but it was too late to back out now, I figured. As we walked down to where Mr. Harkins was working on the baler, I could see Hank had a strange look on his face as well.

"Morning boys," Mr. Harkins said as he saw us come walking up. "How come you didn't drive the tractor down here Pete? We're wasting good daylight as it is. Gotta get this hay in the barn quick as we can. Heard on the weather last night it might rain in the next couple of days. One of you boys run back up and get the tractor while I finish greasing up this here baler."

"We need to talk to you, Mr. Harkins," I said as he leaned back over the baler where he was finishing up with the lube job. I was beginning to think he hadn't heard me when he finally rose up and looked our way.

"What is it that can't wait till we get this hay baled?" he asked.

By then I was wondering if I ought to just go get the tractor and get started with the baling. I looked over at Hank, but he was looking at me, so I just blurted it out.

"We figure we ought to be due a raise," I said. "I've been working for you for three years and I ain't never got a raise. "

Old man Harkins just looked at us with a blank expression on his face, and if you knew Mr. Harkins, you'd know he about had the market cornered on blank expressions. Never knew what he was thinking.

"Figure you're due a raise, do you?" He asked.

I didn't trust myself to speak, so I just nodded.

"Why don't we talk about it after we get the hay crop in?" He said.

Well there it was, time to put up or shut up. I figured if we waited till the hay crop was in, then all our leverage for a raise was gone. Had to be now or never to my way of thinking. I looked over at Hank, but he wasn't helping at all. His face had sort of a pinched look about it like he had just tasted something real sour. No help there that I could see.

"We figure we need a raise before we start baling hay," I finally said.

Old man Harkins got down from where he was working on the baler and sat on the metal frame that served as a support for the tongue. He took off his old hat, he wore the kind that looked like an Army helmet, but had a fabric cover on it. Sort of a tan color and had a little brim that ran all the way around. He had several of them hanging in the shop building right by the door. He took his handkerchief out of his hip pocket and started mopping the sweat from his face.

"How much of a raise you boys figure you need?" He asked.

Now we were finally getting somewhere looked like. "We figure we're worth a dollar an hour," I said, looking over at Hank. At least he nodded his head that time.

"A dollar an hour huh," Mr. Harkins said, almost as if he was saying it to his self. "That would be a twenty five cent an hour raise. Don't nobody get that big of a raise that I know of, he said. Tell you what, let's get this hay baled and in the barn, then we'll talk about a raise."

Now there is a thing called stubborn, and a thing called stupid. Right then, I took the stubborn course and did something stupid.

"We ain't gonna bale any hay until we get a raise to a dollar an hour, I said." Then silence that seemed to stretch up to longer than a minute. Finally Mr. Harkins looked over at Hank. "You feel like that too Hank?"

It took a while for Hank to get his Adams apple back in the right place so he could talk, but when he did I was right proud of him. "Yea," he said, as he nodded his head, sort of squeaky, but he said it. Silence again. Old man Harkins put his hat back on and started to climb back up on the baler. When he got both feet up on the side of the baler, he turned and looked down at us still standing there not knowing what to think.

"Sure have enjoyed having you boys work for me," he said. "I'll make out checks for what I owe you and leave them hanging on the clip by the shop door. You all just drop by and pick them up next time you're by this way." With that, he turned and went back to working on the baler.

"What just happened here?" Hank asked as we walked slowly back across the hay field to the shop building. "Did we just get fired?"

" I guess we did at that," I said.

I had a queasy feeling like I might lose my breakfast or something. On the way back to town, neither of us could think of anything to say. What went wrong, I wondered? How was old man Harkins gonna get all that hay baled and in the barn? What was I gonna do for spending money without a job? I really liked working for Mr. Harkins. How stupid could a boy be? By now, I was wishing I had never thought of asking for a raise.

"What you doing home in the middle of the morning?" Dad wanted to know.

I had just slunk in the back door hoping I could get to my room without having to answer a bunch of questions. Didn't look like that was gonna be the case though. Dad was sitting at the kitchen table with a cup of coffee when I came in the door. Didn't look like I was gonna avoid it, so I sat down across from him and started chewing on a piece of toast from the plate Mom had just set on the table.

"Got fired," I said.

"What!! What do you mean you got fired? Mr. Harkins fired you? What did you do to get yourself fired?"

"I didn't do anything except ask for a raise," I said.

"Mr. Harkins fired you for asking for a raise? Why would he do that? Why wouldn't he just say no if he didn't think you deserved a raise?"

"What's that about getting fired?"

Mom had just come back into the kitchen and caught the tail end of the conversation.

"Pete said Mr. Harkins fired him for asking for a raise," my dad said. "That sure don't sound like Mr. Harkins. You sure there wasn't more to it than just asking for a raise Pete?"

Parents! Couldn't get a thing by 'em. Dad had seen through the raise thing just as soon as I'd said I got fired.

"You want to tell us what really happened Pete?" he asked.

So I told it just the way it happened. When I was through, my dad got up and poured his self another cup of coffee.

"Here's the way it is Pete," he began. "You were probably right in asking for a raise. You've worked for Mr. Harkins long enough to deserve a raise. At least to have a right to ask for one. But you see Pete, you went about it all wrong. First off, you picked a bad time to ask for a raise. Mr. Harkins was bound to feel like you thought you had him over a barrel. Then you demanded a certain amount of a raise which was wrong to boot. It was okay to ask for a dollar an hour, but it wasn't okay to insist on it. If you weren't happy with what the raise was gonna be, then you would have the right to either take the raise that was offered, or look for another job."

"But he didn't offer any raise at all," I shot back.

"But he did say he was willing to talk about a raise, which probably meant he was prepared to give you one. He just wanted to do it at a more opportune time, that's all."

Bad as I hated to admit it, my dad was making a lot of sense. Too late now though. Right now, I was joining the ranks of the unemployed.

The rest of that Sunday passed slowly for me. After lunch, I curled up on the couch with a western book and a glass of Kool Aid. I read for a couple of hours, then I must have fallen asleep because I awoke to someone hollering my name.

"Pete! Get up! Someone wants to talk to you on the phone."

It was my little sister Virginia. She thought she had to be the one to answer the phone every time it rang.

"Hello," I mumbled, still half asleep.

"That you Pete," the voice on the other end of the line asked? "This is Lloyd Harkins."

I was suddenly fully awake. What was Mr. Harkins doing calling me when he had just fired me that same morning?

"Thought you might know of a couple of guys that need a job," he said. "I got a couple of jobs baling and hauling hay that I need a couple of guys for. Job pays seventy-five cents an hour for a new hand, but if a boy had a little experience, I might be willing to pay as high as eighty-five cents an hour. You know any boys that might like to have them jobs Pete?" he asked. Eighty-five cents an hour, you say. Now that was more like it.

"Yes sir, Mr. Harkins. I know a boy that would like to have one of them jobs. When would he need to be there to work?"

"I figure with all the time already lost today, we might have to work all the way through the night to get that hay baled and in the barn. So the quicker he could get out here, the sooner we could get started," he replied. "Oh, by the way Pete. Stop by and pick up Hank on the way out here. I just got off the phone with him." Then I heard the click as he hung up the phone.

Hank had a big grin on his face when I pulled into the yard. He was holding a brown paper bag that looked to have enough food in it to last a week. He had taken old man Harkins at his word about working all night.

"You ready?" I asked as he got into the car.

"Yea, I'm ready," he said. "Just promise me one thing though."

"What's that," I said.

"Please don't ask for another raise when we get out there," he replied. We were still laughing as we turned the corner at Opal's Café and headed west out to the farm.

I've gotten a lot of raises over the years. At times, the raise I received was not as much as I thought I deserved, and at other times, it was more than I expected. I've even negotiated a raise on more than one occasion. But regardless of how it has worked out, every time I have gotten a raise, the episode with Mr. Harkins has come to my mind. I've even told that story a few times over the years to folks that I have given raises. Incidents such as the one with old man Harkins are just a part of growing up. The trick is to learn the lesson that is sometime hidden within all of the hullabaloo. I didn't learn all the things I got a chance to learn, but with Dad's help, Mr. Harkins taught me the correct way to ask for a raise.

I look back fondly on the time I worked for Mr. Harkins. That job helped teach me a sense of responsibility and helped me to succeed in many of my life's ambitions. I'm thankful I had that experience to draw on over the years.

The End

The Watermelon Heist

What is better than a big, sweet, juicy watermelon on a hot summer day? Not a thing that I can think of, and that is exactly what Davey and I were thinking that hot August afternoon in 1958. That's why we knew we had to do it. We had been talking about it ever since we overheard a couple of high school boys talking about stealing watermelons out at Old Man Harkins' orchard. The thought of those big, juicy watermelons just lying there for the taking was more of a temptation than we could endure.

Oh, we knew it was stealing, but for some reason, since we knew the high school boys were doing it, it didn't seem so bad a thing, you know what I mean? They had looked on it as a trick more than a crime and I was inclined to do the same. After all, what right did a couple of nine year old boys have to be second guessing a bunch of high school guys?

We had heard a few days earlier, that someone had shot at some boys with a shotgun as they were attempting to steal a watermelon at the orchard, but that just made it more of an adventure for us. We had it all figured out; at least we thought we did. Here's how we planned for the watermelon stealing caper to go down. We would meet down by the train depot about an hour before dark. Old Man Harkins' orchard was about five miles out of town, so we figured to be there just as it was getting full dark. We would each bring a toe sack, (burlap bag to you city folks), to carry the watermelons in while pedaling our bikes back to town. I even thought of a pocket knife to cut the melons with. We would bring them back to Main Street where there was a street light and sit on the sidewalk and eat them. Pretty simple plan if you ask me. Not much of a chance anything could go wrong the way I had it figured.

We eased along the county road to the orchard just taking our time so it would be full dark when we got there. We were just riding along shooting the bull like a couple of guys will do when we saw the lights of a car come over the hill toward us about a mile away. Since we surely didn't want anyone to spot us and be able to remember seeing us later on, we eased our bikes into the tall Johnson grass alongside of the road to wait for the car to go by. I recognized the car right off as the red and white 1957 Mercury that Old Man Harkins had just purchased a few months earlier. This little caper was beginning to look like it was going to be easier than even we had thought. Old Man Harkins was headed somewhere and wouldn't even be home when we got the watermelons. We couldn't believe our good luck.

We eased slowly along the side of the road nearest the house as we went by. That way, the tall Johnson grass would hide us from view if anyone happened to be looking that way from up at the house that sat about a hundred yards off the road to the south. We knew Old

Man Harkins was headed to town, but Mrs. Harkins or somebody else might be home and we surely didn't want to be spotted. The orchard was another quarter of a mile west of the house but on the same side of the road.

We hid our bikes in the tall grass beside the road and eased under the orchard fence. It wasn't long before we could see the big watermelons just lying in rows on the ground among the vines. We each picked one out and using the pocket knife, cut it from the vine. The one I picked was so heavy it was all I could do to carry it back to the road after I rolled it into the toe sack. Davey had a big one as well and we exchanged big grins as we gathered up our bikes and helped each other tie the ends of the toe sacks to the handlebars. We had just finished that chore and were getting ready to head back to town when the voice came clear as a bell from a spot just inside the fence and about twenty feet behind us.

"What you boys think you're doing?" the voice said. I nearly jumped out of my jeans it scared me so bad. Davey was looking at me, and by the faint light of the rising moon, I could see a sort of sick look on his face.

"Let's get out of here!" I hollered. We took off like the devil himself was after us and as we hit full speed, I could hear the voice call again.

"You boys better stop stealing my watermelons," the voice said. I could see the beam of a powerful flashlight searching the darkness for us. I just pedaled that much faster. I could just see us getting caught and ending up in the hoosegow at Sulphur. My dad was gonna kill me for sure. It was just about then that Davey hollered at me. "He's coming after us," he shouted. I looked back and could see headlights coming out of the orchard and when they got to the road, they turned our direction. I figured our goose was cooked when Davey all of a sudden made a sharp turn to the left and rode into the open gate of a hayfield. We pulled our bikes into the tall grass along the fence and lay down as close to the ground as we could get. The lights turned out to be the lights of a tractor and we could see it plainly as it eased along the road toward our position. When it got even with the open gate it stopped and just sat there. We could see a man sitting on the tractor but the light wasn't good enough to make out who it was. My heart was in my throat. It looked like he was going to turn into the hayfield, and if he did, we were caught sure as the world. When the tractor started slowly down the road again, I could feel the air escaping between my clenched teeth. I hadn't realized I had been holding my breath.

We took the opportunity to ease down the fence row in the direction of town, all the while watching the tractor make its way down the road ahead of us. We followed along for about a quarter of a mile then stopped and hid in the grass again when the tractor stopped. As we watched from our hiding place, the tractor made a U-turn in the road and headed back our way. I was just beginning to feel like we had gotten by with it when the tractor stopped on the road even with our hiding place in the tall grass. I glanced at Davey, and when I looked back toward the road, my heart skipped a beat. The man was getting down from the tractor! Instinctively, we both hunkered down farther into the grass as the man stood there in the road in front of the tractor. I could feel the blood pounding in my head as I strained to hold my breath.

Holy crap!!! The man was walking toward the exact place on the fence line where we were hidden. When he finally stopped, he was directly in front of us and about three or four feet on the road side of the fence. I knew he hadn't seen us or he wouldn't have been just standing there not saying anything. He must have had some idea we were close by though as he stood and appeared to be listening.

All of a sudden, I could hear a sound like a zipper being unzipped and then the unmistakable sound of water splashing in the grass not three feet in front of my face. He was relieving himself right in front of us!! When he finished, the zipper sound again, then silence. I had held my breath just about as long as I could. My head felt like it was about to burst when he finally turned and walked back to the tractor. When the tractor passed our position and was about fifty feet down the road, I just let it go. I gasped for breath for at least two or three minutes and I could see Davey was doing the same thing. We hustled the bikes along the fence until we came to the open gate at the far end of the field. Just as we mounted up on the road again, we could see the tractor turn into the hay field at the other gate where we had first hidden in the grass.

We rode those bikes about as hard as we could the entire five miles back to Mill Creek. When we finally untied the watermelon sacks from the handlebars and laid the watermelons on the sidewalk under the street light, I could finally begin to breath normally. We had pulled it off! We really had!! Those high school guys didn't have a thing on us! We were both feeling pretty good about ourselves along about then. I took the pocket knife out of my pocket and handed it to Davey. "You do the honors," I said.

I looked on as Davey positioned the knife and cut cleanly along the center of the melon. He turned the melon over and repeated the process on the other side. I could already taste the sweet red meat of that watermelon on my tongue. As Davey finished the second cut and the melon fell apart into two identical halves there it lay in all its glory.

What? NO! NO! NO! It can't be!! There lay the

watermelon and it was as green as a gourd. Green! Can you believe it? After all the trouble we took to get those melons. Packing them all the way from the orchard back to town at the threat of getting caught. Almost losing consciousness from holding my breath. I just couldn't believe it. I picked up the knife from the sidewalk where Davey had laid it and cut the second melon. Same thing!! Green as it could be.

We just sat there looking at each other in disbelief. I could see the corners of Davey's mouth begin to turn up. Before long, it turned into the makings of a smile. We looked at each other and just broke out laughing. All of a sudden, it was the funniest thing I had ever heard of. We laughed 'til we couldn't laugh anymore. The joke had been on us after all.

The old saying is that crime doesn't pay, and at least in this instance, I would have to agree that it was true. We really didn't see it as a crime just a practical joke, you might say. A joke that backfired in our case. As the years went by and we got old enough to have a better understanding of life, I came to believe that Old Man Harkins got a bigger kick out of trying to catch guys stealing watermelons than we got out of trying to do it without getting caught. Why else would he plant so many watermelons every year? Most of them just rotted in the field after he had picked all he wanted.

Years after that August night in 1958, I worked for Mr. Harkins as a part time job while I attended high school in Mill Creek. I never told him about stealing the watermelons that night and he never mentioned it either. For some reason though, I always figured he knew. By the way, it was Mrs. Harkins in the Mercury that night. Seems she was going to get her hair fixed.

Don't ever hear of kids stealing watermelons these days. What we hear about is drugs, robbing liquor stores, and pornography. I'm not trying to say that one crime is worse than another, but when was the last time you heard of a kid getting sent to prison for stealing watermelons? I did learn a powerful lesson that night. That's the key to the entire thing. You have to learn. Some do, some don't. I sometimes wonder what would have happened if Old Man Harkins had caught us that night. I believe he knew where we were the entire time and could have caught us if he wanted to. But then that would have spoiled the fun, now wouldn't it?

The End

The Appaloosa

Louis Helms bought him from a man that needed money in the worst way. At least that's the story I got. The way I heard it told, this man wouldn't be selling the horse at all if he wasn't in dire straits for a little cash money. Why, if he didn't need the money so bad and needing it right now like he did, you couldn't have bought the horse for twice what he was asking. It became apparent to Louis, in short order, that the real reason the fellar was selling the appaloosa was because he had a mean streak in him. Not the man, the horse.

Chief was a big horse. He stood about fifteen and a half hands tall and weighed close to thirteen hundred pounds would be my guess. He was a four year old the first time I laid eyes on him. Pretty cuss on the outside, but mighty ornery on the inside as I was soon to find out. Louis couldn't do a thing with him, and I ended up buying him for a song. The first time I got on old Chief was just outside the barn at Louis's place the day I bought him. Jasper was with me and he had hauled a gentle mare down to Louis's in the trailer. The plan was to leave the pickup and trailer there and ride the five miles back to town along the gravel road just to get the appaloosa used to being ridden. I wouldn't have given a nickel for that plan two seconds after my rear hit the saddle for the first time.

Chief stood there quietly while I threw the saddle on him and cinched it up tight. This didn't look to me like it was gonna be any kind of a problem at all. I led him around a little to get him used to the feel of the saddle on his back, then put my foot in the stirrup and swung into the seat. That's when the whole world seemed to blow up. The first time he swapped ends, he almost lost me. I finally managed to get my posterior back firmly in the saddle on about the fourth or fifth jump. From there on it was a battle. With both Jasper and Louis yelling encouragement, I hung on to old Chief as he bucked all over the area in front of the big barn. I'll admit I was all over the saddle for the first few minutes, but the longer he bucked, the more confidence I gained. After about ten minutes of non- stop bucking, he finally quit and just stood there with sweat dripping from his tired body to the ground. I was just grateful for a second or two to catch my breath as well.

We started out along the gravel road leading back to town with Jasper in the lead on the gentle mare. Chief was doing pretty well just following along behind the mare, and after a mile or so, I began to loosen up and give him a little free rein. Bad Idea!! As soon as he felt he had an opportunity to get his head down, here he went again. He bucked from one bar-ditch to the other for a hundred yards or so up the road. Finally, he wore down again and just stopped in the middle of the road. It didn't matter what I did, he wasn't gonna move. After a few minutes, Jasper took the halter lead and old Chief fell right in behind the mare when he jerked on the rope. I was soon to learn that the sudden fit of pitching was gonna be a constant thing with Chief. Just about the time you thought he was through with the bucking and let your guard down, here he would go again.

I kept Chief in the corral up at the old Ozment place because it had a lean-to shed and feed house attached to it. There was also a water faucet right outside the corral that worked most of the time. It was pretty bad about throwing the breaker in the well house if I used it much, but it beat hauling water in the back of the truck from somewhere else.

I rode him every day. At least all the days it didn't rain or I didn't get hung up doing something else I couldn't get out of. It would take fifteen or twenty minutes most days to get a bridle on Chief. He purely hated a bridle. Didn't seem to mind the saddle too much, but he hated anything on his head. I tried every kind of bit I could think of and finally settled on a hackamore. He seemed to tolerate it a little better once I got it on him, but it was about as much trouble to get on his head as anything else.

Chief was a pretty horse. Folks would stand and just watch as I rode by on him. Jasper allowed as how I'd never make a usable mount out of him.

"Got a mean streak in him for sure," he'd say. "Be lucky if that horse don't hurt you bad someday when you ain't ready for one of his antics." It wasn't long until Chief proved him right.

It was a warm day and I was just moseying along on Chief headed for the gate going into the meadow pasture east of town. I figured to give him a good workout in the meadow where there weren't any trees or anything else in the way. There were a few bois 'de arc trees in the pasture just after going through the gate, but past that, the meadow was a hundred acres or so of just rolling grassland. I stopped and got off at the gate and gave Chief a pat on the neck. He was acting mighty gentle for some reason that afternoon and I wanted to reward him for it. With the gate closed behind me, I put my foot in the stirrup to mount and before my rear hit the saddle, the bottom fell out of it.

I had one foot in the stirrup and the other one dangling as I tried desperately to find the off side stirrup. Meanwhile, Chief was bucking straight toward the Bois 'de arc trees with seemingly every intent to rake me off his back under the thorny tree limbs. I found the stirrup just as he ran in under the low hanging tree limbs and managed to throw my other leg over the saddle. There I hung, one foot in the stirrup and one hand grasping the saddle horn as I hunkered down as low as I could hunker against the side of the saddle. I don't have a clue how I managed to hang on as he ran on under the trees and out into the meadow. I could feel the limbs whipping the back of my neck and shoulders as we cleared the last of the bois 'de arc trees. When clear of the timber, I just turned loose and fell into the soft grass of the meadow. I could see Chief running and bucking for all he was worth toward the far end of the pasture.

I just lay there and watched the soft white clouds drift slowly across the summer sky. My shirt was hanging in tatters from my body and I could feel the wetness of blood on my bare chest and stomach. The skin was knocked off the knuckles of my left hand that had been holding onto the saddle horn. I didn't remember that happening at all. I knew then that Jasper was right. I was never gonna be able to trust Chief. If I kept him, I would always be afraid he would do something that might end up getting me hurt or killed. Or even worse, somebody else. I made up my mind as I lay there in the meadow that day, that I was gonna get rid of him.

When I had regained my strength, I walked down the

meadow to where Chief was quietly grazing on the lush grass. He just stood and waited while I gathered up the reins. One rein was broken where he had stepped on it in his run across the pasture, but I had no intention of riding him anyway. I led Chief back to the Ozment place and turned him loose in the corral with a bucket of feed and a trough full of cold, clean water. I had no intention of riding him again and had in mind to take him to the next horse sale at Sulphur, Oklahoma. I thought I'd had my last bad experience with Chief and all that was left was to take him to the sale and be done with it. Little did I know that Chief had not quite finished with me and there would be one more little adventure awaiting me before I saw the last of him.

It was a Monday afternoon in August 1965 and it was horse sale night at Sulphur. The sale was held every other Monday night all year as long as the weather was fitting. I arrived at the corral early in case I had any unexpected trouble. It had come to my attention a few days earlier that I had never loaded Chief in a trailer and I had no idea how he would respond. I had ridden him from Louis Helms' place the day I bought him, and had never had occasion to haul him anywhere.

The trailer I was using was a sixteen foot, double axel trailer and it didn't have a top cover on it. The sides were made of strong pipe and I didn't figure to have any kind of a problem once I had Chief in the trailer and the back gate closed and latched. The problem, I figured, was getting him to jump up into the trailer in the first place.

I fastened a stout lead rope onto the ring of Chief's halter and tied him to the corral fence while I backed the trailer into position. When I led him up to the back of the trailer, he didn't seem the least bit concerned. He stepped up into the trailer like he had been doing it every day, but when he saw he was trapped inside the thing with no place to go, he ran backwards out of that trailer as fast as he could, nearly jerking me off my feet in the process. After he had time to calm down a little I tried again. He would walk right up to the back of the trailer, but he wouldn't step up into it. I tried and tried to get him to jump up into the trailer, but try as I might, he was just not going to do it. I always figured I was as long on patience as the next guy, but I finally decided I was gonna have to take a different approach if I was ever gonna get him into the trailer.

I attached a lariat rope onto the lead rope of the halter, then led Chief up to the trailer again. Then I ran the rope up to the front of the trailer, around one of the support pipes and then back to the back of the trailer. Standing on the ground behind him, I would pull on the rope and at the same time give him a pop on the rear end with a little buggy whip I carried behind the seat of the truck for just such occasions as this. Old Chief danced around a little then all of a sudden he jumped up into the trailer. I slammed and latched the back gate before he could change his mind. When he saw he was trapped again, he ran backward like he had done before but was brought up short by the latched back gate. When his rear end hit the gate, he lunged forward, and with a mighty leap, cleared the front of the trailer and landed with his front feet in the bed of the truck. His hind legs were hanging inside the trailer still and I just knew he was gonna kill himself or at the least injure himself badly.

His flailing back hooves finally found purchase on one of the bars that made up the front of the trailer, and he flung himself completely into the back of the truck. With another lunge, he was out of the truck bed and running free down the road toward the cattle guard which he cleared with a soaring leap. I stood and watched him go out of sight around a bend in the gravel road.

I was stunned to say the least. I just stood there and gazed at the bent tailgate and scratched sides of my truck with a blank look on my face. What had just happened here? It had all happened so fast, I was having more than a little trouble making sense of it all.

I found Chief grazing quietly by the side of the road some five miles from the Ozment place. The lariat was still attached to the halter lead and trailing behind him. He followed along calmly behind the truck as I led him back to the barn. The horse sale would have to wait for another day. I was gonna have to do a little more thinking about how I was gonna get him to the sale without killing him. The leap from the trailer didn't appear to have done him any harm, but I surely didn't want to try that again.

Monday night two weeks later found me back at the corral with the intention of taking Chief to the horse sale. This time though, I was a little better prepared. I had borrowed a sixteen foot trailer with a steel top on it and I knew if I ever got him into that thing, he was gonna stay there 'til I opened the gate and let him out. Much the same as before, I ran a rope up to the front of the trailer and around a pipe, then back to the back so I could put a little pull on him as I popped him with the whip. Chief jumped into the trailer on about the second pop of the whip and I quickly fastened him in. He was banging his head on the steel top as he tried unsuccessfully to repeat his escape of two weeks earlier. I couldn't help but laugh at his futile attempts to escape his prison.

Even though I bought him for a song, I still lost money on him after he chased all the handlers out of the sale ring when they ran him in. He was bought by a company that canned and sold horse meat to the market in France and I was glad he did. I hated to see him go that way, but I surely didn't want anyone to buy him and then have him kill or cripple them.

I know there are some really good appaloosa horses, seen a bunch of 'em myself. For my part though, you can have all of them. Old Chief ruined me for appaloosa horses. In my case, one bad apple spoiled the barrel you might say. Occasionally I'll see a pretty Appaloosa in somebody's pasture and Chief will come back to mind. He was the darndest horse I was ever around. You know the place in Revelations where they talk about the seven horsemen? When the fourth seal was opened, there appeared the Spector of Death and he was riding a pale horse. I'm amazed it wasn't an appaloosa.

My daddy always told me; "Son," he'd say. "There ain't a soul that hasn't made mistakes. The key is learning from them mistakes. If you do that, you'll be alright." I learned something from Chief. Me and appaloosa horses don't set well with each other. I wouldn't have wished him on anybody. Come to think of it, I wonder why Louis sold him to me in the first place him knowing what he was like and all. He must have misunderstood the Golden Rule, I expect. He must have thought it said "Do unto others as others have done unto you." The man that was so hard up for cash money did unto Louis and Louis did unto me. I surely would have passed up on selling Old Chief if someone other than the packers had bought him at the sale that night, I surely would.

The End

The Legend of Sadie's Gold

The legend of Sadie's gold is based very loosely on a person I knew when I was growing up. It is a story of how things might have been and could have been. In all likelihood, there is a lot of truth to the legend, but since I have no firsthand knowledge of how things really were, I am writing the story the way I want it to be. Here's how my imagination tells me it went down.

Sadie Johnson had been a widow for many years when I first met her. She had lived in the old ramshackle house with her husband Emerson since he went to work for Old Man Darby in 1948. They never had anything more than barely enough to eat and occasionally a few dollars for a new set of clothes for each of them. That's why Sadie never got around to having any children. She just didn't see how they could possibly raise children the way they ought to be raised when they were just barely keeping skin and bones together the way things were. Then in 1953, on a beautiful spring day, Old Man Darby brought Emerson home slung across the saddle of his horse. She kept him alive for most of a week, but he had something busted inside of him that she just couldn't fix.

They laid him to rest under the only good sized tree within a quarter of a mile of the house. The old ground was so rocky, the three cowboys assigned to dig the grave stopped at just over four feet deep. They figured if anything wanted to go to enough trouble to dig through the rocks and hard clay to get to Emerson's body, it could just have him. Outside of the three cowboys, the only other people at the graveside service were Old Man Darby, his raisin-faced wife Clarabelle, and Mr. Clermont from town. John Clermont owned the only grocery store in Mill Creek and had been delivering the few things the Johnsons purchased once a month for the past five years. He figured he lost money on the groceries every time he made the eight mile trip from town each month, but Sadie had asked him to do it so he did. That's just the kind of man he was.

John Clermont was just about the only person in Mill Creek that had any dealings with the Johnsons, so he figured he needed to be at the service and maybe say a few words over old Emerson. Otherwise, Old Man Darby was just likely to drop him in the hole and send him on his way without even the benefit of a prayer. When they had all gathered around the open grave, John read a few verses from the Bible and closed with John 14:1. When he glanced at Sadie, she just nodded her head so he figured he had done all he could do.

After the short service, Sadie started to gather what few belongings she wanted to take with her. She had already asked John for a ride to town and he was waiting patiently beside the truck while she packed. When Mr. Darby saw what she was doing, he laid a hand on her shoulder.

"You don't have to go anywhere, Mrs. Johnson," he said. "You're welcome to stay in this house as long as you want to. I intend to give you half of Emerson's pay every month as long as you want to stay."

Sadie just sat down on the rock stoop and stared out toward where the cowboys were filling in the grave with the loose rock and clay. She hated to leave him there, in the cold ground like that with nobody for company except the coyotes and rattlesnakes. But what about her? Did her allegiance to Emerson mean she was supposed to stay here by herself until she died? But then, she wouldn't really be alone, would she? She had her cats, and Emerson was just a little way from the house any time she wanted to go down and talk to him. All of a sudden, she made up her mind.

"You go on John," she said. "You bring me some vittles next time you're by this way. I just feel like I ought to stay here in case Emerson needs me."

"Now Mrs. Johnson," John said. "Emerson ain't gonna need a thing. I can about guarantee you he won't. Why don't you let me take you to town so you can have a good place to stay? You might make some friends and learn some new things to do like sewing or something. I hear tell some of the ladies get together every so often and make a quilt or some such thing. You hear what I'm saying, Mrs. Johnson?"

"I hear you John and I'm much beholden to you," she answered. "But you run on now and bring me some groceries next time you come by. I'll be just fine."

John mused on her decision all the way back to town. Half of Emerson's pay uh? Now I just wonder how much money that will be a month? It shocked him that Darby had been even that generous. Probably not enough to even buy groceries to keep one person alive, he thought. Little did he know, but that situation was about to change for the better, and rather quickly considering the source of the change.

The weeks and the months went by and John religiously took the few groceries by to Sadie every couple of weeks. She always paid him cash money, but he could tell it took about all she had every time to pay the small bill for the groceries. And that was with him putting in a few extra things each time and conveniently forgetting to add them to the bill.

The letter came addressed to Mr. and Mrs. Emerson Johnson, general delivery, Mill Creek Oklahoma, and the postmistress brought it over to the store for him to take to Sadie the next time he went out. Rather official looking letter, he thought. Monarch Oil and Gas Exploration Company, the return address on the envelope read. Now that was a perplexing thing, wasn't it? What in the world could Monarch Oil Company be wanting with Sadie Johnson. He figured he might find out sooner than later since he was gonna take some groceries out to Sadie that very afternoon.

Sadie took the envelope and opened it with shaking hands. John couldn't help but notice how she had gone down in the few short months since Emerson's death. The pounds had melted from her already thin body until she looked like she was about ready to join him on the rocky hillside.

It was all he could do to stand there quietly as she extracted the folded paper from the envelope and began to painstakingly read the words. After a couple of minutes she lowered the paper and looked over at him.

"John," she said. "Would you mind to read this thing to me? I just can't seem to be able to get my mind around all them fine sounding words." John took the letter and began to read.

"Dear Mr. and Mrs. Johnson," the letter began. "It is our distinct honor to inform you that the

Monarch Oil Company has struck oil on the allotment members of your family leased to us in 1937. Since you are the only remaining family we have been able to locate, be advised that the royalty payments on the oil taken from the lease will be made to this address quarterly. If you would prefer other arrangement be made, please notify the Monarch Oil and Gas Exploration Company immediately upon receipt of this notice."

The notice was signed by a Mr. AJ Latimer, President, Monarch Oil Company. John looked over at Sadie to gauge her reaction to the notice he had just read. She was standing there with a dazed look on her face. The implications of what the notice said was just beginning to register with her.

"How much money do you reckon Mr. Latimer is talking about John?" She asked. "You think it might be as much or more than half of Emerson's pay is a month?"

"Hard to tell," John answered. "Best I can see is you'll just have to wait 'til the first check comes in the mail to find out, I reckon. I'll be sure to bring it out to you first thing when it comes in."

Over the next couple of months, John forgot all about the anticipated check. He had taken groceries out to Sadie a couple of times, but the last time he went by, neither of them mentioned the check. Now, just as he was gathering up the usual grocery items to take to Sadie, little Jimmy Snodgrass came running into the store.

"Miss Mabel down at the post office said you'd likely give me a free pop if I brought this here letter to you," he said. "Was she lying?"

"No, she sure as heck wasn't," John replied. "You just pick out any soda pop you want out of the box there Jimmy. I'm much obliged to you for bringing this letter over here to me." He took the letter Jimmy was holding out toward him and he could see right away it was from the Monarch Oil Company. His hands trembled as he opened the envelope. He just didn't feel right opening the letter and it not addressed to him, but Sadie had given him instructions to open it and cash the check that was inside if there was one. She wanted the cash money brought to her when he came out with the groceries.

Just as he was about to discover what the envelope held, old Mrs. Brumley from up the street came in the door. He knew as soon as he saw her enter that the envelope was just going to have to wait for later. Mrs. Brumley came in every week at about the same time, and it was the matter of an hour or more to get her waited on. She cooked supper every night for her two bachelor sons that worked at the mill outside of town. They were both in their thirties and neither had ever been married. Not surprising with her waiting on them hand and foot and cooking for them every day like she did. It was a small miracle that they had ever moved out of the house at all.

Mrs. Brumley always had a list, and on that list was the beginning of the menu for every meal she was going to cook the next week. It was a custom for John to follow her around the store helping her fill in the missing blanks on her menu list.

"What do you think would go good with liver and onions on Monday John?" she would ask. "Or, do you think the boys would like turnip greens with the roast on Tuesday?" At times, it was all John could do to keep from telling her he didn't give a good rat's @#%@& what the boys would or would not like. Like the good merchant he was though, he never failed to answer with a smile, albeit a pasted on one at times. Today was no different, and a little more than an hour later, he was free to once again try to find out what treasures were hiding inside the envelope.

When he drew what was obviously a check from the envelope, he had to look twice before it began to sink in. $3,643.23 was the amount of the check printed there in bold numbers for all to see! More than thirty-six hundred dollars!! He couldn't believe what he was seeing. Why, he didn't have the cash money to cash a check that big! What was he going to do? All he could do was take the check by to Sadie when he took the groceries and get her to sign the thing. Then he would have to take it all the way to the bank in Tishomingo to get it cashed. One thing for sure, this was turning out to be a lot more trouble than he had anticipated when he had agreed to cash the checks for her.

Later that same afternoon, he stood on Sadie's porch and waited for her to quit looking at the check. She had been staring at it for more than a minute when she finally looked up with a disbelieving look on her face.

"Is this check for three hundred and something dollars or three thousand and something dollars John?" She asked.

"That there check is for over three thousand dollars," John replied. "Closer to four thousand as a matter of fact. I didn't have enough money on hand to cash the thing. You'll have to sign it and let me take it to Tish to the bank."

"I don't trust them banks," Sadie replied. "You can just wait 'til you get the money to cash the thing and then bring it to me."

John knew it was no use talking to her about it anymore so after she signed the check, he drove slowly back to Mill Creek. He would drive to Tish the next day and cash the check when he did his normal deposit for the week.

The checks came once a quarter just like clockwork

and they never varied over a few dollars one way or the other. John would have Sadie sign the checks and then take them to Tishomingo to cash. He would give her the cash money, then she would pay him what she owed him for the groceries. As time went on and the years passed, Sadie's health began to fail. Each time he would go by, John could see she was going downhill and was in poorer health than the last time he saw her.

"Why don't you move to town, Sadie"' he would ask. "You don't have any business way off out here in the boonies by yourself. What if you was to fall and break a leg or something? What would you do? You'd be dead before anybody found you, that's what."

"I've been here too long now John," she'd reply. "I wouldn't fit in there in town. Too many people all crowded together. I'm afraid I couldn't breathe all crowded up like that."

"Why don't you let me take you to Tish so you can deposit the money in the bank so it's safe?" he asked one day. "You are going to want to leave that money to somebody, so it needs to be where they can get to it. You need to write a letter or something telling who you want to have your stuff if something happens to you. I can take you over to Tishomingo and have old man Bensen write it up for you. He's a lawyer, you know."

"I ain't got nobody to leave anything to," she answered. "I might just leave it to you if I had anything to leave. You're the only one ever done anything for me. No need talking about it now though. I ain't fixin to go nowhere for some time. I've just been down on my feed a little. I expect I'll be fine in a day or two."

It was the last time he saw her alive. He knew something was wrong before he ever got out of the truck. The front door was closed despite the nearly ninety degree temperature and there was not a cat in sight. It had been two weeks since they had the talk and this was the first chance he had to get away and bring her out some groceries.

The old worn boards squeaked when he stepped up onto the porch. He caught the smell before he even opened the door. She was lying in the bed with her hands folded over her stomach and she had been dead for most of a week, he figured. She was dressed in her best dress, the one she wore to Emerson's funeral. Looked like she had deliberately gotten dressed and then just lay down on the bed to die. He felt a tear come into his eye and he shook his head to clear his mind. She was gonna have to be buried, he knew, and the sooner the better.

Old Doc Newsome was working in his garden when John drove up. What was John Clermont doing calling on him in the middle of the day on a working day, he wondered?

"I need you to go with me Doc," John said as he walked up to where Doc was leaning on his hoe handle. "Sadie Johnson is dead. I found her just lying on her bed like someone had laid her out for burying."

"Sadie, heh?" Doc exclaimed. "Don't surprise me any, her living out there all by herself like that. Likely just grieved herself to death. What good is it going to do for me to go out there for if she's already dead?"

"I need you to declare her dead before we bury her, you old cuss. I can't just go and bury her without somebody pronouncing her dead, now can I?"

"Alright, I pronounce her dead," Doc replied. "Now does that suit you?"

"Just get in the truck Doc, John said. We'll go by and pick up a few of the guys loafing on the spit and whittle bench to dig the grave. We've got to get her in the ground before she gets any riper."

"Okay, I was just funning with you John," Doc replied.

Let me get my bag and a death certificate form and I'll be right with you."

It was getting on to mid-afternoon by the time they arrived back at Sadie's shack. Old man Darby met them there and he had a couple of cowboys with him to help dig the grave. It never occurred to John to question how Darby had found out about Sadie's death until weeks later. By then, it was too late to ask. With the help of the two cowboys, the three loafers from town got the grave dug in just over three hours. While the grave was being dug, John and old man Darby knocked together a wooden casket from the boards they found in the old ramshackle barn back of the house. It wasn't much, but it was better than nothing, John figured.

Just before dark, with Sadie safely in the ground beside Emerson and with the signed death certificate in hand, John drove slowly back to town. It had been a trying day and he was glad it was almost over. What would happen to Sadie's things, he wondered? And what about all that money he had been taking to her over the years? It had been more than fifteen years since the day he delivered the first check from Monarch Oil Company, and in all that time, the checks had come every quarter. The dollar amount of the checks had grown over the years as well. The last check, he remembered, had been for more than five thousand dollars. All that money must just be lying around in the house, hidden somewhere so casual eyes wouldn't see it. As far as he knew, the only people who knew about the money besides himself, was Sadie and the president of the bank at Tishomingo. Just to be on the safe side, he stopped and put a chain and padlock on the gate going into the lane to Sadie's house. No need taking a chance on someone driving the two miles through the pasture to the shack just out of curiosity before he had time to get back down there and look around a little.

It was almost noon the next day when John stopped to rest. He had been searching through every nook and cranny, through every chest and box in the house since before 7:00 o'clock that morning and so far hadn't found not one red cent of the money. It had to be there. Where else could it be? He knew for a fact that Sadie hadn't been off the place in more than fifteen years. He had brought all the money to her himself. So where could it be? Then it dawned on him. She must have buried it somewhere close by. That's what she did, she buried it. But where? He started walking in a wide circle around the shack just looking for some kind of evidence where the ground had been disturbed. Where someone had dug a hole or moved a rock or anything that might lead to where the money was hidden. When he had covered all the area within fifty yards of the house with no luck, he sat back down on the porch to think.

He had spent most of an hour the night before trying to figure the amount of the checks that he had cashed for Sadie over the years. He had run through a whole roll of adding machine paper before he was satisfied that he was within a couple of thousand dollars of the total. The amount shocked him when he first saw it, but he knew it was a lot of money. $190,000 was a lot of money, but if he wasn't mistaken, that was just about what should be hidden somewhere close to the old shack. The more he thought of it, the more he became obsessed with finding it.

Just before sundown, he dragged his tired body into the truck and headed to town. He spent a restless night tossing and turning and finally slept fitfully for a couple of hours before dawn. By 8:00 o'clock, he was back at the shack and ready to begin searching again. It was Sunday, and if he didn't find the money today, it would be the next Saturday before he could get back out there again.

He started about fifty yards from the house and worked farther out in an ever widening circle. By the time he was a quarter of a mile from the house, he knew it was useless. Why kid himself. He wasn't going to find the money. Maybe someone had already found the money before he started looking for it. He didn't believe that for a minute. Nobody even knew about the money. At least nobody that would come out here looking for it. It had to be there somewhere.

The next week dragged by like the week before Christmas for a kid. He couldn't get interested in the store at all, he just went through the motions. By the time Friday afternoon rolled around, he had all he could take so he closed up early and drove the eight miles to the gate leading up to Sadie's shack. His heart fell into his boots when he saw the chain on the gate had been cut and was lying on the ground. The car tracks were clearly visible in the gravel of the road. There had been a rain earlier in the week and the car or pickup or whatever it was had been here since the rain. It was beginning to look like he wasn't the only one that knew about the money after all.

John didn't find the money that weekend or the next. Or the next either for that matter. After the third weekend in a row of crawling through rocks and brush looking for the money, reality finally began to set in. The money was taking over his life. He had to stop this nonsense of spending all his spare time out here looking for something that likely wasn't even there. He had been neglecting the store and the customers were beginning to complain about the bare shelves and the poor service. As he drove out of the gate onto the highway that third weekend, he made up his mind that the search for the money was over for him.

As time passed, the story of Sadie's money begin to get around. First one, then another spent time out at the shack looking for it. Somehow, the story changed from a stash of money to a stash of gold. Sadie's gold, they called it. Before long, all the country within a quarter of a mile around the shack was pockmarked with dirt piles from all the digging. Any piece of ground that remotely looked like it had been disturbed was shoveled up and gone through. It took about a year, but finally the mystery of the missing money began to lose its allure. Fewer and fewer gold seekers ventured out to the shack. Old man Darby had erected a steel gate at the road and the only way to get to the shack was walk the two miles through the pasture. Finally, the shack and surrounding country was again alone with nature. The only sound to be heard was the sound of the never ending wind blowing through the rocks on the ridge behind the house.

Occasionally, even today, somebody with a metal detector will walk the two miles to where the crumbling shack sits lonely in the hollow below the rocky ridge. They walk where countless others have walked in a vain attempt to locate the missing treasure.

Will Sadie's gold ever be found? Nobody knows. If you are ever down that way, why don't you spend a few hours in the quiet solitude of Sadie's homestead? Just drive the eight miles south out of Mill Creek to the lane leading to the shack. You'll know it by the big metal gate across the lane with the huge padlock on it. The two mile walk to the shack doesn't take long and before you know it, the place comes into view right over a low hill leading down into the hollow. The old shack is still standing, though the roof has fallen in. The pockmarked earth is still visible where countless shovels have overturned the rocky soil looking for the gold.

How do I know all of this? Because I too have spent time looking for Sadie's gold. I know it wasn't gold, but rather huge stacks of greenbacks, likely some of which were silver certificates. I believe to this day that the money is still there. Will it ever be found? I doubt it after all this time. Where could it be hidden so that hordes of lookers couldn't find it? As far as I can see, the only place within a half mile of the shack that wasn't disturbed by the searchers is Emerson's and Sadie's graves. Hold on!! Why didn't I think of that before. Surely Sadie wouldn't have hidden all that money in Emerson's grave, would she? Naw, surely not!!

The End

How Dead Man's Lane Got Its Name

You know where it is don't you? It's the little gravel road off state highway #1 south of Mill Creek, Oklahoma. It heads east and if you follow it a couple of miles, it runs into what was old highway #7, the last gravel state highway in the whole state. I heard several variations of the story while growing up in Mill Creek in the 1950's. Shine Waller told me the story the first time I heard it and I still believe what he told me is the correct version of what happened. Here's what he had to say.

"It was in 1932 as well as I can recall," he said. "It was in the summer, but I don't recollect the day or even the month. It was, however, a Saturday night that it happened on. At least it happened between dark on that Saturday night and daylight the next morning. You see, old man Wright had been down around Milburn, Oklahoma all night hanging out with some of his buddies down that way."

The story Shine told me was that they had been coon huntin all night and Mr. Wright was just making his way home about daylight when he found the body. Other variations of the story allowed as how old man Wright had likely been out drinking all night and probably wasn't in any condition to recall what happened at all that night.

"I remember Coley coming in the station that Sunday morning," Shine said. "He had a sort of sick look about him and I asked him what was wrong."

"I believe I just killed a man," Coley said. "He's laying at the side of the road down on the cut-off road south of here. I reckon I ran over him, near as I can tell."

"What man?" Shine asked. "Who was it? You shore he was dead?"

"He shore enough was after I got through running over him," Coley answered. "Face all puffed up and blood running out of his mouth. Yea, I'd say he was dead alright. Gave me the creeps just looking at him."

"What did you do with him?" Shine wanted to know. "You call the sheriff or anything?"

"I come right up here just as fast as I could," Coley replied. "I wasn't about to drive all the way to Tishomingo to tell no sheriff. I figured you might tell me what I ought to do. You think they'll send me to prison for running over that fellow, Shine?"

"That would be a hard thing to tell, Coley," Shine answered. "It might depend on whether it was an accident or not. Why you asking me about stuff like that anyway? I ain't no lawman."

"You're the next best thing to a lawman," Coley said. "Why folks come to you all the time for advice. I know they do cause I seen 'em do it myself."

"Well, I'll tell you what we're gonna do," Shine said. Quick as I can get Ruth up here to watch the station, we're gonna drive back down there and see about this here dead fellow, that's what we're gonna do." With that being said, he went to the back door and commenced to holler for Ruth.

They could see the truck as soon as they turned off the highway. Appeared like somebody else had found the body as well. When they got closer, they could tell the truck was the old green Dodge that Wilbur Harris tooled around in. Wilbur was standing beside the truck looking down at the body lying half in and half out of the bar ditch.

"What you make of that fellar, Wilbur?" Shine asked. "You ever seen him before?"

Wilbur looked up with a funny look on his face. "I seen that fellar down by the train depot just yesterday while I was getting my oil changed at Emory's Station, " he replied.

"Getting your oil changed at Emory's was you," Shine shot back. "Why, I thought you didn't have the money to get your oil changed at Emory's. I know he don't take no credit like I do. After all the times I changed your oil on credit, you go to Emory's the first time you have a little cash money and let him change your oil. I'm a good mind to cut you off."

"Now Shine," Wilbur replied. "I got to spread my business around a little, now don't I? First thing you know, if folks don't spread their business around, you'll be the only station in town and then you'd likely charge a dollar and a half for an oil change."

"Would you fellars just shut up and tell me what to do about this here dead man?" Coley exclaimed. "He ain't just gonna go away, that's for sure."

Before they could reply, another car turned off the highway and sped down to where they had the road blocked beside the dead man. Shine was the first to recognize County Sheriff Floyd Allen as he got out of the car.

"Got a call about an hour ago that there was a dead man on this road," Floyd said. "You fellars got anything to say about that?"

When Coley saw that Shine or Wilbur weren't gonna to say anything, he walked around to where Sheriff Allen was standing, looking down at the body.

"I might have run over that man this morning Sheriff. I was coming back from Milburn along this road about daylight and felt my truck hit something. When I stopped and got out, I saw this here fellar laying right where he is now. I swear I never saw him standing in the road though."

Sheriff Allen squatted down by the body and commenced to go through the dead man's pockets. After a thorough search, he stood back up. "They ain't a thing in his pockets, no identification or nothing," he said. "You sure you fellars haven't already gone through his pockets and took his money or anything?"

All three of the onlookers shook their heads in the negative. "What do you take us for anyway?" Wilbur said with a hurt look on his face. "What kind of a fellar would steal from a dead man?"

"Well, help me get him in the trunk of my car," Sheriff Allen said. "I'll take him to the funeral home in Tishomingo and then start trying to get a lead on who he might be." When nobody made a move, he had to repeat the request. "Get hold of his feet Coley," he said. "I'll get his shoulders." After some huffing and puffing, they finally got the dead man into the trunk of the car.

"You gonna file any charges on me Sheriff?" Coley wanted to know. "I swear I didn't see a thing until I felt the bump."

"Not right now anyway," Sheriff Allen replied. "He

was likely already dead before you ran over him if you ran over him at all. Let's wait and see what the judge has to say."

It was a Tuesday afternoon and it had been over a week since the dead man had been found. Nobody had heard a word form Sheriff Allen, or anybody else for that matter. Coley was beginning to breathe a little easier since he figured no news was good news. He had been at the station most of the afternoon and was just about to head home for supper when Shine got up from where he had been sitting on an upturned pop crate to go wait on a customer who had just pulled in at the gas pumps.

"Why, hello Sheriff," Coley heard him say. "What brings you up to this part of the county? Hear anything about that dead man we found?"

Coley got up and walked outside just in time to hear the sheriff's reply.

"I checked out Wilbur's story and sure enough, there were several folks saw the man down around the depot that day or the day before. Likely came in on a freight and intended to go out the same way. More than likely headed to Dallas to try to find work or at least be able to eat at one of the soup kitchens. I can't figure what he would be doing down on that cut-off road. I got me a good feeling he was dropped off where you guys found him. Somebody killed him for what little he had on him and dumped his body on the gravel road. Another thing you boys might be interested in knowing. That fellow had been sexually molested."

"What do you mean, sexually molested?" Coley said with a blank look on his face.

"I mean sexually molested. What do you not understand about sexually molested?"

Coley's face started to turn red as the meaning of the sheriff's words began to sink in.

"You don't think somebody local would have done that?" do you Sheriff.

"Well, it would have been somebody who had a car or a pickup truck or something," Sheriff Allen replied. "Had to have gotten him down there some way. What I'm thinking is that somebody just passing through must have spotted him after dark and thinking he was a local, knocked him over the head and robbed him. I bet he didn't have twenty cents on him. I don't know if he was molested before or after he was killed."

"He's probably got a family somewhere, but with so many folks riding the rails these days, it would take a miracle if we could ever trace him back to anywhere. I put out a notice to all the sheriffs around to see if they know of anyone missing, but so far, haven't turned up a thing."

"Sounds like you ain't gonna charge me with nothing," Coley said. "Sure is a load off my shoulders if you ain't. I ain't thought of nothing else since you took off with that body."

"I found the tire tracks on his jeans on the right leg below the knee," Sheriff Allen replied. "You ran over him alright, it appears like, but he was already dead when you did. You wouldn't have killed him anyway by running over his leg. You better start paying more attention though when you're driving. Next time, you might not be so lucky."

As summer turned to fall, and other things started to take attention away from thoughts of the dead man, things pretty much returned to normal for the three of them. The talk on the spit and whittle bench down in front of Clementine's Grocery had long since moved on to other issues, like what kind of basketball team the Bullfrogs were likely to have, and what the price of cattle feed was gonna be if the winter got bad like everyone was expecting. By October, it had been over a month since Shine had even heard the dead man mentioned.

One Thursday afternoon not long before Thanksgiving, Carlton Bates walked into the station with a copy of the county paper in his hand.

"You see the article in the paper about the dead man you guys found?" he asked. "It's right here in the paper on page 2."

Shine took the paper Carlton was handing to him and turned to page 2 and began to read.

John Doe killing put in cold case file

The case of the unidentified dead man found on a cut-off road in northern Johnston County last summer has been officially placed in the cold case file. Although technically, the case is still open, no more time is being allocated to trying to find the dead man's identity. "Like many cases across the country," Sheriff Allen stated, "there is not much likelihood this case will ever be solved. We'll keep it open for a while to see if anything turns up, but I don't hold out much hope." In this journalist's opinion, this is just another of the sad endings common to the times. With so many folks on the move because of the depression, families will likely be split up for years to come. Who knows, sometime in the future, someone may happen along and inquire about the dead man. Until then, he will continue to be known as just another John Doe.

And so, the story of Dead Man's lane came to be. Before long, everybody around Mill Creek, Oklahoma started calling the road "Dead Man's Lane." I heard it called that no more than a year ago. When the county began to officially name the county roads for the 911 directory, I was curious as to what that little stretch of road would be called. Would it officially be called "Dead Man's lane," or would it finally receive a more civil moniker? I happened to be down that way recently and noticed a new looking sign at the entrance to Dead Man's lane. It was the new 911 official name and it read "Rocky Road."

Although the dusty gravel road now has a new name, it has been known as Dead Man's Lane for more than seventy-five years. Seems a shame to change it after all this time but progress is not to be stopped. The next time you take that road though, you might want to pay close attention to where you are going, especially at night. I hear the ghost of the dead man still walks that road on stormy and windy nights. It's as if his spirit is still hunting the justice it was denied in 1932. Will he be upset with the name change? I don't think I want to chance it. I'm taking the long way around!!!

The End

Shotguns and Cat Head Biscuits

Eastern Oklahoma is pretty country. Almost everyone will agree with that opinion. The mountains green with pine and oak, the clear streams teeming with fish, and the lush meadows where you can spot deer and an occasional elk grazing on the nutritious grasses and legumes.

The area has a history of moonshine running and bootleg whisky dating back to the prohibition days of the early 20th century. There are a lot of areas that are sparsely settled, and in these areas it is a good idea, even today, to be cautious if you are roaming around in the woods. You just might stumble onto something you don't want to know about and even more important, something somebody else doesn't want you to see.

The inhabitants of these areas are fiercely independent, and mostly just want to be left alone. They are, for the most part, hard living and hardworking folks, that might on occasion, bend the law a little to suit their way of living and thinking. They are family oriented and almost clannish when it comes to protecting what they feel rightfully belongs to them. It was into this country that I ventured on several weekends in the late 1960s and early 1970s just trying to make a little extra money.

It was pretty early on a Saturday morning in October 1969, and I had been on the road since well before daylight. I was headed for the John's Valley area to try to buy some horses. I was pulling a 20 foot trailer and my objective was to have six horses in that trailer and headed back to Mill Creek, Oklahoma before dark. It was my second trip to this general vicinity and I had made a good haul the first time. Nearly every open spot alongside the narrow highway would have at least one horse grazing on the lush green grass and sometimes a dozen or more. I was buying almost any kind of horse I could get for a good price. The old ones and the mean ones, I was selling at the horse sale in Sulphur and the good ones I would finish out and sell at a good profit. The export buyers were giving as much as fifty cents a pound for horses to ship to France for human consumption, and the dog food buyers were paying almost as much for the old broken down horses. The previous weekend I had bought five horses for a total of eleven hundred dollars, and sold them at the horse sale that Monday night for twenty-six hundred. Pretty good wages for two days work, I'd say.

That particular morning I was headed back to a farm where I had seen four horses in a little trap close to an old frame house. I had in mind to try to buy them horses. It was just after seven in the morning when I pulled through the gate leading down toward the house and barn. I was afraid I was too early, but then I spotted a column of smoke coming out of the chimney. Two Black and Tan hounds came out to greet me and the baying sounded good to me. I'd just about bet those two hounds had treed many a coon in the creek bottom I could see winding off to the southeast. I pulled the Ford truck up behind an old John Deere tractor and had started to open the door to get out when I heard the voice.

"State your business," the voice said. I turned to look out the back glass of the truck and could see an old bearded gentleman standing alongside the truck about where the rear quarter panel started.

"I'm looking to buy some horses," I said. "Saw your horses there in the trap when I went by last week. You interested in selling them horses?"

"Not for sale," he replied. "Now if that's all you got to say, I'd thank you to get off my property."

About that time a rather large lady with a flour covered apron came out onto the front porch. "Who's that out there with you Clem?" she hollered. "Breakfast is about ready. Whoever that is, invite them in to breakfast. Now don't tarry around none Clem Hollis, you get in here to breakfast now and bring your friend there with you."

Well I just looked at Clem as he grimaced like he was trying to swallow something that was too big for his pie hole. You could tell he hated to do it in the worst way, but he finally managed to grunt it out. "You may as well come on in to breakfast before Gertrude runs me and you both off," he said. With that, he turned and headed for the house in the long strides common to mountain folks.

We washed up at a little stand just inside the kitchen door. I could smell the wonderful smell of coffee brewing along with the softer aroma of homemade biscuits hot from the oven. As I followed Clem into the kitchen, it was like walking into a different world. There were three tall boys of the teenage variety sitting on the far side of the biggest dining room table I had ever seen. As big as the table was, there was hardly an empty spot on its vast expanse that wasn't occupied with some dish filled with food. Along with the biscuits, there was a large platter of ham slices, another full of bacon strips, and right in the center of the table was a bowl of gigantic proportion filled with scrambled eggs. I'll bet there were at least four dozen eggs in that bowl. About that time, in came Mrs. Hollis with a dishpan sized pan of the loveliest flapjacks I ever did see.

"Well what are you men waiting on?" she asked. "Go ahead, sit down. I'll just get some coffee cups. Now you sit right there at this end of the table Mr. uh, uh, I don't believe I caught your name," she said as she stood and looked me over with her hands on her massive hips.

"Just call me Pete," I answered. "This is about the most impressive breakfast I believe I've ever seen, Mrs. Hollis."

"Well, thank you Pete," she replied. "Now sit down there and as soon as Clem gets around to offering thanks, we'll eat."

Clem took the chair at the opposite end of the table and when Mrs. Hollis and I were both seated, he bowed his head and began. It was the best prayer I can ever remember hearing prayed before a meal.

"Lord God of Abraham," he began. "As we gather here at this here table filled with your bounty, we thank you for your abundant charity. We thank you Lord for you finding a woman for Jeb Crowe Lord, you know how long he's looked. Lord, we are most appreciative for you fixin it where we could tree them three coons last night for we can sure use the money them hides will bring. We ask you Lord to be with my sister Bessie when it comes her time to birth so it won't be too hard on her Lord. Lord

bless this stranger among us and make his stay with us short and seldom to repeat. Amen."

"Clem Hollis, you old cantankerous fool," Gertrude began. "The Lord is gonna strike you down for bad-mouthing a guest at our table. I'd be ashamed ifen I was you."

Clem never paid her no more mind than if she wasn't there. He helped himself to a big helping of ham and passed it off to the nearest boy. One by one, the boys helped themselves to ham and passed it on. When it came to me, I took a piece and handed the platter to Mrs. Hollis. She just looked at me and wouldn't take that platter.

"Just sit it on the table boy," Clem said.

I sat the platter on the table and I had no sooner took my hand off it 'til Mrs. Hollis picked it up and after spearing a big hunk of ham with her fork, sat the platter right back down where it started from. The eggs were next and I began to see the pattern. Nobody was taking anything until Mr. Hollis had first taken some of it. It went that way all the way from the egg platter through the biscuit pan and the flapjacks. When everybody had been served in that manner, Mrs. Hollis nodded her head and the boys began to wolf down the food like it was the last meal they ever expected to eat. I soon followed suit, but a little more slowly.

Folks have different cultures and different ways of going about things, I know, but that breakfast was about as strange a meal as I ever ate. Nobody was allowed to pass anything to Mrs. Hollis, she helped herself from what she could reach. I moved the pan of biscuits closer to her so she could reach it and was rewarded with a fleeting smile I almost missed. The food was delicious, and the coffee even better. I could see a coffee grinder sitting on the shelf by the stove and then I knew why the coffee was so good. Fresh ground coffee just can't be beat.

When everyone was finished and just sitting there sipping coffee, Mrs. Hollis looked over at me.

"What brings you out this way Pete?" she asked. "Not many strangers venture into our neck of the woods these days."

"I was looking to buy some horses," I answered. "Reckon I come to the wrong place though since you folks don't have any horses for sale."

"Well now," she said. "I don't know about that. "You aim to pay for horses with cash money Pete?"

I hated to let them folks know I had cash money on me, but it was looking like I might get a chance to buy them horses after all, so I went ahead and played out my hand.

"I've got cash money to pay for horses providing I can get a bill of sale for them," I said.

It was then that Clem joined into the conversation. "I don't reckon we got any horses for sale," he said.

"Now Clem," Mrs. Hollis said. "You was just saying last week that you had a mind to take them horses to the sale over at Antlers and sell them. They ain't doing us one bit of good standing out there eating their heads off."

"I figured to sell them horses to a neighbor or someone around here close," he replied. "Not to some stranger that happened along the road and ate up all my vittles." He had the ghost of a smile on his face when he said it though, so I thought I'd test the water a little bit. I hadn't looked the horses over too good, but I'd seen enough to know they were pretty good looking five or six year old geldings.

"If them horses are broke to ride, I'll give two hundred dollars a head for 'em," I said. You'd have thought I'd slapped Mrs. Hollis by the look on Clem's face.

"Two hundred dollars!" he exclaimed. "Why them horses are worth twice that if they're worth a penny."

"I might take a harder look at them when we go back out, but I can't give that for them," I said.

We followed Clem out the door and to the trap where the horses were grazing on the rich grass. They all looked up as we approached and before long we were petting them over the fence. Nice gentle horses, I could see.

"They all ride good?" I asked.

"Just like the lead horse in a rodeo parade," Clem answered. "I'll have the boys saddle 'em up and work 'em a little if you want me to."

"Naw, I don't see any need for that," I said. "I'll tell you what. I'll give you a thousand dollars cash for all four of them right now. I've got the cash money right here on me."

When Clem began to look dubious, Gertrude took him by the arm and led him off a little way. I could see them talking and Gertrude was doing most of the talking. Finally, Clem nodded his head and they walked back over to where me and them three tall lads were waiting beside the fence.

"I'm gonna do business with you," he said. I'll just go in and make out a bill of sale. You pay the money to Mrs. Hollis now, and don't be trying to short change her any, she knows her money real good."

When I had the bill of sale in my pocket and Mrs. Hollis had her huge hand around the ten, one hundred dollar bills, I was set to go. I had one other favor to ask though before I left. "Is it alright if I leave these horses here 'til this afternoon?" I asked. "I aim to try to buy a couple more horses and I don't want these four to have to stand in the trailer all day."

"I'll just run them in the lot by the barn," Clem said. "Just back up to the breezeway when you come back and you can run them right up into the trailer. We may not be here when you come back. We may go to town and pick up a few things we've been waiting on some cash money to buy."

I left them standing there when I drove off. Not one of them answered the wave I sent their way as I turned onto the gravel road and headed east. Strange folks, I figured. I had me four good horses at any rate and I knew I was going to make some pretty good money on them too.

I didn't have very good luck that afternoon and it was getting on to late in the afternoon before I finally managed to buy a couple of two year old fillies from a family near Cloudy, Oklahoma. Sure enough, when I arrived back at the Hollis place, there was not a soul in sight. I backed the trailer up to the breezeway like Clem told me to do and walked into the open center aisle of the barn. I had intended to drive the four horses into the aisle way from the lot when I heard a noise in one of the stalls on the north side of the center aisle. My glance naturally went that way and I nearly jumped out of my boots. Protruding through a crack between the boards were the twin barrels of a shotgun.

"Just hold her right where you're at," a voice said. I wasn't about to move a muscle. The shotgun barrels disappeared and then a big man that looked to be a carbon copy of Clem Hollis stepped out into the aisle. The shotgun was pointed right at my belt buckle.

"Who are you and what are you doing here?" he asked. "Looks to me like you was fixin to steal some horses from the looks of things."

"I've got a bill of sale for them four horses in the lot," I said. "I bought them off of Clem Hollis just this morning."

"Bill of sale, you say!" he answered. "Suppose you just

pitch that bill of sale right here to me so I can get a look at it," he said.

Since it didn't appear that I had much choice, I took the bill of sale out of my jacket pocket and pitched it onto the ground in front of him.

"You better hope this bill of sale is in Clem's writing," he said. "If it ain't, we're going take a little trip over to see the sheriff in Antlers." He picked the paper up off the ground and studied it for at least a minute. "This here appears to be Clem's hand," he said. The shotgun barrels tilted down toward the ground ever so slightly. I'm Sol Hollis, Clem's brother," he said. "I was just over here getting me some feed for my chickens when I saw you turn in at the gate. I'm right sorry I held a gun on you but you just can't tell these days. Let me help you load them nags."

I kept the four geldings for more than a month just getting them used to the saddle again. I sold one of them to a man down around Tishomingo for five hundred dollars and took the other three to the sale at Marietta, Oklahoma. The three of them sold for seventeen hundred and fifty dollars.

I bought horses over in the eastern part of the state for more than two years off and on. I never ran across another family like the Hollises. It took me several months to get over the feeling I got just looking at that double barrel shotgun sticking from between the boards that day. It took me longer than that to get over the best breakfast I ever ate. If you happen to be down towards John's Valley and you see a weather beaten old frame house with a barn and lot just west of it, look at the name on the mailbox. If it belongs to the Hollis's, I guarantee you that you can get the best home cooking you ever had in that old kitchen with the massive table. I wouldn't recommend it, however. It could be hazardous to one's health to spend much time around there. I ask you to stop on the road though and say a prayer. Ask God to provide a tree full of coons for Clem and the boys to skin. Ask Him also to bless Mrs. Hollis. She's about as heavy laden as your apt to find when it comes to caring for them boys and old Clem. I owe the purchase of them horses to her. I would never have gotten them if she hadn't talked Clem into selling them. Take a big whiff of the air before you go on your way. That aroma you smell is the fresh ground coffee perking and the cat-head biscuits baking in the huge oven. If you see any horses around the place, give me a call. I just might go and try to deal for them.

The End

Busted Up

The sun shining on my back felt really good as I rode along. It was one of the lazy summer days, not too hot and not too windy. That kind of day was a rare commodity that summer of 1975. It was a tough summer for me and an even tougher summer for Darlene. We had been married less than a year, and it had been the busiest year of my life. I was working rotating shifts at the tire plant in Ardmore, Oklahoma and Darlene was taking a full load of college classes and working two jobs on top of that. Then, the two of us were taking care of a 200 head cow and calf operation as well. We thought we had all we could do and then her dad got sick.

It started out as not too much of anything to get too worried about, but as time went on it became apparent that if something wasn't done, he just wasn't going to make it. He had checked into the hospital at Ada, Oklahoma and walked in under his own power the day he checked in. The longer he stayed, the sicker he became and all the test they ran failed to identify the problem. By the end of a week there, he knew we were going to have to get him to another facility or he was going to die.

We checked him out against the advice of the hospital staff and took him in an ambulance to Scott & White Hospital in Temple Texas. In a couple of hours the verdict was clear. He had an abscess on his spinal column and a bad valve in his heart. He spent two months in that hospital, but was finally able to come home and recuperate. It was during that two months' time that I got into a really bad situation on the ranch.

With Darlene and her mom both staying in Temple to be with her dad, I was left to take care of the stock and continue to work. Luckily, there wasn't much to do in the summer with the cattle that required more than one person. That Saturday afternoon though, would prove to be the exception to the rule.

I was just riding along enjoying the nice day and looking over the cattle. I had decided to ride a big sorrel mare I called Lady that had just recovered from a bad wire cut on her leg. She was a good roping horse, but I was a little skeptical of her stability after the bad cut. I enjoyed riding her though, and not expecting anything more than a few hours riding and checking on stock, had decided to give her some exercise. I was at the very south end of the east pasture, as far from the house as I could possibly get when I spotted a big yellow cow that was crippling along pretty slowly. As I got closer, I could see she had gotten some baling wire wrapped around her right hind leg just above the ankle. It had pulled tight and was in danger of cutting off the circulation to her hoof. I knew I had to do something about it.

One thing you learn pretty quickly when messing with stock is that you always need to be prepared. You never know when you are likely to find a cow or calf that has a wound that needs doctoring, a horn that needs trimming, or in this case, wire wrapped around a hoof that must be taken care of. I always kept a pair of cutters, a tube of disinfectant ointment, and a bottle of wound spray in the little saddle bag on my saddle. The way the old cow was moving around, it didn't look to be too big a job to just rope her and snub her up to a tree short enough to get the wire cut off her leg. Problem was, that old cow had a lot more get up and go to her than she or I either one thought she had.

With the loop over my shoulder, I rode slowly toward where that big yellow cow was grazing along with four or five yearlings. I had decided to tie on solid to the saddle horn and let Lady do the work of holding the cow while I cut the wire loose. When I got pretty close, she smelled a rat and busted out of the bunch in a run for the timber. Old Lady took out after her like her tail was on fire.

I had a loop built and was just about to let it fly when the old cow took an abrupt turn to the right. I could see she was going to make the timber if I didn't do something, so I nabbed the loop on her just as she turned. Lady didn't have time to turn and get set before that big old cow hit the end of the rope, and she was at right angles to the cow when the slack went out of the rope. Unfortunately, the full force of that thousand pound cow hitting the end of the rope was centered right on that bad leg. Down she went with me under her.

I felt the crushing weight of the horse as she landed on me and heard the distinct snap of bones breaking. Then everything went black.

I awoke with a dizzy feeling in my head. I couldn't have been out very long, judging by the angle of the sun, and when I managed to raise my head for a look around, I could see Lady standing about twenty feet away holding steady with the yellow cow straining on the other end of the rope. I knew I was in trouble and was hurt, but I didn't know just how badly I was injured. When I tried to sit up, the pain made me pass out again. When I came to that time, I remembered thinking I was gonna just lay right there and die. Darlene was in Temple, Texas and nobody else was likely to even come to the house let alone way back here in the southernmost part of the pasture. I figured I was sure enough a goner.

I've heard that a man will do things he doesn't think he can do to benefit someone else or something else before he will try to do it to help himself, and that's just what happened to me. The longer I lay there, the more I knew I had to do something to get Lady loose from that cow. I just couldn't get it straight in my head what that something was gonna be until I remembered my pocket knife there in my jeans pocket. I eased around on my side until I could reach the knife and finally managed to extract it from my pocket. Then I just fell back and rested again until the pain subsided to the point I thought I might try again to sit up. I made it that time, but I was trembling pretty badly and the sweat was pouring from my face by the time I got it done.

I was as weak as a kitten, but I could feel the determination building inside. I was gonna cut that rope if it was the last thing I did. Shakily, I got to my knees and balanced there for a few seconds until my head began to clear. Then, with the help of a slender persimmon sapling, I made it to my feet and stood there swaying like a drunkard. I felt like the slightest wind would blow me off my feet. After a couple of minutes, I began to re-gain my equilibrium and took a couple of hesitant steps toward the horse. The farther I walked the more stable I became and by the time I had walked the half dozen steps and took hold of the saddle horn, most all the dizziness had vanished. I could see I wasn't gonna be able to loosen the rope from the saddle horn, so I opened the knife and cut it loose. That yellow cow took off in a cloud of dust and disappeared around a corner of the timber with the rope dragging along behind. I knew it was only a matter of time until that rope caught on something and the cow would be trapped and sentenced to a terrible death of starvation. I would have to worry about that later. The first order of business now that the cow was free, was getting back to the house and then to the hospital.

I led Lady over to a fairly tall rock and after a few tries, was finally able to crawl up on top of it. Once standing on the rock, I could get my foot into the stirrup. I gritted my teeth and slung my leg over the saddle and just flopped down onto it. All I could see for a minute or two was black circles in front of my eyes. I could feel Lady began to walk and all I could do was trust she was going in the right direction.

I fell in and out of consciousness as she walked and it seemed like she walked for an hour. When I finally felt her stop, I opened my eyes and could see she had stopped right in front of the saddle shed at the barn. Now to get off. I tried a few times to swing my leg over the saddle but could never quite get it done. Finally, I just leaned down as far as he could lean and turned loose. When I hit the ground, pain shot through my body like someone was carving me up with a dull knife.

I must have passed out again because when I woke up, the sun was hanging low in the western sky. I crawled a few yards, then managed to get to my feet. It took a while, but I managed to walk to the house and eased down into a chair by the phone.

Buster Dunn answered the phone on the second ring. Buster was a friend of mine and lived just on the north edge of Tishomingo, Oklahoma, about eight miles from the ranch. He was there in less than fifteen minutes and in another fifteen we were pulling up to the emergency entrance of the hospital in Tishomingo. X-rays revealed a broken collarbone and three cracked ribs along with some pretty good bruises and pulled muscles. A fair sized knot on the back of my head finished off the list of ailments.

Buster drove me back home and cooked a steak supper for the both of us. I don't know what I would have done without him. After Buster left, I washed up as best I could with a washcloth and eased down on the bed. I managed to sleep a little and by daylight was feeling considerably better. I spent the day just lazing around and after a lunch of left over steak and a baked potato, decided I would try to take a bath. I took off the harness that kept the collar bone in place and that was my undoing. I ran the tub full of hot water and finally managed to ease down into it. And there I was. The hot bath water felt good and I lay there until it began to get cool. I was ready to get out of the tub and dry off but there was one small problem. I couldn't get out of the tub. Without the harness on, I couldn't put any pressure whatsoever on that broken clavicle, and since I couldn't, I was as trapped as if I had been caught in a huge mouse trap.

Now what was I gonna do? I was sure in a fix. Maybe the worst one I had ever been in. I could see the article in the paper now. ***"Man starves to death in bathtub, but died a clean death."***

Darlene wasn't due home at all, I was going to drive to Temple when I got off work the following Friday night. She would call on the phone, I knew, but when I didn't answer, she would just think I was out doing something around the place. What were the chances of someone dropping by? I began to look at the possibilities. The only one I could think of that might come by was my dad and he wasn't likely to come near the house. He came down and looked at the cattle on a pretty regular basis, but he might or might not come to the house. Even if he did, he probably wouldn't hear me holler. I couldn't holler very loud anyway without causing the pain to flare up again. It looked like a pretty hopeless situation as far as I could tell. At least I wouldn't starve for water, all I had to do was turn on the faucet with his toes and let it run until it got the tub full enough for the water to run into my mouth. I got tickled just thinking about it and when I laughed it felt like my insides were going to blow up.

It was now full dark and I had been in the tub for about four hours. The skin on my hands was all wrinkled and this was beginning to get serious. I tried a few more times to get out of the tub, but just couldn't make it. I finally managed to wiggle the stopper out of the tub with my toes and the water began to run out.

When I began to air dry, I started to feel a little better and despite my predicament, I drifted off to sleep. I awoke with a start. What had waked me up? Then I heard it, a pounding on the door. I hollered as loud as I could and could feel the cracked ribs come apart but I grimaced and hollered again.

"Pete, hey Pete," somebody hollered. "You in there Pete?"

"I'm in here," I managed to holler. "I'm in the bathroom! Come and help me!"

I could hear the footsteps coming down the hall and the bathroom door opened to reveal my dad standing there with a quizzical look on his face.

"What in the world happened to you?" he asked. "I heard a horse fell on you."

"Help me out of this bathtub but be careful, I've got a broken collarbone and some broke ribs," I said. I could see my dad was trying hard to keep the grin off his face. I realized I must have been a funny sight, trapped in the bathtub in my birthday suit like that, but this was no time for jokes.

With some dry clothes and a belly full of vittles, I was as good as new in a couple of hours. My dad promised to get some help and take care of the yellow cow the next day.

After my dad left, I called Darlene in Temple and told her what happened. She insisted I stay with her Granddad and Granny until I got to where I could take care of myself and that is just what I did for two whole weeks. It was nice to have someone cook for me and wash my clothes and everything though they routed me out of bed every morning bright and early for breakfast. If I slept in a little I could hear them discussing what might be wrong with me sleeping so much, so I tried to get up when I smelled the biscuits cooking.

Darlene's dad finally recovered and came home from the hospital. He had a new heart valve; I heard it was from a pig, and a clean bill of health though it took him a while to regain his strength.

I won't ever forget that summer of 1975. I won't forget the friendship of Buster Dunn and all he did for me that day when the horse fell on me. It is my hope to get the chance to help someone in the same way some day to sort of payback and get even. A friend is more valuable than gold when you need one and I needed one that day. I always sympathize with anyone I see wearing the shoulder harness that signifies a broken collarbone. I know what they are going through. I sometimes get the urge when I see someone with a broken collarbone to warn them to stay out of the bathtub if they are alone.

1975 was a rough year. Tough times and how we handle them tend to define us though. Better times are sure to follow and they did for me back then. The next year, our son was born, and the next year, a daughter. We were a family and the strength of the family has seen us through both good times and not so good times ever since. The addition of still yet another daughter later in our lives made our family complete. Now, as grandchildren fill our lives, I sometimes let my mind wander back to the early days of our marriage and how things were. In retrospect, 1975 was a pretty good year. It was a year we got to spend together and witness the healing hand of God in our lives. I know I wouldn't take anything for it. I would just as soon not have to spend another afternoon in the bathtub again though. Come by and see us if you're by this way Buster. I'd like to see you again and thank you properly for what you did for me back in the summer of 1975.

The End

Epilogue

Mill Creek, Oklahoma was not much different from a hundred other small towns in Oklahoma in the 1950s and 1960s. The lifestyle that these little towns provided is a thing of the past and will never be seen again. Oh, I realize there are still small towns scattered around like there was back then, but the lifestyle is not the same as it was then. Better cars, better roads, and more money to spend have changed them from what they were. Wal-Mart and the fast food franchises scattered around played a big part in the evolution of small town life as well. Folks can drive to the nearest Wal-Mart in about a half hour from almost anywhere these days.

You know what I miss more than anything? Drive-in movies. Whatever happened to them anyway? It was a tradition to go to the drive-in movie on Saturday night when I was a teenager. Just another of the things that have passed by never to be seen again in most places. I've seen a few still in existence in my travels around the country, but for the most part, they are a thing of the past.

When was the last time you went unannounced to someone's house that wasn't a relative just to visit? That wouldn't be considered proper etiquette today. It happened all the time when I was a kid. Now we see folks at Wal-Mart and maybe at church. We are all too busy to stop and chat anyway. Got to get to the next thing on the list of things to do.

I'm glad things have changed. In all seriousness, life is much easier for most folks than it was fifty or sixty years ago and that is a good thing. Let's just don't let our values and the really important things in life go the way of the drive in movie.

I hope you enjoyed "Black Cotton II." You all come see us, you hear?

Ted L. Pittman

About the Author

Ted Pittman lived the stories in Black Cotton II. A baby boomer born into the family of a World War II veteran, he grew up in the small town of Mill Creek Oklahoma during the 1950s and 1960s. The Oklahoma of his youth was characterized by editorials and books such as "The Grapes Of Wrath" which depicted Oklahomans as mainly illiterate and uncultured.

Growing up in rural Oklahoma in that era defined a generation of Americans that have their roots planted firmly in the free soil of this great nation. Ted and his lovely wife Darlene have raised their family in the general area that is home to the characters in "Black Cotton II.

"Black Cotton II" is Ted's fourth book to be published. There are thousands of his books in print. He has written about life in Oklahoma in the post war years of the 1950s and 1960s. His historical fiction novel, "Son Of The Red Earth" is based on a true story set in the Great Depression years of the 1930s.

"Bellwood Cowboy" chronicles the life of one of

Oklahoma's most prolific citizens, Artie Quinton, who worked for the sprawling Daube Ranch in south central Oklahoma for half a century. He is one of the old time cowboys that did it for a living.

Ted's interest outside of writing include fishing and the outdoors. Walking in the Chickasaw National Recreation Area near his home, boating on beautiful Arbuckle lake, and spending time with the family. Ted and Darlene have four children and eleven grandchildren. He has been a business manager for forty years.

Try these books by Ted L. Pittman

Black Cotton

One night when Julie was about four years old, I was at the horse sale at Sulphur, Oklahoma with Bill Suggs and Louis Helms and outside before the sale started, we overheard some guys talking about coon hunting and such. We eased up a little closer so we could hear what was being said. They were talking about a ridgerunner coon down around Mead Oklahoma, near the Texas border that no dog could tree. Talking about how big and smart this coon was and how he had made the best coon dogs from all over the country look silly. Now a ridgerunner coon is not like an ordinary coon. They are a different breed of coon, lighter in color than a regular coon, much bigger, and with legs about half again as long as a regular coon.

It's not unusual for a ridgerunner coon to weigh as much as thirty pounds when fully grown. They were likely as not to just cut across open country to get to another creek or stretch of timber when dogs were on their trail. A regular coon would never do that.

As they continued to brag about this coon and how this old ridgerunner would never be treed, I stepped up in the middle of them and just said it real slow like so they were sure to hear what I said.

"I got a little Blue Tic dog that can tree that ridgerunner," I said. Total silence for a minute. Then one of the guys drawled, "how much money you got?"

"I don't hunt for money, just for fun," I replied.

"You don't understand," he said. "There has been guys bring dogs down to hunt this coon that were grand champion coon dogs, field trial champions and such. The best coon dogs there is in this country and none of them could tree this coon."

"Julie can," I said.

Well, the guy took my phone number and promised to call me the next day to talk some more about it. As we walked on into the sale barn, Bill allowed as how I might just have cut off more than I could chew. Or in this case, more than Julie could chew. Had I spoken too soon? Did I really have too much faith in Julie? I figured I was about to find out.

Son Of The Red Earth

When Lugnut returned to the cave in the rocks, the first thing he saw was the dirty breakfast dishes still sitting by the dead fire. Dad gum that boy! When was he gonna learn some responsibility? He stepped out of the cave and hollered a couple of times. Where could that boy be? After a couple of minutes, when he got no answer, he ventured down to the creek. When he saw the pile of clothes laying on the rock, he felt his stomach tighten and the fear began to set in. Something was mighty wrong here. Something had happened to Jorney. Carefully, he looked over the scene. The muddy footprints on the rock. The disturbed dirt track heading off toward the south. Before long, he could identify two different sets of footprints. The story was there to read. Two men had somehow surprised Jorney and taken him with them. One of them stepping mighty heavy. His first instinct was to head for town. They would surely take him to the nearest town to collect the reward money. As he continued to follow the plain trail, it was easy to see they were headed away from town, not toward it. He sat down on a rock to think. No need rushing off into anything. That wasn't gonna help Jorney. Might as well get back to the cave and gather up some grub and such to take with him. This might turn into a long ordeal. There was no telling where the two men were headed and how far they would go before they stopped. It looked to have been several hours since they had taken Jorney. The muddy tracks on the rocks were completely dry.

With his pack on his back, Lugnut headed south following the tracks. He was having to go a lot slower than the two men, he knew, what with having to hunt around occasionally for the trail. They weren't taking many pains to hide the trail, but the rocky ground and the brush they were going through, made staying on it a challenge. By the time it was too dark to see the tracks, he figured he had covered upward of six miles. As he made his meager camp, the feeling of dread that had accompanied him all day begin to get stronger. He should have stayed around camp instead of going off to town like that. He shouldn't have left the boy all alone like he did. He slept but little and was on the trail again as soon as it was light enough to see. His old bones were mighty sore from all the traveling the day before, but that was the least of the things on his mind as he continued to make his way south. The country had begun to open up a little and the trail was there as plain as day. He found where they had camped about a mile south of his camp and from there he could see that there were three sets of tracks now. He figured they must have carried Jorney to this point, and then let him walk. By the time the sun had started its downward journey toward the western horizon, he was hidden in the brush looking down on the cabin in the hidden valley.

Bellwood Cowboy

The little house Artie and Ag moved into, (the first house they shared in their married life) was a little house made out of ship-lap boards an inch thick and six inches wide just stood up on a boxboard floor and nailed together. There was not even a step at the door, you just walked up to the wall, opened the door, and stepped into the house. With the men working in the feedlot coming in and out that door all day, it was a constant job just to keep the floors mopped. The house was ten foot wide and thirty foot long, and was divided up into three ten foot by ten foot rooms. Artie and Ag were in the north room, the middle room served as a kitchen, and the south room housed three cowboys. The kitchen had a little wood cook stove and boxboard cabinets. The stovepipe was a little too short to reach all the way through the roof, so they had to sit the stove up on bricks to get the stovepipe above the roofline. The inside walls were just the ship-lap boards, no wallpaper or anything on them.

Ag cooked three meals a day, by herself, sometimes for as many as twenty cowboys, depending on how many might be working close by. She never knew, when she started a meal, how many there would be there to eat it. Artie said Ag told him later that the first cake she baked when they were at the feedlot looked so bad that she took it over the hill and threw it away, not wanting him to see it. Artie already knew about it, however. He was riding pasture one day shortly after she threw the cake away and he saw it there in the grass and figured out what must have happened. She really was an excellent cook.

The Legend of Greybull (Expected to be released in 2012)

Billy held out his hand. "I'm Billy Ramsey", he said. "Looking forward to playing next year."

"You're going to have to get a lot bigger and a lot tougher than you are now if you're going to play football at the high school level." The smirk was still on his face. By that time, half the team was standing just watching what was taking place.

"Little runt like you won't last the first day of two-a-days, be my guess," he said. "You wouldn't hardly make a pimple on a football players butt." With that, he reached over and pushed Billy backwards. Billy just happened to be standing right in front of the bench loaded with spare gear, and when he staggered back, the bench caught him right behind the knees and over the bench he went to land flat on his back on the muddy ground. Gear went flying every which way as he fought to regain his feet. Then Coach Phelps did the last thing you would have expected him to do. He just started walking toward the field house whistling softly to himself. He didn't turn and look when he heard Maddy Palmer's grunt of surprise as Billy picked him up over his head. A little smile crossed his lips when he heard Maddy hollering as Billy, with Maddy held at arm's length over his head, walked over to the fifty five gallon barrel that served as a trash container. He whistled louder to hide Maddy's curses as Billy stuffed him head first down into the trash barrel. He did manage to steal a look in that direction just before he closed the field house door behind him. What he saw was Maddy with his legs sticking out of the trash barrel kicking wildly as the rest of the team stood around and laughed. They were laughing so hard they could hardly stand. He saw Billy calmly making his way to the side exit that led to the street. This bunch of guys were going to get a rude awakening when Billy Ramsey joined them the next year, he knew. For that matter, so would the entire state of Rhode Island if he was any judge.

Printed in the USA
CPSIA information can be obtained
at www.ICGtesting.com
LVHW092118260823
756397LV00006B/64